AF442785

CODE NAME:
VIRGO

USA *TODAY* BESTSELLING AUTHOR

JANIE CROUCH

CODE NAME: VIRGO • SPECIAL EDITION

To Chasidy.
If you liked the back you ought to get a huge kick out of the front.
Thank you for all your help and encouragement.

CHAPTER ONE

FIVE YEARS *Ago*

The Navy SEALs trained you to within an inch of your life. Harrison "Sarge" McEwan knew that first hand.

Almost everyone had heard of the twenty-four-week BUD/S—Basic Underwater Demolition and SEAL—training and the infamous Hell Week SEAL candidates went through to weed out anyone who couldn't hack it.

But that was really only the beginning.

You still had months of training ahead of you before you officially earned your Trident: training in combat diving, land warfare, weapons, maritime operations, small unit tactics, demolitions, cold weather survival, parachute operations, and medical skills.

Only after that, oh yeah, and another full year of making sure you had all that information locked tightly in your head —training until all of it became muscle memory—did you become a SEAL.

Sarge had been in the Navy for the past seventeen years and a SEAL the past eleven. There wasn't much someone could throw at him that he hadn't been trained to handle.

But that day's circumstances were one of those things.

Standing down.

Any trained soldier, anyone with a warrior mind-set, would tell you that the most difficult missions weren't necessarily the ones where you looked death in the eye. The hardest ones were where you geared yourself up to do whatever needed to be done only for the mission to be canceled at the last minute.

That's what had happened to his team today there in the middle of the Czech Republic.

They'd been seconds away from infiltrating a building—fully armed, prepared to kill—when they'd been told to stop. The hostage situation had been resolved through more diplomatic means.

They'd immediately backed out silently, no one aware they'd been there, especially since they weren't officially supposed to be in the area at all. No lives lost, but the sudden reverse had left a shit-ton of adrenaline pumping through their systems.

After they'd debriefed, Sarge and his team had been given some downtime to make up for the powers-that-be jerking their chains. Most of the guys had hit the bars. The liquor was cheap in Eastern Europe, and so were the women. They would spend their time drinking and fucking the frustration out of their systems.

Normally, he'd join the guys at the bar if only to babysit more than anything else. He was older than the majority of the team. Less rowdy. He made sure no one went too far off the deep end.

But today, he needed to be away from people, a chance to get out of his own head. No one was surprised by him going off on his own. Sarge wasn't exactly a people person.

They were in Prague, the canceled mission having been about a hundred miles south of there. The Navy had sent him all over the world, but that was a new location for him. He spent a few hours walking around the tourist trap areas of the city, then as the sun set, he found himself off the beaten path. The buildings weren't quite as clean there, the electricity a little more sketchy.

Another good thing about being a Navy SEAL was your training gave you confidence to go where most tourists wouldn't want to venture. He was pretty far from Pražský hrad—Prague's famous castle—or the Charles Bridge, another favorite of travelers.

And while he wasn't worried about handling any trouble if it came his way, he wasn't trying to attract it either. He kept his head down so it looked as if his eyes were on the ground, although he still took in everything going on around him.

And that was when Sarge saw her.

A girl, she had to be a teenager, sitting on the lowest windowsill of an old house, reading a ratty paperback as night fell on the city. The book was falling apart in her hands, kept together only by her grasp on it. He would have walked by without giving her much thought if it weren't for that book.

He wondered what she was reading the way only someone who loved books could do. He didn't see a lot of young people reading paperbacks anymore—which made him feel so fucking old—they tended to be too plugged into electronic devices. So seeing her gave him a little hope that he wasn't completely over the hill yet.

He had barely passed by on the other side of the street when he heard her cry out. He spun out of instinct to find two men had joined her—one older, one younger. One of them had thrown her to the ground from her perch.

She got back up, pieces of paperback clutched in her hands, and said something to the men he couldn't hear. The younger guy, maybe in his mid-twenties, backhanded her.

All the adrenaline he had spent the past few hours attempting to get rid of came rushing back as her face jerked to the side.

This was not his problem, not his business. He knew that going over to help her could make the situation worse in the long run.

He had learned that growing up on their farm in Iowa when he'd found a butterfly attempting to make it out of its chrysalis. It had been struggling so hard he'd decided to help it, and cut the outer shell just a little with his pocketknife.

But in the end, his help meant the butterfly didn't develop the muscles needed to survive once it was out. The butterfly had died because its wings were too weak to fly.

Helping this girl now might save her from a beating, but could very likely cause bigger problems for her now or in the future, which was the last thing Sarge wanted to do.

But when the young man hit her again and she fell to the ground, paperback flying, his legs started moving on their own, walking toward the trouble. He could take out both men, permanently, but that would cause more problems also —international problems.

Sarge knew the second they saw him. All three of them froze.

It was his size. He knew how to downplay both his status as an American and his size at six foot three and two hundred twenty pounds of muscle. But right now, he wasn't trying to downplay anything.

By the time he crossed the street, the two men had turned and walked away, the young one giving the girl one last glare. He stopped before he reached her, watching as she got off the ground and picked up the pieces of her book.

Her eyes, the clearest fucking blue he'd ever seen, met his. Her brown hair fell around her shoulder as she wiped a little bit of blood from the corner of her mouth.

He didn't say anything. He doubted she spoke English. He just nodded and then turned back the way he'd come, hoping he hadn't made her life worse.

"Thank you."

He could have sworn he heard the words as he turned away, but he didn't look back. It was better for her if he left her completely alone.

He forced himself to walk back toward the touristy part of town and grab a bite to eat. That was better than the plan he wanted to pursue—tracking down those assholes and teaching them what it was like to get a hit by someone bigger than them.

Not his problem. He had to say it almost as a mantra as he walked.

He nursed a watered-down beer as he read his own paperback at an outdoor table facing the Charles Bridge a couple hours later when he blinked and did a double take.

It was the girl again.

She looked different. Her brown hair was pulled to the side over her face, covering those distinctive blue eyes. Her makeup and posture were different too— she was making sure not to draw attention to herself.

Sarge took a sip of beer and watched.

She almost seemed to be lost, walking a little bit in one direction, then turning in the other, not making eye contact with anyone or trying to interact with them. But when she passed by one couple a little too closely, he realized what she was doing.

She was pickpocketing them. He chuckled to himself.

He watched over the next hour, switching from beer to coffee, as she found three different marks. There was no better place to find tourists not paying attention and caught up in the romance of the Vltava River than there.

And she was good at what she did. Small, quick, unmemorable...as long as she kept those blue eyes downcast.

Then he showed up—the younger asshole from earlier. He waited in the near darkness of one corner of the bridge. As soon as the girl saw him, she ran her earnings over to him.

By the look on his face, it wasn't enough. He grabbed her

arm with enough force to leave bruises, jerked her closer, and whispered something. She nodded and pulled away quickly.

Whatever he'd said put her into a near-panic. Twice in the next twenty minutes, she tried to lift another wallet but was almost caught. Her movements were too jerky. Plus, it was getting later, the shops were closing, and people were more scarce and naturally more suspicious.

Sarge kept his head down and his book in front of him so it didn't look like he was watching as the guy signaled for her to come back over to him. An overweight, balding man stood next to him.

He knew by her hesitant steps and the sly smile he gave the overweight guy, that the asshole had just become the girl's pimp for the night.

God fucking damn it.

Once again, he told himself not to go over there—literally or figuratively. This was a situation he couldn't do anything about in the very limited time he had in Prague. But still, he found himself paying for his meal, ready to move.

The girl wasn't interested in spending time with the fat man; that was obvious. It was also obvious that she wasn't going to have a choice in the situation.

Sarge scrubbed a hand down his face as Asshole pushed her closer to the fat man. She didn't pull away, but she hunched her shoulders like she was hoping she could disappear into the medieval-aged bricks.

Once again, he found himself rushing somewhere he had no business going.

Asshole saw Sarge first, his eyes narrowing. This time, he wasn't going to walk away.

"This has nothing to do with you," he said in surprisingly good English when Sarge got within earshot. "Go back to your business."

The girl's head flew up at his words, those striking eyes growing wide as she saw him. But then she went right back into her hunch, not pulling away from the fat man now holding her arm.

"How much for her for the whole night?" He didn't know any other way of getting her away from there without this ending in a beating for her.

That fucker who'd hit her earlier smirked. "Five hundred."

Sarge kept his cool. "We both know that's not going to happen." Not that he wouldn't have paid five hundred to get her out of this situation, but he knew that would only cause more trouble in the long run. "I'll give you a hundred."

He crossed his arms over his scrawny chest. "For a hundred, you take her back behind the alley, and she'll make you very happy."

"Nikolai," the girl gasped, face flying up again, despair blanketing her features. This obviously wasn't usual business for her.

Sarge wanted to beat Nikolai into the ground.

He smirked. "How about for one hundred and fifty, you both can split her. $75 for each. Yeah? She can take it."

The fat man licked his lips as the girl blanched, breathing so rapidly he thought she might pass out. Fat guy obviously spoke English, looking excited because he was getting a bargain.

He was done with this shit.

He crossed his arms over his own chest, mimicking Nikolai's posture, but he had at least fifty pounds of muscle on him. "How about I pay you one hundred and fifty, I get her the whole night in my hotel room, and I don't beat the shit out of you?" He looked over at the fat man. "Out of either of you. My final offer."

The fat man turned and left. Good. Fucking pervert.

Nikolai didn't like his solution. He obviously wanted the girl to be as humiliated as possible.

"What are you going to do with her all night?

"That's between her and me." Sarge grabbed the cash out of his wallet and slammed it against his chest. "Don't look for her again until the morning."

Nikolai folded the money slowly. "You like my feisty girl? Fine, you have her all night. But I'll escort you to the hotel to make sure you get there safely."

So much for his plan of sending her on her way as soon as Nikolai was gone. He wanted to beat this little shit until he dragged his ass home crying for his mama.

"Fine by me," Sarge said.

The girl was silent, all but dragged her feet as they walked the few blocks to his hotel. She sure as hell didn't look very feisty right now. There wasn't anything he could say to reassure her, so he didn't try.

Nikolai had the nerve to walk them all the way to the door of the lobby. "I'll see you in the morning, Bronya. I'm sure you'll have a big tip from your American. Be safe, sister."

Bronya.

Sarge didn't know whether to hope that she was really his sister or not. If she was, maybe she wouldn't be subject to any of Nikolai's own advances. But if he was selling his own sister against her will…what a clusterfuck.

They left him and went inside.

"Do you speak English?" He asked her. He spoke a couple of other languages conversationally, but he didn't necessarily want to make that information public.

"A little," she whispered with no trace of an accent.

"Will Nikolai be waiting to see if you actually go up into the room with me?"

She nodded. "He will wait here at least a couple hours. If I come out early, he will want…"

She faded off. He would want her to give him any money? Obviously. He would want her to find a second John for the night? Probably. He'd want to slap her around some more because he was a dick, and Sarge had spoiled his humiliation plans? Maybe.

He had no idea what he was going to do with her once he got her in his room.

He had absolutely no interest whatsoever in having sex with a traumatized teenager being forced into something she didn't want to do. He had zero people skills, so talking to her to make her feel comfortable wasn't going to happen either.

As usual, all he wanted was to be left alone. But that didn't seem like an option. Not tonight. Not with her.

"I know my word doesn't mean anything to you, but if I promise not to hurt you, not to touch you at all, would you agree to come up to the room with me?"

CHAPTER TWO

The big man was right-- his word didn't mean anything to Bronya.

But she followed him silently into the elevator anyway. She hadn't been lying about Nikolai waiting outside for the next couple of hours. By now, he would've called another member of his crew so that someone was watching both the hotel's front and rear exits.

If he caught her sneaking out of there before morning, she would definitely spend the rest of the night on her knees servicing anyone he could find who would pay. He'd probably offer her body for free to get back at her for turning him down last week.

His father had made it very clear that Nikolai wasn't to touch her unless she wanted it. And Gregory's word was law in their neighborhood. It had kept her out of Nikolai's bed for the past two years. She'd been sixteen when he'd noticed she had breasts and started a haphazard pursuit of her.

Until recently, making her life hell had merely been a random pastime for him. She hadn't crossed his mind often, so he hadn't made trouble for her.

But when she'd turned eighteen a few months ago, she'd publicly shunned him in front of some of his crew. It was then Nikolai had decided to put more effort into making her miserable.

Gregory had always been content with the money her pickpocketing put into his coffers. She'd been doing it since she was little, and she was quite proficient at it. Gregory had also used her for some larger burglaries from time to time.

Bronya was good. She knew how to make herself unnoticed and work it to her advantage. That skill had kept her fed and relatively safe in the seven years since her parents died.

Until Nikolai had decided he wanted her.

She should've slept with him. Pretended to be in love with him. That would've bored him and sent him running.

The moment she said no, Nikolai became obsessed. When he realized she meant her no, that decision backed up by his father's edict, he became vicious.

There had been no leeway anymore if she couldn't bring in enough through her stealing. Suddenly, she was expected to use whatever means she had available—including her body—to bring in the required amount to stay within Gregory's protection. And without Gregory's protection, Bronya wouldn't last long on the streets on her own.

She'd learned to live through it—even when Nikolai went out of his way to pick the least attractive men to sell her to— and she would live through whatever the big man walking down the hall in front of her had planned.

But no, she didn't believe him for a second when he said he wouldn't touch her. Not hurt her? Maybe. He'd seemed upset both times today when Nikolai had been exerting his power over her.

But no one spent one hundred and fifty American dollars for a woman and expected nothing in return.

She glanced at his face as he used the key to open the door. He was a lot more handsome than most of the men she was around—dark hair cut short. A strong jaw with a full day's worth of beard. But mostly, he was just big with wide shoulders—twice the width of hers.

She lowered her gaze when his brown eyes met hers, and she slowly walked into the room. It didn't matter that he didn't repulse her. She still didn't have any choice about being there.

She flinched at the click of the door closing. She was at his mercy. No one was going to help her, not even if she screamed. She'd never been sold to someone for a full night.

Bronya knew what a man could want when he only had fifteen minutes. The thought of the things that could happen when he had a full night… she grabbed the strap of her rucksack across her shoulder, rubbing it between her fingers. Maybe she could use it to…

Then she let it go, dropping her hands to her sides. The bag wouldn't offer much protection against him even if she swung it as hard as she could. All it would do was make him mad, and then she'd still be at his mercy.

With every second he didn't say anything, terror spread further throughout her body. She stood in the corner of the room, afraid to look at him, afraid to run, almost afraid to breathe.

The room was plain but clean. The big bed took up most of it except for a dresser and a small refrigerator. Her gaze dropped to the floor, and she saw his booted feet walk by then heard the creak of the bed as he sat down.

He still didn't say a word, but she knew what sitting at the edge of the bed meant—what he wanted. Maybe he would still keep his promise and not touch her, but it looked as if she would be touching him.

There was no point postponing the inevitable. She swallowed and walked toward him, dropping down on her knees between his feet, reaching for the buckle of his pants.

"Wait, what? No." He stood up so fast she fell backward, blinking up at him.

"That's not what I want," he continued. "There wasn't anywhere else for me to sit, so…"

He was so much bigger standing over her with her lying on the ground, so she scrambled to get back on her feet. "You want me in the bed?"

He rubbed a hand down his face. "I would like for you to sit on the bed, and I will sit on the other side. So we can talk."

Bronya stared at the giant bed then looked back at him. "Talk?"

"Yes, talk."

She sat down on the corner of the bed and looked at him, hoping this was what he wanted, afraid that at any moment, the rather polite American would disappear and a monster would take his place.

He sat down on the opposite side and held out a hand as if to make sure she didn't come over and kneel in front of him again. She wasn't going to do that unless he told her to.

"Your name is Bronya?" he asked. She nodded. "Do you have a last name, a family name?"

"Roch," she responded, surprised enough by the question to tell him the truth.

He nodded. "How old are you?"

She swallowed the bitter ball of despair. That was what the questions were about. The big man didn't want to have sex with a child. She thought about lying, telling him she was younger than she was. Maybe that would save her from his plans.

But all that would accomplish was getting her sent back downstairs to Nikolai. "I'm eighteen."

"Really?"

"Yes. Truly." She closed her eyes, back stiff, ready for a command, for her to resume what she'd started on her knees.

Or maybe he wouldn't speak. Maybe he would snap and

point to himself like Nikolai had to the woman he'd forced to suck him off in front of her and his friends.

But the man didn't move. Once again, he didn't say anything at all.

So she sat there, watching him out of the corner of her eye, without looking like she was watching him.

"How do you speak English so well?" he finally asked.

Bronya wasn't sure why he cared, but the longer he talked, the less time they had for…other things.

"My parents spoke English," she whispered. They'd spoken English almost exclusively for the first few years of her life.

"Spoke? Past tense?"

She nodded. "Yes, they died."

"How long ago?"

"I was almost eleven."

He reached up and rubbed the back of his neck. "You've been…working on the streets since you were eleven?"

She shook her head quickly. "No, not like this. Not…" She waved her arm around her. "Not with men. That has just been in the past few months."

She glanced over at him. He nodded, relief evident in his brown eyes. "You pickpocket."

"Yes. Usually. Only the other"—Bronya waved her arm toward the bed again— "when Nikolai makes me."

His eyes narrowed, and he fell silent again. It still made her nervous. Should she try to say something?

"How did your parents die?" The question came suddenly.

"A car accident." She didn't know why he was asking, and she didn't know why she was telling him the truth, but somehow, she wanted to. "We moved to Czech Republic from Ukraine. My parents were professor and student, but after the civil unrest, we couldn't stay. And there weren't many jobs for a university professor of American literature."

"Your father was a college literature professor and your mother his student?"

She shook her head. "No, Mother was the professor. Father was her student."

For the first time, the man smiled.

"That goes against type. I like it."

She wasn't sure what that meant, so she just nodded.

"Their love of American literature explains a lot about you—your excellent English, and probably the fact that I saw you reading earlier today. Do you have the book you were reading in your bag?"

Bronya swallowed. "No, I don't have it with me." She didn't want him to take it. She'd rather he take her body than her books.

His eyes narrowed. "You're lying. You need to be better at lying if you're going to survive."

He stood up, and fear shut down everything inside her. Now she would get a beating as well as being forced to do whatever he wanted.

"I'm sorry," she whispered.

She flinched as he walked past her, but he didn't stop, didn't grab her, didn't pull her by her hair. Instead, he walked over to the fridge in the corner of the room and opened it. He took out a bottle of water and handed it to her.

"Don't be sorry. Be better at lying." She still waited for the blow, but nothing came. "Drink it." A moment later, a chocolate bar fell in her lap. "And eat that."

She tore open the wrapper immediately. It might end up costing her later, but she didn't care. When was the last time she'd had something like candy? She only got treats like that if she stole them, and usually, they weren't worth the risk.

Bronya had barely finished the last bite when a package of peanuts dropped next to her leg. "Eat that too."

She wasn't going to argue. She hadn't eaten anything since this morning, and the money she would normally set aside to buy food she had given to Nikolai in hopes that she wouldn't be in the position she was currently in.

The man took his seat back on the other side of the bed, and she relaxed a little bit.

"The book you were reading earlier, was it in English?"

She nodded, taking another handful of the nuts.

"I like to read too. Will you tell me what book it is? Maybe I've heard of it. I promise I'm not going to take your book. Let me guess. It was one you got from your parents?"

She slowly lowered her arm and looked over at him. He was the only one who had ever figured out why her book was so precious to her even though it was falling apart.

"Yes. My parents brought their favorite book when we had to flee Ukraine. But the book is for children. Teenagers. That is what Mother taught—adolescent literature. Not books a man would read."

"Try me."

"It is called *The Outsiders*."

He smiled.

Everything about his face changed when he smiled. He was still dangerous and big—someone who could hurt her just because he wanted to, but he looked almost kind when he smiled.

"Stay gold, Ponyboy."

Her eyes grew big. "You know it."

"Of course. S.E. Hinton. It was one of my favorites growing up. I read it in high school, but I read it again a couple of years ago. I've seen the movie too."

She gave him a slight smile. "I read other books. Sometimes people leave them, and I find them and read them, but I always come back to that one as my favorite."

"It's a good one to have as a favorite, Pony Girl."

The corners of her mouth pulled up in a smile, although she didn't let him see it. She'd never been called a nickname before, unless you counted what Nikolai and his men called all women they didn't like. Pony Girl was much better.

He pointed to the food in her lap. "Finish eating. I don't think this hotel has room service and it sure as hell doesn't have Uber Eats, but I can try to have some food delivered if you want. I have some friends who wouldn't mind dropping something by."

Bronya shook her head quickly. The last thing she wanted was his friends joining them. "I'm fine. Thank you."

He nodded. "Then we'll clear out the mini bar. Whatever you don't want tonight, you can take with you in the morning."

She looked over at the small bags of food on the refrigerator. She would gladly take them with her. That would be meals for a couple of days.

"My name is Harrison McEwan, but people call me Sarge. They've called me that as long as I can remember."

Because he seemed to expect it, she repeated after him. "Sarge."

Sarge got up and walked to the other side of the room, folding his arms over his chest and leaning against the wall.

"Let's call this situation what it is, since you seem to be pretty level-headed. We can both agree that I'm bigger and stronger than you, and you don't have anyone coming to help you if I decide to do something to you that you don't want."

She swallowed, her throat dry, but nodded. That was exactly the situation. She'd known it from the first minute.

"And because I can do whatever I want, it's not going to do you any good to resist, is it?"

The food he'd given her soured in her stomach. This was it. This was what Bronya should have been expecting from the beginning, but she'd let herself think the circumstances were different because they'd been talking about books and he'd smiled.

She was an idiot. He was reminding her. She nodded again.

"What I want you to do is to go into the bathroom and take a shower. As long and as hot as you want. I'm not going to come in there. Nobody's going to come in there, but there's nothing I can say to make you believe that right now. The only thing I can do is prove it to you."

Again, she'd be an idiot to believe him.

"And then once you come back out here, with all your clothes on, you are going to sleep in the bed. I'm going to sleep on the floor. And you're going to get a few hours of rest without having to worry about anybody touching you or hurting you in any way. Do you understand?"

Bronya nodded again. She understood what he was saying, but she had no idea if he was telling her the truth.

He rubbed a hand along the stubble on his jaw. "You don't trust me. I get it. But it doesn't matter if you trust me, right? Because I'm going to do what I want to do, and you can't change that. Only accept it."

"Yes," She choked out.

He crossed his arms again. "Then at dawn, you're going to leave here. I won't need to leave until two hours later. You're going to rip your shirt and make sure your hair is a mess. You're going to go back to that bastard Nikolai, and you're going to cry and lie better than you lied to me and tell him that I was horrible. That I hurt you. That I was the worst thing that had ever happened to you."

His eyes narrowed. "Because that's the only way someone like Nikolai is going to be satisfied with what happened here —if he thinks that whatever I did to you was worse than whatever he would have done had he kept you tonight."

"Yes," she said again. The big man—Sarge—was right. That was the only way Nikolai would be satisfied.

"Good. Then we have a plan."

The rest of the night went exactly as he said it would. She

took a shower, enjoying the wonderful pressure and unlimited hot water, although her eyes were glued to the door the entire time.

But he never came in.

Bronya got dressed afterward and went back into the room. She found Sarge lying on the floor, the corner of the covers pulled back on the bed so she could get in. So she did. She didn't sleep much, still not completely able to trust him, but he never moved from his place on the floor.

And at dawn, she did what he said…tore her own shirt, and went crying to Nikolai, telling him how horrible the American had been as the weight of the food he'd given her pulled on her rucksack and slid in around the book he hadn't taken from her.

Nikolai asked if he'd given her a tip, and she'd said no. She expected Nikolai to search her, prepared to lie about stealing the food, but he didn't. He nodded. He asked her if Sarge wanted her again the next night, but she told Nikolai no. That Sarge was leaving at eight that morning.

That was her mistake.

At eight o'clock, Nikolai and his crew dragged her back to the hotel. Nikolai kept a hard grip on her arm, making her watch as his men forced Sarge into a back alley when he came out of the hotel.

Sarge's brown eyes met hers as Nikolai walked up to him as his men held him. Sarge wasn't even putting up a fight.

"Bronya says you didn't tip her. It wasn't very nice not to tip my feisty girl."

She couldn't say anything, couldn't do anything, as Nikolai's five men beat Sarge and didn't stop until he lay on the ground barely conscious.

Nikolai reached into Sarge's pocket and took his wallet. He grabbed the cash and dropped the rest by Sarge's bleeding face.

He walked back and handed her a twenty-dollar bill. "Your tip. Sounds like you earned it."

They walked away, but her feet felt glued to the ground as she stared at the wounded man who'd been nothing but kind to her.

Nikolai snapped his fingers and spoke in Czech. "Bronya. You did good, but let's go. Leave the American trash."

She saw one of Sarge's eyes flutter open, but she didn't have any choice. All he would see was her walking away.

CHAPTER THREE

TWO YEARS *Ago*

Sarge touched the small scar that ran along his left eyebrow as he crossed the Charles Bridge. He hadn't returned to Prague for three years. He wasn't sure what he was doing back there now.

That wasn't true; he knew why he was there. He had just finished an operation for the security company he now worked for, Zodiac Tactical. His new boss and former SEAL teammate, Ian DeRose, had sent him to head up a kidnap and rescue mission, ironically not far from the village where their SEAL team had been told to stand down in a similar situation three years ago.

The day he'd met Bronya.

This time, there had been no standing down, no resolution via diplomatic measures. This mission, like most Zodiac Tactical handled, didn't involve governments or military. Sarge and his team had been sent in to ensure the recovery and safety of a billionaire's kidnapped nine-year-old son.

Everything had gone according to plan if you didn't count the two dead bad guys. The kid had been reunited with his parents. No one on his team had been hurt.

Those were the types of missions they handled as part of the company Ian had started last year. He'd been with him from the beginning and was part of his inner circle. Sarge loved the work they did.

He'd always thought he'd be a lifer in the Navy, but fucking up his knee during a routine training exercise had ended his special forces career. It wasn't so bad that it affected him too much in everyday life, but it was enough that he couldn't be a SEAL anymore. Deciding not to re-up hadn't been hard. He'd been in twenty years, so he got out.

Zodiac Tactical had given him a job and a purpose. Ian trusted him to handle things for him—things like this mission —and he did. He liked being part of a team that got things done when normal routes or law enforcement couldn't.

In short, Zodiac Tactical kicked ass.

And while Sarge had participated in a number of Zodiac missions in the past year, Ian had also sent him on this one because he knew about Sarge's obsession with Prague, although he didn't know why.

Ian thought it was because of the beating Sarge had taken three years ago, the one that had given him the scar at the edge of his eyebrow. He thought he still had unfinished business there.

He touched the scar again, faded to the point where it could hardly be seen. He did still have unfinished business there, although not revenge on some thugs like Ian thought.

He had thought about his business there every day for the past three years. Had read *The Outsiders* way more times than any grown man should, and he wondered what other books her parents had taught her about.

To Kill a Mockingbird? Little Women? The Lion, the Witch and the Wardrobe?

He'd read them all. A grown-ass man reading *Are You There God? It's Me, Margaret* probably seemed strange to damned near everyone. There'd definitely been too much adolescent literature in his life these past three years, that was for sure.

Especially since after what had happened, Sarge could only be called a fool for thinking of her at all. Or the damned books she loved so much.

Definitely a fool after she'd led Nikolai and his buddies right to him that morning. A fool for taking a beating he had the training and skill to stop because she would've been the one to pay the price.

And looking for her now in every possible person who could be her size? That made him a complete dumbass.

Yet, here he was.

Sarge spotted her near sundown, still casing potential marks like she had been three years ago. Her hair was a little longer, pulled back into an inconspicuous braid, wisps hanging out to hide her face and those striking eyes. She was dressed like everyone around her—jeans, lightweight dark jacket, shoes that allowed her to move quickly.

He had no doubt if she was caught and had to run she'd shed the jacket and let down her hair, giving herself a different appearance in a few mere seconds.

She would run from him when she eventually saw him. She had too much self-preservation, too much intelligence, not to. Not that it would make any difference.

He'd still catch her.

He watched her for two solid hours. She wasn't the only one who knew how to blend in and make themselves less noticeable.

She'd gotten better at pickpocketing, and she'd already been good when he'd studied her before. She chose her marks well, kept her body relaxed and nonthreatening, and used her petite stature to her advantage.

Nobody ever suspected a thing. She knew exactly when to crouch down to tie her shoe to keep out of a line of sight.

Knew what people to bypass and what people to concentrate on.

Properly trained and off the street, she could be a huge asset for a business like Zodiac Tactical. Some of what their company handled needed someone with a deft touch who could disappear into a crowd. And they had an office in Paris.

Offering a beautiful thief a job was not why Sarge was there.

Why the fuck was he there?

He was about to turn away, about to walk away from Bronya for good, when she made a face from where she was standing at the edge of the bridge and pressed a hand to her side.

She was hurt.

He watched her now, mindful of that, and could see the slightest stiffness in her posture when she was resting. She ignored it when casing a mark, but he could tell she was in pain.

He was so intent on studying her, figuring out how badly she'd been hurt that he forgot to make sure she didn't notice him. He knew the exact second she did.

She'd turned to follow a well-off couple so wrapped up in each other that they would never notice her, then froze as she spotted him, letting a prime mark get away. Her eyes narrowed, then grew large as she recognized him. Then she turned, smart enough not to run, but knowing she needed to get out of there.

He'd been watching her long enough to know which way she'd be going and turned the opposite direction so he could double back to cut her off. She would look behind her and think she'd lost him.

Using his long legs to his advantage, Sarge walked quickly along the side of the bridge, careful not to draw undue attention to himself. He ducked into an alley—the same alley where Nikolai had offered to sell him Bronya. Once he was in the dimness, he ran, getting to the other end moments before she did.

She'd already ditched her jacket and let down her hair like he'd expected. She was looking over her other shoulder, in the direction from which he should've been coming, when he grabbed her arm and pulled her into the alley, trapping her between the wall and his body.

"Hello, Bronya."

Those striking baby blues blinked up at him. "What? How...?"

"You need to vary your routine more. I've been watching you the past couple hours. This is where you go when you want a break."

"I'll scream."

"Will you?" Sarge kept his arms on either side of her, pinning her in, but didn't press up against her. He didn't know how bad her injuries were. "Do you want to bring the police here? Have them take us both in for statements? Make sure they know what you look like?"

Her mouth popped shut. They both knew she wasn't going to scream.

"How badly are you hurt?" He asked her. "I saw you flinch at certain movements."

She turned her face away. "I'm not hurt."

"I see you still haven't gotten much better at lying."

She glared up at him. "I'm not hurt enough for it to be any of your business."

That fire in her eyes sent him shifting back a little even though he wanted to press closer. It was way too alluring for someone who was a decade and a half younger than him. She may not be a teenager anymore, but that didn't mean he was going to be one of the men who used her.

"But you're hurt enough for it to bother you. What happened?"

She shrugged. "I was running and needed to jump over a banister. I hit it wrong and bruised my ribs."

He wanted to ask for more info. Who had she been running from? Police? Nikolai?

He wanted to ask if her life had gotten any better since he'd seen her last. She looked okay. Intelligence and wariness simmered in her eyes, not defeat or blankness. But she was obviously still in a shitty situation.

"What do you want, Sarge?"

She remembered his name. Why the fuck that mattered to him, he had no idea. But it did.

"I want a repeat of three years ago."

He didn't know who was more surprised by his words, him or her. They definitely hadn't been what he expected to say.

"Minus the part where you bring your boss and his goons to kick the shit out of me," He added.

She stiffened. "Do you want revenge? To beat them? To beat me?"

The hell of it all was that she looked prepared to take the beating if that's what she had to do. Maybe that was part of her life now.

"What if I told you that I could have stopped what Nikolai's men did? That I was trained to do exactly that, even at five-to-one odds?"

"Then why didn't you?"

He eased a little forward. "Because I knew who he was going to take it out on if I fought back. I have a couple of brothers who I scuffled with all the time growing up. I know how to take a beating." Much better than someone of her size would.

"Why would you do that for me?" she whispered.

That was the question, wasn't it? Sarge didn't have an answer.

"Where I come from, men protect women," I finally said.

"My father always protected my mother, my brothers protect those who need it too."

She looked down then back up at him. "I didn't lead Nikolai to you that day. He tricked me. But I'm sorry. I should've done more to stop it."

"No harm done."

She reached up and touched the small scar above his eyebrow. "Some harm done."

He stepped back farther at the touch of her fingers on his face. Damn it, why was she affecting him so much more today? For three years, he'd thought about her, and not one bit of it had been sexual.

But now...everything about her was affecting him differently.

Sex wasn't why he was there. But at least now he was figuring out what had brought him to this particular area of Prague. His subconscious had known all along.

He dropped his arms from either side of her, a little surprised when she didn't bolt immediately.

"Will Nikolai be coming by for his daily take soon?"

She shook her head. "Probably not him, but someone, yes."

"Do you have enough?" The thought of someone forcing her to sell her body again sent rage coursing through him.

"Yes."

"Do you want to make more? Like I said, I'd like a repeat of three years ago. I'll pay one hundred fifty dollars if you come up to my room for the whole night, and I promise not to touch you."

"Why?" she whispered, still right in front of him as if his arms still had her caged. "Last time, you were trying to save me from Nikolai. Why this time?"

"I want to offer you a job."

CHAPTER
FOUR

Sarge was in trouble, and Bronwyn was finally going to have the chance to rescue him for once. She didn't think this day would ever come.

Not that a Paris bar with two women hitting on him was much of a dangerous situation. Still, he looked…panicked. Which was pretty hilarious, given that the bar where they'd all gotten together held at least a dozen Zodiac Tactical employees. All trained to handle multiple sorts of dangerous situations with deadly force.

So was Sarge himself.

Sarge was quite safe, not that you could tell by the look on his face as the two women, both with American accents, fawned all over him.

She hadn't known he was going to show up today at the Paris Zodiac office. He hadn't visited once in the entire year she'd been working there. Ian DeRose, the owner of Zodiac, had been around a few times, plus a number of people high up in the company. But not Sarge.

She hadn't known what to expect when she'd finally made it to Paris six months after Sarge found her in Prague for the second time. She'd walked into a nice office on the outskirts of the city, the card he'd given her clutched in her bloody hand. She'd handed it to the lady sitting at the desk and expected to be laughed at and turned away. Instead, she'd asked her to wait while she punched the code written on the card into her computer.

Within a few minutes, she'd been shown into the back, then subsequently hired, fed, clothed, and trained.

Bronya Roch had died. Bronwyn Rourke had been born.

She watched Sarge now as he smiled awkwardly when one of the women slid a little closer, laughing at something he said that couldn't possibly be that funny. He turned to face the bar, and both women turned with him.

He had no idea what she'd done, the risk she had taken by trusting him. She could never return to Prague. Ever. She'd die a horrible death as soon as Nikolai got word she was back. And he would. He would look for her forever.

But he wouldn't find her. She became more confident of that each day that passed. Became more confident in herself with each day of training Zodiac provided.

She would never be under Nikolai's control again.

Granted, she had spent the first few months in Paris looking over her shoulder every second, even knowing that Nikolai and Gregory didn't have ties there.

If the job with Zodiac hadn't existed, if Sarge had been tricking her, she wouldn't have made it. She knew that without a doubt. She owed Sarge everything she had become in the past year.

This life where she lived with the freedom to answer only to herself, never forced to do things she didn't want to do? She owed that to him.

And she guessed she could start her repayment with his rescue.

From two beautiful women.

The woman on the left side of him touched his wrist, and

she narrowed her eyes as she picked up speed, crossing toward them from her table near the door.

Bronwyn didn't like to see any other woman touching Sarge, which was ridiculous, of course. Their relationship wasn't like that. Their relationship didn't exist at all.

He'd always been handsome to her. Even when she was eighteen and terrified, she'd been able to recognize the good looks of his dark hair, strong jaw, and deep eyes. Meeting him again at twenty-one, she'd been even more aware of his appeal. And now, at almost twenty-three and no longer living in constant survival mode, she could see what was obvious to the two American women flanking him.

Even with his back turned to her, she knew his eyes were the shade of melted honey, clear with intelligence. His big body was formidable—long legs, broad shoulders—but not something he used to make others feel smaller unless he deliberately decided to. The stubble on his jaw did nothing to hide his handsome features. If anything, it accentuated them.

But that handsomeness was rugged, honed, like the man himself. There was nothing pretty about him.

Given that he had paid for two full nights with her in a hotel, Sarge had never shown any sort of physical interest in her whatsoever. But she still didn't like that woman's fingers on his arm.

Her training at Zodiac Tactical had taught her multiple ways she could break her hand, multiple ways that she could do much worse than merely break a bone. She'd actually excelled at it over the past few months. It ended up that her dexterity when it came to picking pockets also translated into close-quarter fighting. She now knew multiple ways to take down men twice her size.

Too bad she couldn't use it to take out these women.

She walked up behind Sarge and placed a possessive hand on his shoulder. She had to remind herself that this was an act as she felt the firm muscles under her fingers. "Sweetheart, I leave you alone for a few minutes and you make all sorts of… friends."

Insecurity hit her as he spun in her direction. Did he want to be rescued? Worse, did he remember her? So much about her had changed since he'd seen her eighteen months ago, including her name.

But all that melted away when he gave her a smile. A real smile.

"Hey, Pony Girl."

That nickname combined with his deep voice did something to her insides that she wasn't sure she'd ever feel. The women on either side of him who'd also turned around, scoffed.

"Pony Girl? What kind of nickname is that?" the laughing one asked.

"Must be because she looks like a horse," the one now closer to receiving a broken hand replied. They both giggled.

Bronwyn looked them over. They were everything she was never going to be. Feminine with ample breasts almost falling out of their tops, makeup skillfully applied to draw attention to their best features.

She'd lived my entire life trying to ensure she didn't draw the attention of others. She wouldn't know how to draw attention if she tried. And no amount of makeup was going to give her their figures.

But Sarge wasn't responding to them at all. He was only looking at her. Waiting to see what she would do.

So she said the first thing that came to mind. "Do you want to dance?"

"With you? Absolutely."

The women sulked as he set his beer down and didn't say another word to them, taking Bronwyn's hand and leading her out to the dance floor.

The area wasn't very big, and a number of couples were

already on it. The song playing was an upbeat pop song that she'd heard before but had no idea how to dance to.

What had she been thinking? She could feel the women staring at them as she glanced over at the dancing couples, hoping she could copy some of their moves. That's what she had done my whole life—mimic others.

But she had no experience dancing whatsoever. Sarge might decide he was better off with the bimbos at the bar when he saw her try. They'd know how to dance.

She'd only made one small awkward swing of her hips when his arm came around her waist, and he pulled her up against his body, his other hand reaching out and grabbing hers.

"Slow is the only way I know how to dance, so it'll have to do." They began an unhurried sway that somehow worked with the song's upbeat tempo.

One of his hands cupped hers, and her other landed on his shoulder. Her nose barely came up to the middle of his chest, and she found herself wanting to burrow in against him.

But, of course, that would make things a lot more awkward.

"Yeah, this is good," she said. "I'm not much of a dancer."

"Thanks for the assist with the double trouble over there. I wasn't sure if I was supposed to pick one or if they were going to double-team me."

She couldn't help but laugh a little. "I think most guys would consider both acceptable alternatives."

"Maybe. But those women aren't my type. I don't do casual sex."

Neither did she, although probably for very different reasons.

He swayed them back and forth. She could feel his big hand on her waist. "I didn't know you were in Paris until I saw you as everyone was leaving the Zodiac facility this afternoon."

"I came in yesterday. I watched you doing some training, but I wasn't sure if you would want to talk to me. Bronwyn."

She grimaced. "Yeah. I changed my name when I first got here. Thought it might be a little bit more common than Bronya. And Roch got changed to Rourke."

To my surprise, he nodded. "Those are both good choices. With your lack of an accent, the name won't label you as Eastern European."

She looked up at him. "You're not mad at me for lying to the place where you got me the job?"

They kept swaying. "All I did was approve the employment code that got you in the door. You making your way up the chain and proving your skills are valuable and that you could handle it? That was all on you."

Bronwyn forced herself not to focus on his fingers making small circles on her waist. "I never really understood how that code worked. I wasn't sure that the job was real until I got to the Paris office."

He shrugged. "All the core team members of Zodiac Tactical have a code that we can give contacts, people who might be useful to the company on a contractor or employment basis. So we're all able to connect people to the business if we feel it's appropriate."

After a year with Zodiac, understanding how the company worked, the business they did, she could understand the policy. More than one person she worked with there in Paris had been recruited by a core member.

On paper, Zodiac Tactical was labeled security contractors, a private military company. It had been started by billionaire Ian DeRose three years ago, and thanks to his own military background and the team he'd surrounded himself with—people like Sarge—it had grown into one of the largest and most respected security organizations.

Zodiac did a little bit of everything: risk consulting, intelligence gathering, private and corporate guarding, international hostage negotiation and rescue. But not just for the rich who could afford it. Zodiac helped those in need whether they could pay or not.

And she was part of this organization. It meant everything to her.

"Thank you," she whispered up at Sarge. "Thank you for giving me a chance."

"Thank you for rescuing me tonight. I'm not good with people, even ones like them." He nodded his head toward the two women who were still glaring at them. "Especially ones like them."

"If they bother you any more, I can take them out in the parking lot and teach them a lesson. I've got the training for it now."

He smiled, and little dimples appeared on either side of his jaw that she wanted to reach up and touch. "I've heard you've become one of the most skilled full-time employees we have in this office. And I saw you sparring. It was pretty damn impressive, and I already knew how quick you were."

Her fingers smoothed out the material of his shirt on his shoulder. "It ends up what I knew about fighting was wrong. I thought the strongest and biggest person would always win. But that's not the case."

"No, it's not," he said. "The smartest person wins the fight. You use what you have to your advantage. And you have a lot of advantages."

His words sent a heat through her. He admired her. It was almost inconceivable. "I haven't had to use any of those skills on a mission yet."

Bronwyn wished she'd had them when she'd lived in Prague. It would've made my life a lot easier.

"Good," he said, "I hope you never have to."

"It turns out I like stealing from bad guys." She smiled up at him. "Rather than tourists who aren't paying attention."

"Your supervisor showed me your file today. It looks like you've been doing some good work. Important work."

She was never going to be a bodyguard like many of the people on the Paris team—she didn't have the size or patience for it. But her ability to get in and out of places unnoticed and to liberate or retrieve needed items had been put to good use the past couple of months after her supervisors had made sure she was trained properly and trustworthy. She'd done her best to prove that.

The music changed, but they kept dancing. "I'm going to Marrakesh next month."

Was it her imagination or did he pull her slightly closer? "I know. I was on the conference call when the mission got approved. You be careful."

She would be breaking into the office of a museum to retrieve stolen data. It would be the first mission where she was the lead.

"So you already knew I was going? You already knew for sure I was an employee here, even with the name change?"

He nodded. "The inner team discusses all important missions. So yes. And yes, I've known you were here since that code was first entered."

"I'm surprised I haven't seen you before now. I expected to." She shrugged. "I thought you worked here."

"No. You needed a chance to make a fresh start on your own. To make your own decisions without anybody else around. I hope you've been able to do that."

She had, and it was because of him. But...she'd thought he'd be a part of the process more and been strangely disappointed when he wasn't.

"I have eight hundred dollars for you," she blurted out. It had been the first thing she'd saved and it was sitting in a drawer in her kitchen.

"Eight hundred dollars?" he said with a laugh. "What for?"

"For the two nights at one hundred and fifty dollars and for the five hundred dollars you gave me to help get me out of Prague that second night."

It hadn't been enough, and she had paid the price with blood and terror, but he didn't need to know that.

"I never expected you to pay back that money. There's no need."

"I want to," she said. "Please. I don't know how to explain it, but it's important to me."

"You don't want to be in anyone's debt again."

Relief flowed through her. He understood. "Yes."

"Then yes, I'll accept it."

They danced the same way through a couple more songs, and soon the Zodiac team members were all heading home after enjoying an evening together. Sarge and Bronwyn found themselves outside in the cool Paris night air.

"Can I walk you home?" he asked.

She wanted him to walk her home. She wanted to show him the tiny flat she lived in. She wanted to show him all the books she had on her shelves and her own kitchen with dishes and even her own bathroom. She wanted Sarge to see what her life had become.

And...she wanted him to stay with her tonight.

She knew her fellow employees at Zodiac thought she was distant and maybe conceited. She kept to herself and never dated. She wasn't interested in anyone romantically, only in making herself the best Zodiac employee she could and in carving out a future for herself. Sex, romance… They had no place in her life.

But for the first time in years, maybe ever, she wanted a man.

This man.

"Yes, walking me home would be great. I'm not far from here."

They talked about literature on the way, not her parents' books, but current favorites of their own. In the past few months, she'd spent all her free time reading. Evidently, he had too.

He climbed silently behind her up the four flights of stairs to her flat. She smiled as she let him inside and showed him all her private treasures—candles, a collection of sunglasses, her beloved books, including the ragged copy of *The Outsiders* sitting proudly on the shelf.

If he thought it all ridiculous, he never let her know.

She gave him the eight hundred dollars in cash. He respected her enough to take it without argument and put it in his pocket.

The studio apartment was tiny, and she didn't have anywhere for them to sit comfortably. She had just one chair at her small table; the only other option was the bed on the other side of the room.

She gestured toward it. "Want to sit?"

"I should probably go."

"You don't have to go." The words came out in a rush. "I mean, I'd like you to stay. Here. With me. Tonight."

He closed his eyes and let out a breath. "I can't."

"Can't or not interested?" It took all her nerve to ask that, but she needed to know.

He opened his eyes. "Actually, neither option."

She tilted her head as she studied him. "Doesn't that mean you can and you are interested?"

He crossed the few feet between them more silently than someone his size should be able to. He cupped her cheeks. "Yes, it means both those things. But I'm wheels up in a couple hours, and some rushed quickie wouldn't be right for either of us. You deserve more, Pony Girl. Better."

He knew that the rushed quickies she hadn't wanted were all she'd ever had. She hated that he knew it almost as much as she hated that it was the truth.

Bronwyn nodded, keeping her eyes down. "I understand."

He stepped back, letting go of her face. "In a few months, there're going to be some transfer opportunities into the Denver office. Maybe you'd consider trying out the United States for a while. I'd like that."

That would mean seeing him on a regular basis. She smiled. "I've always wanted to see the USA. I'll definitely look into it."

"Good." He smiled too. Those dimples. "Good luck on the Marrakesh mission. They're not going to know what hit them. You'll be perfect."

"I've been training every day to make sure of it."

He nodded, and they stood there looking at each other for a long minute.

"Close your eyes," he whispered.

She did, amazed that there wasn't a single bit of hesitation or fear in the action. This was Sarge. He'd gone out of his way to never hurt her.

His lips brushed against hers. Softly, gently. Not quite a full kiss, but a promise of more to come.

Her first real kiss ever. He couldn't possibly know that.

"It was nice to meet you tonight, Bronwyn Rourke. I hope to get to know you better in the future."

With one more brush of his lips against hers, he was gone.

CHAPTER
FIVE

BRONWYN WAS IN AFRICA.

Morocco was in North Africa, so it wasn't the Africa most people thought of. No rhinos or elephants here. But a lot of desert.

Still, she was in Africa.

A couple of months from now, she'd be in America if everything went as planned. Transferring to the Denver office.

At that point, she would have been to three out of seven continents. Maybe she should make it a goal to get to all seven sometime in her life. A bucket-list item. She'd learned that term pretty recently.

Maybe Sarge would visit a couple continents with her. Asia. South America.

She hadn't heard anything from him since he'd left Paris three weeks ago, but she hadn't expected to. He knew she'd be spending every spare minute preparing for this mission. A lot of pieces had to fall into place perfectly in order for this to work.

"How you liking Africa so far?" The voice of Jenna Franklin, tech support for the mission, came through the earpiece she was wearing.

"Currently, it's a little underwhelming," she whispered.

Jenna and Bronwyn had become almost friends over the past month as they prepared for this operation. She was also based in Denver. Yet another reason to go there.

Not that she needed another one.

"Hanging out in that tiny section of closet for hours can't be fun. Glad you're not claustrophobic."

Being cramped in here for three hours to wait for the small museum on the first floor to close was more uncomfortable than anything else. But she didn't mind. Uncomfortable she could do.

"Boring but manageable. I'll have to come back to Morocco sometime and take in more sights. Have you ever been here?"

"No. I don't really travel."

"You mean outside of the USA?"

"I don't travel anywhere. Zodiac lets me work from a computer command center in my house. It's why I took the job, because I wouldn't have to go into an office. I...I don't like to go outside. It's complicated."

"Oh." There was obviously so much more to the story than she was saying, but Bronwyn didn't want to push. She knew what it was like to have things you didn't want to discuss.

"Yeah."

"Do you mind that everyone calls your team the nerds?" She wanted to change the subject, but as soon as the words were out of her mouth, she realized that new topic might be just as bad.

But Jenna laughed. "No. It's a badge of honor—nobody means it with any disrespect. Plus, we actually gave ourselves the nickname. Everyone else merely makes sure it never dies."

They fell into silence, and she took turns tightening and loosening different muscle groups in her cramped space.

"Did you have any problem switching the keycard with Omar Zeroual?" Jenna asked.

That was why this mission had been deemed perfect for her. It required someone who could pickpocket a key card without being caught, hide in a tiny section of a storage closet, not get spotted by any security cameras or guards, and get the data that had been stolen via corporate espionage out of the safe. Make it out then hand it off.

All skills she'd already had that Zodiac had honed in the past year.

"Not at all. I would've thought he would've been more on edge, given that he stole the drive to begin with."

"Overconfident. That's brought down a lot of people."

They fell into silence again, and she waited, keeping her mind focused on what she needed to do next.

She would not mess this up. She would prove herself a valuable member of this team. When Sarge read the report of this mission, and she knew he would, he would see that he'd been right to recruit her.

It was another hour before Jenna spoke again. "Okay, Bronwyn, you're clear to go."

"Roger that."

She eased out of her tiny hiding place, stretching to get the blood flowing correctly to her body parts. Jenna and her team were electronically hijacking the cameras, so she wouldn't be spotted. They were also using infrared to let her know where the guards were.

She had studied the blueprint of this building so she could make her way around in the dark, which she did. She couldn't use any sort of light that might be visible through the windows.

Bronwyn made her way down multiple hallways, stopping when Jenna told her to, sometimes rerouting in a different direction. A very close call with a guard forced her to hide in a stairwell and got her heart racing, but he didn't notice her.

She was dressed from head to foot in black, her hair tucked under a beanie. If anyone caught sight of her, they wouldn't be able to tell her gender or age. Given the sociopolitical climate of this area—part of what she'd studied to prepare for the mission—the average person who might catch a glimpse of her would assume she was male. Another reason she'd been chosen.

Because she could be mistaken for a boy. Sigh. But not something to think about now.

She made it to the office and used the key card—plus a code a different member of Zodiac had accessed last week—to open the safe.

She stared at the contents of the safe a little longer than she should have. Stacks of cash, some jewelry, and various papers filled up the space around what she was there for. More wealth than she had ever seen or thought would ever be kept in one place.

If she grabbed the necklace—diamonds—and money, she would never have to worry about being poor again. She could do whatever she wanted. Go wherever she wanted.

Except Denver.

If she grabbed anything but the computer drive out of that safe, her time with Zodiac would be over. Her time with Sarge would never start.

"You good, Bron?" Jenna asked in her ear. "Is it there? You seem frozen."

She switched out the small computer drive and shut the safe. "I've got it. I'm on my way out."

"Roger that."

She directed her back through the hallways to avoid the guards. A tiny window in the staff breakroom on the first floor was her way out. Another Zodiac team member had changed the hinges a couple weeks ago so that it opened much wider than it should've. But it was still too narrow for almost anyone to fit through.

Almost anyone. She climbed onto the table and shimmied her way through, catching herself with her arms and rolling into the alley on the outside. A moment later, she was on her feet and walking away from the building.

"I'm out."

"Roger. You're still clear. Change appearance at next block."

She removed the beanie and wrapped a scarf around her head. She turned her jacket inside out, so she wasn't in all black. She never stopped walking the whole time.

"Outlaw is standing by at the rendezvous spot. Great job, Bronwyn," Jenna said. Mark Outlawson—everyone called him Outlaw—worked for Zodiac as a contractor. He would've been her backup if she'd gotten into trouble in the building.

But she hadn't gotten into trouble. She'd done the job they'd given her. She couldn't stop smiling. "Thanks. That was actually fun. You missed out."

She chuckled. "I'll leave the adventuring to you adventurous types. I'm quite happy here with my computers."

She stayed in Bronwyn's ear until she met Outlaw in the lobby of her hotel a few blocks from the museum. She handed off the computer drive without making any eye contact with him at all. If anyone saw them, they wouldn't have noticed a thing.

Outlaw would get the drive out of the country and back into the correct hands. If someone had caught sight of her in the museum, they definitely wouldn't be looking for anyone his size, and now she wouldn't have any incriminating evidence on her.

"Outlaw reports he has possession. You're done, Bronwyn."

"Thanks for guiding me, Jenna."

"My pleasure. Congrats on a successful mission. We'll talk more at debriefing tomorrow."

The earpiece clicked off. She was still smiling as she rode up the elevator to her room. She would fly out tomorrow, back to Paris, but tonight, she was on her own.

She would call Sarge. She would let him know how it went. She knew she couldn't use any specifics over an unsecure line, but maybe she could talk through the temptation she'd run up against when she'd opened that safe.

Sarge would understand. She'd always hated that he knew her past, but that would come in handy now.

Bronwyn opened her fancy hotel room door with the key card, still smiling. She wasn't sure she'd ever think of a hotel room without them reminding her of Sarge. This was the only one I'd ever been in without him.

She flipped on the light switch, but the light didn't turn on. She went over to the smaller lamp by the desk.

It didn't turn on either.

She was a second too slow, too complacent, too secure in her own newfound skills.

That one second cost her everything.

She hit the wall of the hotel room with a force that stunned her. She fought back, but there were at least two attackers, both equally as trained as she was. One caught her kick, the other pushed her back up against the wall, restraining her arms behind her back so she couldn't move.

She must have been spotted. Maybe earlier today? Omar Zeroual was a millionaire. Maybe he had sources they didn't know about. At least she didn't still have the drive on her.

Bronwyn felt a sharp pinch in her bicep. She threw her head backward to try to catch the one holding her, but that just got her slammed harder against the coolness of the wallpaper.

"No bruises," another man said from the other side of the

room. "I have a message that needs to be delivered to your boss."

The guy holding her spun her around to face the man who had spoken. She couldn't make out any of his features in the darkness where he sat on her bed.

"Telephones work better for messages," She spat out at him.

"I was informed you were feisty. Obviously true."

What the hell was going on? If these weren't Omar Zeroual's men, who were they?

And why was the room spinning?

"I'm not interested in passing along any messages." She struggled not to show her dizziness.

The man shifted on the bed. "We don't need you to pass on a message. You will be the message."

"I don't understand."

Her words came out funny. The spinning increased. They'd given her something. That sharp pinch on her arm had been some sort of injection. She fought harder against the man holding her, but it didn't do any good.

The man spoke again. "I need Ian DeRose to start looking for ghosts. Until I make him one."

"What are you talking about?" If the big man hadn't been holding her upright, she would've slumped to the floor. "I've only met Ian a couple of times. He doesn't really know me. Who are you anyway?"

"My name is Erick Huen. I'm an old friend of Ian's. But who I am doesn't matter right now. Only you. You're young and pretty, and you work for him. You'll do just fine."

He stood up and walked closer. He was much smaller than the man holding her, but that didn't make her any less afraid.

"Unfortunately, this process is going to be…uncomfortable for you." He was close enough now that she could see him; she didn't recognize him at all. She understood less and less as whatever they'd given her made her feel as if she was living outside her own body. He reached to brush a strand of hair away from her face. She didn't attempt to move from him.

"You're prettier than I thought. Younger. Such a shame you won't be either by the time we're done."

He nodded to the man holding her, and he let go.

She should run. She should fight. She should do something.

But she couldn't.

Her body didn't seem to be hers anymore.

CHAPTER SIX

SARGE DIDN'T LET Bronwyn know he was listening in on the feed between her and Jenna during the mission. He didn't want to make her nervous or put undue pressure on her.

But he wanted to be available if anything went wrong, to be able to lend immediate assistance from half a world away. If Bronwyn panicked, he wanted to be in her ear to provide support.

Hell, he wanted to be in Marrakesh ready to step in if needed. He had almost inserted himself into the mission. But that would've brought up way too many questions. Not only from the Paris office, but from his own friends there in Denver.

He was high up enough that he wouldn't have needed to explain himself, but his silence would've raised more questions.

Sarge never wanted anyone at Zodiac—especially Bronwyn—to think she hadn't made it on her own. Truly, all he'd done was get her in the door.

And check up on her nearly daily since. That was one of

the advantages of his position in the company. Access to all forms, reports, and footage.

But she had been the one to succeed since she'd arrived in Paris. She'd worked hard, constantly learning and improving. Every single supervisor had been impressed by her work ethic, intelligence, and, of course, nimble little fingers that could take whatever she wanted without anyone noticing.

He listened silently in his office as the mission in Marrakesh unfolded perfectly. Bronwyn had kept her wits about her even when a guard came way too close. She'd gotten into and out of the safe and made the transfer to Outlaw like she'd been doing this sort of thing for years.

He was so fucking proud of her. It was almost a fatherly pride, except despite the more than a fifteen-year age gap between them, there was nothing fatherly about the way he felt toward her.

He'd known it the second their lips had touched in the apartment. Hell, he'd known it for a long time before that.

His nickname in the Navy may have been Sarge, which had started as a joke since the Navy didn't have a sergeant ranking, but his code name at Zodiac was Virgo. He did happen to be born in September under that star sign, but that wasn't why he'd been given Virgo as his moniker.

Virgos were known for being practical, honest, and people who took their commitments seriously. He could've been the Virgo poster child.

The Zodiac Tactical code names might have been haphazardly created by Ian DeRose's housekeeper/mother figure, but the one she'd chosen for Sarge fit him well. And she hadn't known his birth date.

Virgos were also stubborn. He hadn't escaped that trait either. But his stubbornness when it came to Bronwyn was to give her all the time she needed. He could wait. He could wait until Bronwyn was ready. See if they fit together the way he hoped they would.

He heard Jenna's congratulations to Bronwyn for a successful mission and shut down his computer with a smile on his face. Bronwyn had done it. Not that he'd had any doubts she would.

He was still smiling as he fell asleep with eyes as blue as the sky filling his vision.

———

Sarge's smile was gone eighteen hours later.

"Why am I just hearing about this now?" Ian barked into the phone at his ear.

He was only halfway listening, waiting with coffee mug in hand to see how he needed to be involved. He'd stayed up half the night listening in on Bronwyn's mission then had put in a full day and evening at work. He'd been about to go home when Landon Black, another one of Ian's right-hand men, and he had been called to the conference room by one of Ian's assistants.

He made a beeline for the coffeepot. Zodiac had offices all over the world, and there was always something that needed to be handled. It was like being back in the SEALs—they had to be prepared for anything.

"Do we have people still there?" Ian continued.

Sarge took a sip of his black brew. Ian was worried. He scrubbed a hand across his forehead as he and Landon looked at each other. For once, Landon didn't have a half smile on his face. Whatever was going down wasn't good.

"Send everything you have on Rourke. And the transcript of the Marrakesh mission. Have Outlaw report in on the hour and get more boots on the ground immediately."

He set down his coffee at Ian's words, caffeine no longer needed to get him firing on all cylinders. Adrenaline coursed through his veins at the sound of Bronwyn's name and the details of her mission.

Something had happened in the hours since he'd stopped listening.

"What's up, boss?" Landon asked when Ian dropped his cell phone down onto the table in front of him.

"The mission in Marrakesh went south."

Sarge had to stop himself from contradicting him. If that mission had gone any further north, it would've been knocking on Santa Claus's door. It had not gone south.

But he shouldn't know that, should he?

"What happened? Is someone down?" Landon asked.

Is someone down?

That was the important question. Was Bronwyn down?

Ian touched a button, and screens silently slid up in front of each of them from the conference table. A few moments later, electronic files appeared on the screen…details of the Marrakesh mission, the transcripts Ian had demanded that he'd already heard, and a large picture of Bronwyn with those blue eyes.

"Bronwyn Rourke didn't show up at her exit point from Marrakesh six hours ago."

He blew out a silent breath. There wasn't a dead body. That was the most important thing.

"Rourke." Landon sped through her file. Sarge didn't need to look at it. He was already aware of the contents of everything on the screen in front of him. "I remember us approving the mission last month. Rookie but with exceptionally high marks. Mission success probability was high."

"Looking over this transcript, mission was a success. She did her job perfectly."

Damned right she did.

"The drive was handed off without any problem in the hotel lobby," Sarge interjected. Both his friends nodded.

"From there, she should've been fine. Gone up to her room and laid low until time to leave," Landon said.

Ian nodded. "Jenna and the tech team are working their angles. There was no footage in the hotel lobby, which is one of the reasons that hotel was chosen for use, so that's a dead end. The nerds are checking to make sure she wasn't spotted in the building she robbed. Outlaw is there too, poking around in person. So far, nothing unusual."

"She's a complete noob," Landon said as he flipped through one of the files. "Are we sure she didn't get lost or lose track of time or something? Marrakesh is a maze."

Sarge didn't say anything. As a leader at Zodiac, he'd be pissed if that were the case, but as a man, he'd be nothing but thrilled if she'd just gotten caught up in the moment.

"She's yours, right, Sarge?" Ian asked. "Got any insight?"

Mine. He grimaced. "I knew she'd be useful based on observation of her pickpocketing skills and ability to blend into a crowd when I saw her in Europe. I gave her the Paris office address eighteen months ago and didn't have much contact after that."

All true, but not the whole truth.

Ian looked up from his screen. "Any concerns we should be aware of?"

"No. Except for maybe she's young." Way too young for him to have kissed her or to be thinking about anything else. Maybe he needed to put a halt on her transfer to Denver. Having her on the same continent was a mistake. This situation might prove it.

"Roger that," Ian responded. "The team is going to run the normal drills—check hospitals, keep trying her cell, focus to make sure she wasn't caught after the handoff. Let's hope this was a rookie mistake and we have her back in pocket in a few hours."

A few hours later, they had no new data. But they did have a shit-ton more questions, and Sarge didn't like any of them.

Both Jenna and Outlaw were on video conference with them.

"She seemed fine at the handoff." There was the slight delay in Outlaw's words since he was on the other side of the world. "Didn't give any duress signal."

"The drive was legit." Jenna looked into the camera. "Team has already cracked it. And there's been no sign that the bad guys are aware it's missing yet."

"How do you know?"

"The replacement drive has a virus that will put them back to the stone ages." Jenna's smile was vicious for such a small and generally nice woman. "If they connect it to any computer linked to their network, they're going to feel it hard. But there's been no sign of that all day."

Landon leaned back in his chair. "We're way past the point where she could've gotten lost or spent too much time in the shops."

Sarge didn't say anything, but nobody expected him to. He'd never been the most talkative person in a room.

"I've been going over her file." Ian looked at him. "I know you recruited her based on her unusual skill set. Those skills are also the reason she was chosen to lead this mission. A thief who can blend in without trying."

"Yes." True, although he'd recruited her to get her out of that hellhole of a situation, not necessarily because of her skills.

"She didn't give us much info for her file. Name. Date of birth. That's about it. She didn't have an address, no known kin, no tax ID number. We were paying her under the table until Jenna built her IDs."

Jenna ran a hand through her shoulder-length black hair. "And, full disclosure, there was no record of a Bronwyn Rourke when I built her ID. I wanted to make sure I wasn't linking into further problems, so I did an extensive search of that name in most of Western Europe."

She hadn't been looking in Eastern Europe, although it wouldn't have mattered. Jenna wouldn't have found a Bronwyn Rourke even if she'd gone farther east.

He shrugged. "She's not the first Zodiac contractor to use an alias."

Everyone murmured agreement. The entire rogue subsection of the company consisted of team members who had pasts that needed to stay buried. Granted, most of them weren't used for normal missions, but Zodiac had never shied away from people with secrets.

Hell, Ian had his own secrets.

"Was there anything about the mission that struck anyone as odd?" Ian asked. "I've read the transcripts. Bronwyn was in that closet a long fucking time."

"She seemed to handle it okay," Jenna responded. "No claustrophobia or any indication she was under duress. The only time I wondered if—never mind."

"What?" Ian, Landon, and Sarge all said at the same time.

"I'm not trying to say this is what I think happened," Jenna prefaced. "I've gotten to know Bronwyn over the past couple weeks, and I like her a lot."

Ian looked at her on the screen. "It's okay, Jenna. Speak your mind."

She blew out a breath. "At the safe, Bronwyn paused. It was the only time when I was concerned we might have a problem."

"What do you think that means?" Sarge asked.

She got quieter. "Probably nothing. Forget I said anything."

He saw the slight tic in Ian's eye, but he didn't let any of his impatience show with Jenna. The woman wasn't open about her past, but they all knew it involved enough trauma that she never left her house. He'd only met her in person once, and that was because he'd gone to her.

He took over for Ian. He wasn't the best with people, but

this was important. "Jenna, tell us, even if it looks bad. Nothing is off the table at this point."

"It was Omar Zeroual's safe. He's a criminal, but he's also one of the wealthiest men in Morocco. There had to have been a lot more in that safe than just the drive. Cash, almost definitely. Jewelry, probably. Bonds. All sorts of valuable stuff. Maybe the temptation was too much for her."

Sarge wanted to deny it outright, but he couldn't. The truth was, he wasn't sure he could blame Bronwyn if she'd done exactly what Jenna was insinuating.

Ian looked over at him. "You got an opinion about this theory?"

Sarge kept his eyes steady on Ian's. They had been friends and teammates too long for him to be anything but honest. "It's possible. Like everyone has pointed out, Bronwyn is young and has a history we're not familiar with."

He was familiar with it more than anyone else, and knowing it didn't make the situation less feasible.

Ian nodded. "If she stole from Zeroual, then she's in the wind, and I don't want to waste time and resources looking for her. What does your gut tell you?"

Sarge looked down for a moment to really let himself process the question.

What did his gut tell him? Not what he wanted to be true, but what did he really think was going on there?

Ian didn't rush him for an answer.

He thought about Bronwyn's sincerity in Paris when she'd thanked him for getting her the job at Zodiac. The light in her eye when she'd told him about her training. The feel of her sweet lips against his when he'd kissed her.

But mostly, he thought about the eight hundred dollars sitting in a drawer in his bedroom. She hadn't had to give that to him—Sarge definitely hadn't expected it or wanted it. But it had meant so much to her to pay off her debt.

Without any words at all, that spoke volumes about her honor.

"My gut says she's in trouble. I don't think she took anything out of that safe she hadn't been sent there for. It might have been a temptation, but she resisted."

Ian nodded. "Then we keep looking."

CHAPTER SEVEN

BRONWYN SAT IN A DARK CELL. She didn't remember how she'd gotten there. There was no furniture, no toilet. Only a cold floor, cold walls, and a cold metal door.

The slit in the door opened as it had multiple times before. She blinked at the light, which felt garishly bright against the darkness even though she knew it wasn't.

"Say it."

A male voice. She didn't know who. Not Erick Huen, the man from the hotel. Someone else.

Her answer was the same as it had been each time. "No."

She wouldn't say it. They couldn't force her.

They could keep her there, covered in her own filth, no food, and barely enough water to stay alive, but she would not say it.

The slit in the door slammed closed.

The light was gone. Her bravado went with it. The temptation to call out, to ask the man to come back, to say what they wanted her to say almost overwhelmed her.

She knew what was coming next. It didn't change. It wouldn't change, not until these people got what they wanted. Whatever that was.

I exist only to obey orders. My final mission is to go home.
I exist only to obey orders. My final mission is to go home.
I exist only to obey orders. My final mission is to go home.

Bronwyn gritted her teeth as the recording played from speakers she couldn't see, high in the corners of the room she couldn't reach.

Over and over and over.

It only stopped when they came in to give her the injections or to demand she say the words herself.

Injections happened every two hours. She had forced herself to count the seconds after her third shot, doing her best to ignore the words droning on around her. Seven thousand two hundred seconds. It had taken her nearly as long to figure out exactly how many minutes that was.

Three men came in each time to give her the injection. Two to hold her down, one with the needle.

Four days' worth of shots and the words that never stopped.

She tried to walk around in the darkness, to dilute whatever they were putting into her system, but by day two, she was too weak.

I exist only to obey orders. My final mission is to go home.

Bronwyn was close to breaking.

Maybe she could've withstood the darkness, or lack of food or sleep, or the constant phrases. Maybe she could've withstood whatever it was they were injecting into her that alternated between making her mind feel fuzzy and separated from itself and making her skin itch until she was sure there were bugs all over her.

But she couldn't withstand it all.

She tried. She tried to remember anything from her Zodiac training that would help. She tried to think of what Sarge would do in a situation like this. He would remain strong. He would refuse to say the words. He would keep himself quiet and calm.

Bronwyn wasn't as strong as him. She was weak. She'd always been weak.

She wrapped her arms around herself, covered her ears, and tried to hang on to something. To find something to hope for.

The only thing she had worth hoping for was that Sarge and the rest of the Zodiac team would come rescue her. She'd been gone for four days. By now, they would know she was missing. They would be looking for her.

They wouldn't leave her there.

Sarge wouldn't leave her there.

I exist only to obey orders. My final mission is to go home.

Bronwyn tried to count the seconds as the words continued. Tried not to cry, but her body was on the verge of severe dehydration, so there were no tears available.

She failed at both, rocking herself on the cold, hard floor. She wished she were anywhere else. Even back on the streets with Nikolai. Anything was better than this.

When the three men came back in, she didn't fight. Fighting them had never accomplished anything. She didn't even feel the sting of the injection.

They went away; the words continued. This time, whatever they'd put into her body didn't hurt so much. Or maybe she was getting used to the pain.

Something about the recording changed. The words seemed less jarring, more…something. Easier to listen to. Melodic.

Maybe her mind had completely cracked.

Bronwyn stopped rocking, laying her head on her knees. At least she wasn't hurting anymore.

Nothing hurt.

There was nothing at all.

Nothing.

She breathed in and out to the sound of the words from the speakers. They relaxed her.

Everything inside her brain turned off. She couldn't feel anything. That was good. So much better. Why had she been fighting this?

Eventually, the recording shut off, and the slit in the door opened again.

"Say it." The same male voice. "Say your words."

This time, Bronwyn didn't hesitate. She didn't fight. She didn't remember why she had been fighting.

"I exist only to obey orders. My final mission is to go home."

———

When her mind floated back into her body, she was strapped in a medical chair. This wasn't the first time she'd been in this chair. She'd been there months ago.

No, days ago, not months. Or maybe only hours. Keeping track of time had become impossible.

Everything hurt. Sometimes it did, and sometimes it didn't, but right now, there was pain. Dull throbs radiated through her body as if the blood in her veins was beginning to overheat. She knew it would get worse.

Bronwyn knew she would scream.

But right now, she focused solely on breathing in then back out, keeping herself still. They didn't know she was awake. She was at the point where the pain hadn't overwhelmed her and the drugs hadn't shut down her mind again.

This was the only time she was herself. It wouldn't last long.

"Is she awake?" That was the man from the hotel. Erick Huen.

She didn't open her eyes to look. She needed to learn, see if there was any way to escape.

At least she wasn't still in the darkness.

Why had she hated the darkness? She couldn't remember.

She couldn't remember specifics of anything.

"No," another man responded. Doctor. Bronwyn heard his voice often. Medical stuff she didn't understand.

"We need her awake," Erick whined.

"We're dealing with a complex mix of gene editing and chemical subjugation. It can't be rushed. If she were conscious right now, she'd be in a lot of pain. There's no need to make our subjects suffer unnecessarily."

Suffer. Doctor had no idea.

Breathe in. Breathe out.

"We need to get the message to DeRose. I want him looking over his shoulder, trying to figure out what's happening. I want him confused and scared."

"I would like to remind you that this project is more than your personal vendetta for someone in your past. This is groundbreaking scientific work."

Erick scoffed. "Groundbreaking work in mind control that you would never get approval for legally. My partner and I are what is allowing you to conduct your research. Don't forget that."

There was a long pause. The fire in her blood was getting worse, making it almost impossible to keep silent. But she had to.

"I haven't forgotten," Doctor said. "Just like I haven't forgotten that until we learn more, parts of this experimentation are akin to torture. Don't lose sight of that."

"As long as it's Ian DeRose's people being tortured, I'm pretty sure I don't care."

"I do. We're rushing the process with Bronwyn. We're destroying parts of her memory, and unless I give her this daily drug regimen, the gene editing will be agonizing for her. Look at her blood pressure and pulse rising. If she were awake right now, she'd be screaming."

Almost. It was taking more and more effort not to.

The pain burned through her, scorching her, but it was the only time her mind was clear. The only time her mind was her own. Once he gave her the daily drugs, she wouldn't hurt anymore…but she also wouldn't be herself.

"Will she be ready for London?" Erick asked.

A sigh. "Did you hear anything I just said?"

"Tippens, do what you're paid to do and get me my results. My partner is going to be very upset if you can't come through with what you've promised."

Bronwyn swallowed a moan as the pain spiked. She could feel Dr. Tippens moving around her.

"It will work. And yes, she'll be ready for London. Every skill set she has under our control."

"Good." The glee was clear in Erick's tone. "And once she's outlived her usefulness professionally, we ship her back. She won't be our problem anymore."

The moan she'd been forcing down escaped her lips. She couldn't help it. Something Erick said triggered a memory, but she couldn't focus in on it. But it was bad. So bad.

Bronwyn needed to get out of there. She began pulling at the wrist restraints.

"She's waking up. Let me give her the medication for the pain."

"It won't affect her abilities? London is important. She has to fool them all. DeRose has to think she's working for us."

No. No, she didn't want to trick Ian DeRose. Because that meant tricking Sarge too. She didn't want them to think she'd betrayed them.

She fought harder. Pulling at the wrist restraints that kept her strapped to the medical chair. She yanked as hard as she could, thrashing. She had to get out of there. She had to—

"You'll have your perfect thief, don't worry, Erick. Now, let me do my job. She's obviously in pain."

They thought Bronwyn was pulling because she was in

pain. She was and the pulling was making it worse, but it wasn't enough to make her stop. She had to get out.

She pulled at her wrists again, even when she felt the straps bite into her skin. Even when she felt the tiny pinch of the injection.

If she could get out of the chair, she could use her training, take down the doctor. Tippens, Erick had called him. Dr. Tippens. She could take him down. She didn't know if there were other guards, but she could get past them too.

She would fight.

But she had to go now. Now. She had to go now before...

Before what?

Before...

Bronwyn stopped pulling.

"That's right," Dr. Tippens whispered. "It's already better, isn't it? The drugs work quickly."

The pain was subsiding, manageable. She opened her eyes and looked down at her wrists. One of them was bleeding.

That was important. Her bleeding wrist. She needed to do something with it, but she couldn't remember what.

"Feeling better?" the man next to her asked. He was in a doctor's coat. Was he a doctor? Who was he? Did she know him?

Where was she?

Who was she?

She couldn't seem to answer his question or ask any of her own. Her voice didn't work.

"Say your words, Bronwyn."

The invisible fist that had been around her throat released. She could talk. Nothing hurt. Nothing was confusing. Everything was clear.

"I exist only to obey orders. My final mission is to go home."

"SARGE, we've got something on Bronwyn."

His head jerked up to meet Landon's eyes where he was standing at his office door. Something on Bronwyn would be either very good or very bad. It had been nine days with no word of anything having to do with her.

"A body?" Please, God…

"No." Relief coursed through my veins as he continued. "Ian received some sort of video concerning her. Nerds took it to make sure it wasn't some sort of virus and just gave the all clear. He's waiting on you to watch it."

Sarge left everything at his desk and immediately walked out the door, jaw clenched to the point of pain. A video sent deliberately to Ian concerning Bronwyn couldn't be good.

"What's the word on Omar Zeroual?" He asked as they sped down the hall toward the conference room.

"Nothing new. We have eyes on him twenty-four seven, and there's been nothing to lead us to believe he has Bronwyn. He's busy trying to figure out what the hell happened to his entire computer system when he accessed that drive."

Sarge gave a curt nod. Zeroual had the most reason to want to hurt Bronwyn. If he didn't have her, and they hadn't found her body floating in the Mediterranean, that was a good sign.

Ian was talking to Jenna via one of the conference table screens when they walked in. His lips were tight. "Good. Let's do this."

Sarge knew it was a sign of utmost respect that Ian had waited for him to watch this footage. Zodiac Tactical was his company, built with his money. He hadn't needed to afford Sarge this courtesy, even as a friend.

"Thanks for waiting," he told him.

He gave a curt nod. "Jenna, go ahead."

Jenna didn't look any happier than Ian as they sat around the table, each of them looking at their own screens.

"We received this video via email at zero seven hundred Denver time. We checked it for possible viruses first, but it came back clean. Subject line: A message for Ian DeRose."

"Play it," Ian muttered.

Sarge gripped the table until his knuckles turned white as Jenna became smaller on the screen, making room for the video footage.

Please God, do not let this be a snuff film. Do not let him be looking into those beautiful blue eyes…lifeless.

The video was almost ridiculous, made to be deliberately jarring and annoying. Like something from MTV thirty years ago—logos and colors flashing, discordant sounds on top of music.

"What the fuck?" Ian muttered exactly what he was thinking.

After a few seconds, the obnoxious colors and audio subsided. Sarge sat up straighter in his seat as a video image faded in.

Bronwyn walking on a sidewalk with three men.

She wore a sharp black blazer and pantsuit with heels, her brown hair pulled back in a business ponytail, sunglasses covering her eyes. She looked more mature than he'd ever seen her, for once not trying to blend into the environment around her. The woman on the screen didn't care if people noticed her.

The men walking with her, also dressed in sharp suits and sunglasses, weren't doing anything to keep a low profile either. They all walked with a purpose, although that purpose wasn't explained.

Bronwyn was alive. Right now, that was all Sarge cared about.

A voice, disguised by a modulator, spoke.

"You destroyed what was ours. Now we will take what is yours, piece by piece. We will destroy."

The image of Bronwyn and the men faded to black and was replaced by one word and silence.

Mosaic.

The footage ended, looping to play again.

He looked over at Ian, expecting anger or confusion. Definitely not expecting to see most of the color drained from his friend's tanned cheeks and rage burning in his eyes.

He looked over at Landon, who seemed every bit as disturbed by the footage.

"What the fuck just happened?" Sarge asked when neither Ian nor Landon said a word. "Play it again, Jenna."

Ian nodded, and they watched the clip again. This time, he looked for any sign of...anything from Bronwyn. Distress, anger, tapping Morse code with her fingers. But there was nothing. Nothing more than an emotionless face—Bronwyn's emotionless face—as she walked with purpose toward some unknown goal.

As soon as the footage faded out, he wanted Jenna to play it again so he could look for more nuances, but Ian stopped everything.

"Mosaic," he whispered. "That can't be right. They're done. I ended them more than two years ago."

He looked over at Landon again, this time as if he needed reassurance of the accuracy of his facts.

"Mosaic was that organization you went undercover with law enforcement to stop, right?" Sarge asked.

He nodded. "Yes. I took down the leader personally. Mosaic was destroyed."

Sarge remembered vaguely. Ian had gotten out of the Navy before him. He knew he was doing some undercover work but hadn't known the details. All he'd known was by the time Ian hired him at Zodiac Tactical a few months after that, he was different from the man Sarge had known in the SEALs.

He'd had demons in his eyes. The same ones he had now.

"What exactly is Mosaic, and what do they have to do with Bronwyn?" Right now, it didn't matter if Ian had been incorrect in his assumption that Mosaic had been destroyed the first time or if they'd decided to rebuild and weren't clever enough to come up with a new name.

What mattered was that they were using words like take and destroy while zooming in on footage of Bronwyn.

Ian sat back in his chair, still looking stunned. It was Landon who answered. "Mosaic is a pretty name for a group of ugly people. They were a well-funded domestic terrorist organization into all sorts of criminal activity—drugs, money laundering, weapons sales, information sales. Basically providing bad guys with whatever they needed."

Ian leaned forward, resting his elbows on his knees, combing his fingers through his hair. "It can't be them. It can't be."

He looked like he had seen a ghost. Sarge wasn't sure he'd ever observed him this shaken.

"Ian killed the leader of Mosaic with his own hands," Landon explained when Ian stopped talking. "After that, the organization crumbled."

"Evidently, somebody decided to take the crumbles and

rebuild," he said with a shrug. "Otherwise, what the fuck are we looking at here? And why did they involve Bronwyn?"

"Jenna, what do we know for sure about this footage?" Ian asked, sitting up a little straighter in his seat, finally looking more like the man who'd been their SEAL team leader and owner of a million-dollar security company.

Jenna enlarged herself on the screen. "The email it came from is untraceable. They made sure we wouldn't be able to get any sort of useful data concerning that. But the footage is real. That is definitely Bronwyn walking with those three men. It wasn't doctored."

"How about a timeline?" Sarge asked. "Could this have been in Paris during some of her training and this Mosaic group got hold of it?"

Jenna shook her head on the screen, looking down at something else. "The footage is from London. We have the team working on specifics, but I can tell you that the shadows from the footage match the weather pattern in London over the past three days."

He scrubbed a hand down his face. "What exactly does that mean?"

"Mostly, it means that we're pretty sure she was in London walking with those three dudes sometime in the past seventy-two hours."

"How sure?" Landon asked.

Jenna was typing as she spoke. "If I was going to put a number on it, I would say ninety percent."

They all let out curses under their breaths. They'd run entire missions based on lower-percentage surety from the nerds than that.

"Okay," Sarge said. "What else do we know besides the fact that she's been in London with three guys recently?"

Jenna bit at the corner of her lip. "I'd prefer if you would give us more time to be sure before we make any accusations."

Accusations.

Landon's eyes met his. Accusations meant once again Jenna was afraid Bronwyn was making bad choices.

"Speak your mind, Jenna. We work better knowing all the facts," Landon said, his eyes still on mine.

Sarge gave a nod. He was right; knowing all the facts—even the ugly ones—was always better.

"In the hour since this email was received and cleared for potential electronic threats, I've had the whole tech team on it." Jenna straightened. "Figuring out they were in London was simple. There's a reflection for a couple of seconds in a car that goes by. Paused and zoomed in, you can see the wrought-iron fence and one of the shell-covered huts found in Grosvenor Gardens unique to London."

He nodded. "Okay, fair enough." She hadn't gotten to the accusations part.

"And like I said, based on weather patterns, it holds that this footage was in the past three days."

None of this was her point. "Continue."

"There was office heist in South London twenty-four hours ago. One that would match Bronwyn's skill set. From what we can see from the police report, two people were caught on a security camera from the rear—a large man and smaller woman—both in suits, the woman had a brown ponytail. Not enough details to give the police anything. No arrests were made."

Two caught on camera, not four. But the other two men could've been acting as lookout and driver, not in the building.

"So you think she's working with them?" Sarge asked, doing his best to keep his voice neutral.

Jenna shrugged and shook her head slowly. "This is why I wanted more time before saying anything. When I first heard the voice-over, taking piece by piece and destroying" —her voice deepened to mimic the melodramatic tone on the footage— "my first thought was that Bronwyn was in trouble. That she was being forced to do something against her will."

"Given what I know about the original Mosaic, if this new group is similar, that assumption would probably be accurate," Ian said.

Jenna let out a sigh. "The problem is I ran both of our nonverbal communication software programs on the images of Bronwyn, and nothing about her body language, posture, or movements suggest that she is being coerced in any way. Everything our programs could tell us suggested she wanted to be there."

"Those programs aren't always accurate," Sarge muttered.

Landon raised an eyebrow. "They're accurate more often than they're not."

Sarge threw a hand up. "You heard big bad voice-over guy say they were going to take and destroy. Doesn't that concern anyone but me?"

Jenna pushed her glasses up onto her head. "My thoughts too, but then I wondered if it meant recruitment. That Mosaic was going to take whatever Zodiac employees they could flip and would therefore destroy the company."

He gritted his teeth and remained silent. Jenna had a valid point.

"I'm not taking anything at face value." Ian stood up. "None of it. Not that Mosaic is back, not that Bronwyn is working against us, and definitely not that we have all the facts."

Landon nodded. "This could definitely be someone trying to spook you. You have a lot of enemies."

Ian's face remained neutral. "Handle this," he told Landon. "I need to dig into my other contacts and see what I can find."

He walked out of the room without another word.

Landon looked back at Jenna. "Run everything again. All of it. We continue to assume that Bronwyn is in trouble, even if it doesn't readily appear that way. Report back as soon as you have anything."

She nodded. "Roger that. I'll get everyone on it."

Sarge continued staring at the screen after it went dark.

"What the hell is going on with Ian?" He felt as if there were big chunks of info he was missing. "If Mosaic has formed a two-point-oh version, why does that have him shitting his pants?"

Landon was silent for so long Sarge thought he might not answer.

"Ian paid a high personal price to shut Mosaic down the first time. I don't blame him for not wanting to face them again."

"The claustrophobia?"

Landon crossed his arms over his chest. "You know about that?"

"I know he's the first one out of an elevator and dislikes being in the back seat of a car. He wasn't like that in the SEALs."

"It's Ian's story to tell if he chooses, but yeah, shit got bad for him when he was undercover. Real bad. So if he's a little jumpy at the mention of Mosaic, he has reason to be."

"Whatever this is, it feels personal against him. Somebody wants to spook him." And it looked like they had succeeded.

Landon nodded. "Agreed."

"My big question is, if they're trying to get to Ian, why use Bronwyn?" Sarge asked, clicking so he could watch the footage again. "He doesn't really know her at all. She has no personal ties to him."

"Maybe low-hanging fruit." Landon shrugged. "She's a newer employee, might need money, easier to pick off. Plus, young with those big eyes. She has a fragile look to her sometimes when she doesn't realize it. Pokes all of us where it hurts to think of her being abused in some way."

Sarge was very fucking aware of Bronwyn's fragility. She

hid it well most of the time. She was smart and capable, but pieces of her were still the lost and broken teenager he'd met in Prague.

He watched the footage of her walking with the men. Nothing about that woman on the screen seemed fragile or lost in those moments.

Landon stood. "Look, I know you feel some sort of bond with Bronwyn, but you need to prep yourself for the fact that she may not be one of us anymore. Hell, she may not ever have been one of us. She could've been working an inside angle from the beginning."

Sarge watched her walk with such purpose in her suit and heels. He had to admit, this was not the Bronwyn he knew.

"If I have to take her down, I will."

CHAPTER
NINE

SARGE WATCHED the footage of Bronwyn at least a hundred times in the next twenty-four hours. He watched it in slow motion and at double speed. He watched it backward, in black and white, every way he could think of that might help him see something he'd missed watching it the time before.

He watched it until he knew every second of it from memory. The entire time, hoping Bronwyn would speak to him in some way. Anything to show she was in trouble rather than working for the enemy.

He watched until his eyes turned gritty, then he watched some more. But he never found what he was hoping to see.

As the hours went by, the news didn't get better. Every test the nerds ran on the footage of Bronwyn's body language made it look more like she was guilty. Details that trickled in from London painted a dark picture. The office burglary had been custom made for her abilities. A phone lifted off a businessman then used to gain access to his office and accounts.

Twelve million dollars had been stolen from electronic accounts. Even worse? The accounts hadn't been criminals or businesses. They'd been individuals' savings and retirement accounts. Bronwyn hadn't been stealing from bad guys this time. She'd stolen from people who would get hit hard by the loss.

And every single trail they followed pointed to her doing it willingly.

Shit.

Sarge hadn't seen Ian since he'd left the conference room after they'd watched the video the first time. He was too busy digging into discovering if Mosaic was really back in business to care much about Bronwyn at the moment. He'd shut everyone out of his office, including Landon and him.

He stayed in the office all night the first night, but Sarge knew he would be doing more harm than good if he tried to stay a second night. He was about to walk out of the building and head to his property on the outskirts of the city when he got a message from Jenna.

Might have something on B.

Sarge spun and headed back into the conference room, video calling Jenna on the way. "What have you got?"

"I found something that might be something in the footage." Her words weren't as concise as they normally were, and she looked as exhausted as he felt. "To be honest, I'm not sure if it's legitimate or not."

"Tech stuff or about Bronwyn herself?" At this point, he would take either.

"Bronwyn." He sat down at the table so he could have a bigger screen. Jenna brought up the footage that he now knew by heart and stopped a few seconds in, zooming in on Bronwyn's arm.

"There." A red circle appeared on the screen to show him where to look. "It's some sort of bruise, I think. Here on her right wrist—an abrasion, like she may have been restrained."

Sarge had been so busy looking at Bronwyn's face or in how she held herself when walking with the men that he hadn't caught sight of what Jenna had noticed. "How did I miss that?"

"I don't think you can see it in the version of footage you have. I only saw it when I was looking in a reflection when they walked by that shop. I enhanced that."

He studied the zoomed-in reflection. Calling the quality grainy would be generous. But at one distinct moment, the sun peeked out from behind the clouds at just the right angle, casting a light on Bronwyn's wrist.

Sarge sat up straighter at his desk when he saw the red mark on her skin—as if she'd been tied or handcuffed but had fought against it.

The blemish only lasted for a split second before the bracelet on her wrist slid and covered it.

It was enough for him. If Bronwyn had been restrained to the point of damaging the skin on her wrist, then there was more to all of this than met the eye.

Relief crashed over him. This was enough for him to fight for her. To demand that no one give up.

Jenna showed him the split second of footage again. This time, Sarge was even more convinced.

"I think you're right. This is proof that there is fuckery going on, and we don't have all the facts."

Jenna enlarged herself on the screen. "I agree. And not because of the markings on her skin, but because I don't think Bronwyn would do this . I never should've said anything to make it sound like I thought she was guilty."

Sarge shook his head. "Your job is to present the facts as they are, not as what we want them to be. Regardless of whether she was forced or not, the fact was Bronwyn was in London, and she almost definitely was part of that burglary."

Jenna let out a sigh. "The worst thing is I don't think this is enough to convince anybody else she's innocent. There are too many ways the data can be interpreted."

The markings were too indistinct. And even if they were

conclusive as bruises or abrasions, that didn't mean Bronwyn was being forced against her will.

But it was enough for him. And as long as he was in her corner, he could help manage what people at Zodiac thought. "You're probably right. But it's enough to stop any sort of witch hunt."

"What are you going to do?" Jenna asked.

"I'm not going to give up on her."

———

Sarge didn't give up. There wasn't a single day that he let his faith in Bronwyn slip.

But a month went by with no word from or about her.

He hadn't sat in the Denver office waiting for information to fall into his lap. He'd traveled to Marrakesh to make sure nothing had been missed. He'd gone to London and stood on the very street Bronwyn had walked with those men. He'd looked into the shop window that had provided the reflection that had let them know something wasn't right with Bronwyn's situation.

Neither London nor Marrakesh had yielded much extra info. The scenes were too cold. Sarge talked to multiple people, but no one remembered anything.

Both Landon and Ian were convinced that Bronwyn had flipped. Out of respect for him, they hadn't said so outright, but they were both too logical and tactically minded not to take what was so clearly in front of them at face value. Even the marking on her wrist hadn't convinced them.

Sarge went to Paris on his own dime, taking vacation days. He wanted to see her apartment himself.

It told him everything he needed to know.

Nearly everything in it was gone. All her clothes, all the cash, everything of value. The empty apartment was meant to reaffirm that she had jumped ship and was indeed working for Mosaic.

But standing inside her door after having picked the lock, Sarge knew with one look that she hadn't left her apartment of her own will. Someone had taken her.

Someone who didn't know her well enough to know that she never would have left the copy of *The Outsiders* her parents had given her.

All the other books, she might've left behind, especially if she'd had to travel light or was in a hurry, but not that one. Not under any circumstances.

He grabbed the book. It was coming with him.

"You hang on," he told Bronwyn, as if the pages in his hand were some sort of conduit to her. "You're not alone. I'm coming for you."

That book was never far from his sight as the weeks passed.

Landon and Ian were focused on figuring out what Mosaic 2.0 was up to. There were no more videos or direct threats, no more kidnapped employees, but evidently, this new Mosaic was real and back in business.

Ian no longer had demons in his eyes. Instead, he had determination. Whatever version of Mosaic was coming back, he was committed to defeating it.

And since Mosaic was the only link Sarge had to Bronwyn —they had her, they'd bruised her—he'd been doing everything he could to help Ian.

Plus, they had all the regular aspects of Zodiac Tactical to run. People still needed guarding, international hostage situations needed negotiating, intelligence needed gathering. Their services were still vital, despite where their focus was right then.

But he still spent every spare second looking for any clues he could find about Bronwyn.

There was nothing.

When Ian got a message from some colleagues in Wyoming with information about Mosaic, he and Landon took off to hunt down the details. Sarge didn't go with them since there was no mention of Bronwyn, and Wyoming seemed like the wrong direction to find anything about her.

Whatever info Ian brought back about Mosaic, he would sort through for any angles everyone else missed. Any angles particularly to do with her.

She'd lost everyone important in her life, had been used by the ones she'd been left with. He wasn't going to give up on her. He would keep searching.

Sarge expected Ian and Landon to be back in a day or two—how much intel could they really get from a tiny town in Wyoming from a bunch of guys who taught civilians self-defense and weapon safety, for Christ's sake? But when they'd been there three days and Ian had already nearly gotten himself killed by Mosaic soldiers, he decided it might be time for him to join the party.

He was packing, about to head for the airport, when his computer started making an annoying beeping sound at him. Sarge growled at it. He was shit with computers for the most part, much preferring to have a weapon in his hand than a keyboard. He'd rather be out in the action than at a desk.

Sarge clicked on the mouse to get it to shut the hell up, then stared at the screen as it woke up and showed him why it was making all the commotion.

Because he had told it to.

Because Bronwyn had been spotted.

CHAPTER TEN

BRONWYN WAS IN NEW YORK.

The nerds had had every facial ID software on the market—and some they'd developed themselves—running from cameras all over the world since Bronwyn had disappeared.

Even with full nerd genius behind it, they always knew spotting Bronwyn would be a long shot. There was no way to run the footage from every camera they could access. They'd just gotten very fucking lucky.

He would take it.

The footage had caught Bronwyn in Midtown Manhattan walking alone down a busy sidewalk. She wore a navy blue dress and heels, no sunglasses this time, which had undoubtedly aided in her being identified. Once again, she didn't remind him of the Bronwyn he knew. Nothing about her was trying to blend in or remain invisible.

Of course, it was New York, so there were a lot of businesspeople who looked quite similar. She definitely didn't stick out.

"What do we do?" Jenna asked via phone as Sarge drove to the airport.

"Home in on every camera you have in this area. See if we can pinpoint where she goes."

"We need to tell Ian."

"I will. Can you get someone to find me the quickest flight to New York and text me the boarding pass? I'll call you again when I'm on the ground to get any new updates."

Jenna hung up without another word. Sarge didn't take offense. She wasn't good with people either, and she had a mission.

He immediately called Ian.

"Sarge. What's going on?"

"One of our facial recognition software programs pinged Bronwyn a few hours ago."

"Where?"

"New York. I'm going after her."

He was silent for a long moment.

"I know the chances of finding her are slim," he continued. She could be long gone before he got out of Colorado. "But I also know the chances of me sitting in the office without going fucking crazy are even lower. So I'm going. I'll take personal time if I have to."

Ian let out a sigh. "You don't have to take personal time. Just…watch your back. We found out that Erick Huen is part of Mosaic, which means this is more personal than we first figured."

Sarge muttered a curse under his breath. Erick had been Ian's brother's best friend—and was a psycho bastard. They'd all thought he was dead, but evidently no such luck. Erick's involvement meant exactly what Ian said: this was personal in the worst possible way. Erick wanted revenge for Ian taking down Mosaic the first time.

"Take somebody with you to New York if you want back-up," Ian said. "Report immediately if you have any info."

"Roger."

But that wasn't going to happen. Sarge didn't want

anyone with him if he found Bronwyn. He wanted to be able to talk to her alone and find out what the hell was going on and how he could help.

And if she was making some bad choices, he was going to…help her figure out better ones. Even if that meant kidnapping her for a while.

Sarge disconnected the call without another word. He was on his own. That was how he liked it.

———

Bronwyn was casing the situation for an upcoming heist.

By the time he made it into the city, the nerds had narrowed down her location to a high-end hotel in Midtown Manhattan. Once they knew where to focus, they were able to find out more details.

Bronwyn had been here at least forty-eight hours. The nerds had found all sorts of footage of her in different wigs and outfits, on different floors of the hotel, as well as the lobby. Jenna had sent him the snippets of footage she'd found.

Bronwyn didn't look like the girl he'd known in any of the footage, but he recognized her mannerisms—the way she kept her eyes averted, her body language subtle and unassuming. Now she was blending in the way she'd done in Prague.

She was definitely casing for a heist.

When the nerds cracked the guest list and they saw Peter Kerpar on it, they knew they'd found out whom she was targeting. He was a mid-level criminal from Boston who ran with the Bollini family. Mostly involved with their money laundering and cybersecurity. There were any number of things Bronwyn could want to steal from him. The nerds were digging deeper.

Normally, Sarge wouldn't give a shit if someone like Kerpar got robbed. Zodiac wasn't in the business of protecting criminals. But Kerpar had a lot of security—four guys with him damned near everywhere he went—and if they caught Bronwyn, she'd be in trouble. Dead sort of trouble.

She had to realize that. What could she be about to steal that was worth her life? Was she being blackmailed?

When Kerpar and three-quarters of his entourage sat down at the bar in the hotel lobby, he parked himself in a corner booth and waited for Bronwyn to arrive. This was when she would make her move.

He didn't have to wait long. He forced himself to stay casual, barely looking up from the beer he wasn't drinking as she entered.

Just like old times. Him watching her while she did something dangerous.

She was dressed damned near perfectly. A flirty dress designed to draw attention but not look so risqué that anyone would mistake her for a working girl. Her hair was pulled back and makeup artfully applied to make her blue eyes seem bigger—if that was humanly possible—and to draw attention to her lips. A choker-style necklace adorned her neck, a bracelet on her wrist.

It took every ounce of self-control Sarge had not to march up to her, throw her over his shoulder, and carry her out of there. Get her somewhere safe then work out whatever shit was going on with Mosaic.

But he had no guarantees she didn't have someone else watching her to make sure she did whatever she was being forced to do to Kerpar. The nerds hadn't spotted anyone who fit those parameters, but that didn't mean the person didn't exist.

So Sarge kept his ass in the booth and watched.

Bronwyn was smart, sitting at the opposite end of the bar, waiting for Kerpar to come to her. They chatted for a few minutes, her smiling, him moving closer. Sarge saw the instant when her fingers slipped into his blazer and got his room key. He never noticed a thing. Neither did his shit guards.

She stayed with him long enough at the bar to keep him from getting too suspicious and then stood with a smile, his key card somewhere in that flirty dress.

Had she replaced the key card with an identical fake one? If not, he was definitely going to remember and suspect her when he couldn't find it. She was playing with fire.

As she turned from Kerpar with a smile, she looked in Sarge's direction. There was no way she didn't see him. He didn't duck. Didn't move. Their eyes met, held.

Nothing. There was nothing. Not a hint of recognition in her features as she looked at him. She may have become a good liar, but there was no way she was that good of one. A moment later, their gazes unlocked, and she turned toward the exit.

Sarge immediately sent Jenna a text, standing once Bronwyn was out of the bar, walking in that direction.

He needed to know what floor Kerpar's room was on.

He had a reply before he made it to the door.

1708

Sarge knew where Bronwyn was heading. She would take the elevator, so he took the stairs. Seventeen floors weren't an easy task, but he didn't let it slow him down. By floor twelve, he was fucking glad that they trained every single day at Zodiac to keep in battle-ready shape. You never knew when the battle would find you.

He spotted her as soon as he entered the hallway. She was almost to Kerpar's door. He needed to stop her. He threw his key card down the hall in front of him.

"Excuse me, miss?" Sarge called out. "I think you dropped your key. Is this yours?"

At his voice, she stiffened and turned to him. Again, no recognition in her blank eyes.

"No, I have my key right here." She held up the key she'd stolen from Peter Kerpar.

"My mistake. Enjoy your evening."

Sarge continued walking toward her. She gave him a smile that was as blank as the look in her eyes. She watched him as he traveled toward her, as if she didn't want to turn her back on him. Not necessarily unusual for a woman faced with a strange man in an otherwise deserted hallway.

But he knew the truth. She didn't want there to be anything that identified her as entering this room.

Sarge walked past, breathing in perfume that smelled expensive and not at all the scent he placed with Bronwyn.

What should he do? He couldn't exactly knock her unconscious, throw her over his shoulder, and carry her out of the building. That would draw too much attention.

His phone buzzed in his hand, and he looked down at it.

911. Kerpar is on his way up to his room.

Shit. Sarge needed to get Bronwyn out of there now. She was still standing at the door, and he turned and took a few steps back toward her. "Look, I know you don't know me and this seems weird, but I was wondering if you were interested in having a drink down at the bar."

Her expression didn't change. "Now's not a good time. But maybe tomorrow night? Around nine?"

She was completely blowing him off. This wasn't working, and they were out of time. He needed to try something different.

He stepped closer, into her space, and she stiffened. "Don't have time for an old friend, Pony Girl?"

His words changed something in her. She stiffened further, but not in the same way—not in a need to fight, but something else.

She was in there. Whatever was keeping her from recognizing him wasn't permanent. It didn't have total control.

"I... I..." She couldn't seem to get words out.

"That's right, Pony Girl," Sarge murmured again. "Fight it. Whatever this is. Come back to me."

Those big blue eyes blinked. Then blinked again.

"Sarge?"

She was with him.

"Bronwyn. What the hell is going on? Come on. We've got to get out of here. Peter Kerpar is on his way up to the room. If you go in there now, you're busted."

And by busted, he meant that she was going to take a bullet to the head. Her hand was still on the door handle.

"I… I…" She shook her head back and forth, like she couldn't make a decision.

His phone buzzed again.

Stalled by holding the elevator. ETA 15 seconds

Sarge had to get her out of there. He cupped the back of her neck and brought his forehead against hers. "You have to run, Pony Girl. Save your mission for another time. You can't do it right now. Kerpar is on his way up in the elevator. Run."

She did.

She dashed down the hallway, away from the elevators. He snatched the key card out of her hand and threw it back toward the door. Hopefully, when Kerpar figured out his key was missing and saw the one on the floor, it would alleviate suspicion from her.

He didn't wait to see if the plan would work. He ran behind her. They were barely into the stairwell before he heard Kerpar's obnoxious laughter behind them. So far, so good.

They both bolted down the stairs. She didn't try to say anything else to him. Didn't look at him or acknowledge he was with her in any way. By the time they reached the seventh floor, Sarge was sure no one was following them. The plan had worked.

"Bronwyn, wait."

She kept going.

They made it down another half flight before he grabbed her arm and pressed her up against the wall, trapping her there with his body.

Just like old times.

"What the hell are you doing, mister?"

Those blue eyes were blank again. She didn't recognize him. Jesus. What the fuck was going on?

Sarge pressed up farther against her. "Do you know who I am, Bronwyn?"

She obviously didn't. Her eyes darted around the stairwell.

"Pony Girl, it's me. Sarge. Do you know where you are? Do you know who you are?"

Those eyes flew back to his. "Pony Girl."

"That's right. Do you remember?" He eased back from her slightly.

Once again, he saw recognition in her eyes. He smiled at her.

"That's right? I'm here to help. We'll get you whatever you need. I'm here to take you home."

She stiffened. "Home?"

"Wherever. We'll work out the details later. Zodiac can get you situated wherever will help you most."

"Zodiac." She blinked slowly, and when she opened her eyes, they were dead again.

Shit.

Her hand came up and touched her necklace, then her entire body stiffened. Sarge waited for her to argue.

Instead, she kneed him in the balls at the same time her arm flew out with a punch meant to knock him to the floor. He forced himself to react through the pain, not to double over, protecting himself as she came at him in a series of punches and kicks that were designed to not just take him down, but to make sure he stayed down.

"Bronwyn, stop." Sarge spun to the side then blocked her as she moved around for another attack.

She didn't respond. He grunted as he caught a side kick to the chest followed by a combination punch to the same area.

Fuck. That cracked a rib.

She was fighting as dirty and as strong as she could. He didn't mind a dirty fight, but it was much more difficult to win when he was trying not to hurt his opponent. Eventually, he would lose. That was inevitable.

"Pony Girl. Listen to me." The nickname had been the only thing that had gotten through to her thus far, but it didn't do anything now. She still attacked him with blazing speed and all the skill she'd learned from her Zodiac instructors over the past year.

She came down slightly off-balance from a roundhouse kick, and Sarge seized his chance, locking her in his arms from behind, hoping his strength and size would be a determining factor. He got a headbutt that he was pretty sure broke his nose for his efforts, and she slipped out of his grip.

She followed that up with a right hook to the jaw. The left uppercut, he was able to block, but a kick to the kidneys that would have him pissing blood for a week dropped him to his knees.

She was trying to kill him.

If she had had a weapon, he had no doubt she would have used it already. He was going to have to really fight her if he wanted to survive. He jumped back up and threw out an uppercut of his own, catching her on the jaw and spinning her to the side.

"I don't want to fight you, Pony Girl."

"I exist only to obey orders. My final mission is to go home."

What the hell was that? The words themselves were scary enough, but that monotonous tone to her voice was spooky-clown scary.

They fought some more. Her doing her best to hurt him, and him doing his best not to hurt her but also not get killed in the process.

Sarge wrapped his arms around her again, careful to keep his distance from that headbutting little skull this time then pushed her body face-first up against the wall, using his size against her. She had a lot of skill and a lot of speed, but when it came to size and strength, he had her beat. He still had to pin both her legs and her arms to keep her trapped against the wall.

"Bronwyn, stop fighting. Let me help you," he murmured against her ear, then quickly dodged another headbutt.

Her breathing was ragged. "No. I have to complete my mission. I must or…"

She threw her neck to the side, and from this close up, Sarge was able to get a better look at the necklace around her neck.

What the fuck? It wasn't a necklace at all, at least not jewelry. It had some sort of small spikes that were pointing into her throat.

"Bronwyn, what is that thing? Is it hurting you? I don't understand."

"I have to complete my mission," she said again.

"Bronwyn. Goddammit, hold still." She started struggling against him once more, and he pushed her up harder against the wall. "If they're listening, if they're coming after you, I can get you out. I promise. Please, Pony Girl, I want to take you home."

She stopped struggling at that word—home.

"No. My final mission is to go home. This is not my final mission."

He didn't know what she was talking about. He didn't know how to help her. They both stood there against the wall, breathing hard.

"You have to let me go," she finally said. "It's the only way. I have to complete this mission."

She started repeating the only way, the only way, the only way under her breath.

Sarge stepped back and let her go.

She was right. He didn't have the backup that he needed to help her. And if Mosaic was waiting right outside, he was going to do nothing but get them both killed.

And that necklace, he didn't know what the fuck that was, but it was obviously something being used to control her. Best-case scenario was that he knocked her unconscious, but then he'd have to carry her out through the lobby which was going to do nothing but get him arrested.

It took everything Sarge had to stay still as she turned and fled down the stairs. He didn't want her out of his sight, but she was right.

This was the only way. At least for right now.

BRONWYN SAT in front of the mirror, sweat pouring down her face. She stared at her hand that hovered on the outside of her necklace on the left side.

She fought not to press the injector hidden in the piece of jewelry. Not because of the slight pain she would feel as the needle punctured her skin, but because of what she knew came next.

The emptiness, losing herself.

Pony Girl.

She closed her eyes as she heard Sarge's voice in her head. For a moment, the throbbing stabs in her brain and fire scorching along her skin eased.

She had been programmed to resist anyone saying her name. But Pony Girl was different—not her, but still her. The words had drawn her out of the depth of her mission-induced haze.

Sarge. It had been him. But the rest she could only remember in jagged flashback. Had they run? Had they fought? She couldn't remember.

Pony Girl.

When she gritted her teeth and focused, she could still hear his deep voice in her ear.

That was what was stopping her from pressing the medication into her neck like she'd been trained to do. Like she'd been programmed to do. Like she wanted to do.

The pain would get worse until she pressed it again. She knew that. She knew it would eventually overcome her. But for the first time, Bronwyn had a reason to endure the pain.

Sarge was there in New York.

Right? Was he there?

He would help her.

If he was really there.

She looked at herself in the mirror again. Was this another trick her mind was playing on her? Was she back in the dark cell? Was her mind cracking once again? Maybe Sarge wasn't nearby at all.

The phone on the vanity in front of her buzzed, and Bronwyn lowered her hand from her neck to pick it up.

"Report," a male voice said. She didn't know whose.

"Plan A failed. Switching to Plan B tonight."

Her eyes burned, and her stomach heaved at not providing all the information. Again, she was trained, programmed, to give all pertinent data concerning the mission.

But if Bronwyn did, she would be putting Sarge in danger. So she fought, knowing if the voice on the phone asked for specifics, she wouldn't be able to hold them back.

She swallowed a shaky sob when he didn't.

"Will you be able to complete the mission?"

"Yes." She tried to keep her voice as cold and calm as possible. Any emotion would give away that her conditioning was failing.

"Good. Complete your mission. Press your regimen now."

Bronwyn couldn't disobey a direct order. She brought her hand up to the side of her neck and pressed the button in her necklace, feeling the pinch of the needle entering her skin.

"Finish and report," the man said.

"Yes." Her voice was already steadier. Blanker.

"Say your words," the voice on the phone commanded.

"I exist only to obey orders. My final mission is to go home."

He ended the call, and she replaced the phone on the dresser in front of her.

She tried to keep Sarge's face in her mind, the sound of his voice in her ears. But with every second, it faded until it was gone for good. Bronwyn stared at the face in the mirror until the person staring back at her was no longer familiar either.

———

There wasn't enough time to get the people Sarge would trust most with this situation to New York. Especially since Ian and Landon were up to their necks with Mosaic shit in Wyoming.

He was still on his own. But he knew what Bronwyn's mission was and that she'd make another attempt at robbing Kerpar soon. That gave him at least a slight advantage.

Where he distinctly did not have an advantage was with the woman herself. He had no idea what was going on with her. And he certainly didn't know what that scary-as-fuck necklace was she wore. When he described it to the nerds, they all agreed that it could be some sort of kill switch—something she couldn't control that could end her life if she didn't do what was being required of her.

That would explain a lot. But it wouldn't explain why Sarge should probably be getting looked at by medical professionals right now. Why not tell him her life was in danger rather than do her best to make sure he didn't make it out of that stairwell alive?

Why had there been no recognition whatsoever when

she'd first seen him? Then once she had recognized him, it had been as if she came in and out of her own consciousness.

This had been more than Mosaic holding her life in their hands. More than some sort of blackmail.

He wanted to know what the fuck was going on.

So the plan had changed. Sarge wasn't going to stop her from robbing Peter Kerpar. The guy was scum anyway. He was going to help her. At the same time, he was going to put a tracker on her so they could figure out a game plan.

Ian wasn't going to be thrilled that Sarge had commandeered his private jet to fly out a four-centimeter tracking device a couple hours ago, but he would have to bill him.

Now, he needed to get the tracker on Bronwyn. They knew her mission had to do with Kerpar, so they made sure they had eyes all over the hotel and especially on him. Jenna and her crew were able to hack his phone so that they could know his whereabouts.

Sarge basically spent the next few hours lying around in the hotel, icing his various aches, waiting for Bronwyn to strike. As soon as the nerds got visual confirmation of her breaking in to Kerpar's room again, he would make his move. He'd been gone for a few hours, so Sarge knew she'd be making her attempt soon.

Jenna had been nice enough to load a communication headset in with the tracker he'd be putting on Bronwyn. That way, he could communicate with the nerds, but it wasn't her talking with him now. Evidently, she was spending all of her time and expertise going through Mosaic information Ian had found in fucking Wyoming.

That was fine. He didn't need one of Zodiac's top minds helping him. All Sarge needed was a warm body who could watch video footage and let him know when Bronwyn arrived at Kerpar's room.

He'd show up, not stop her from stealing whatever it was

she wanted, and conveniently place the tracker on her. Hopefully, not getting any more ribs broken in the process.

He didn't need one of Zodiac's top minds helping him, but he had one anyway, just a different kind of brilliant. "You got anything for me, Outlaw? She's got to be making her move soon."

Mark Outlawson was in the Denver office. "Nothing so far, except me being about to stab a pencil through my eye because this is so boring."

Sarge knew the feeling. "Yeah, I don't envy you."

"I feel kind of like this is somehow my fault," he said. "I should have noticed something was wrong in Marrakesh."

"I don't think when you saw her in Marrakesh there was any problem. I think it happened afterward." If there had been something Mark could see, he would've seen it. He was one of the best contractors Zodiac had.

"Either way, I'm glad I can help you get her back. Even if it's desk duty."

"I'd rather have you than some of the nerds. You at least know what I'm looking for."

Sarge heard him pop his gum—the guy truly hated being behind a desk—and that was one of his coping mechanisms. "Some of them aren't so bad. Jenna, for instance. I can't understand why she's working in this department at all. She's sharp enough to be at any Zodiac office in the world."

"She has her reasons. Believe me. The Linear Tactical team helped get her out of a pretty bad hostage situation a while ago, but I don't have many details, and I don't want to press her if she doesn't want to talk about it."

"Yeah. I worked security for Cade Conner who is friends with those guys."

"The singer?"

"Yeah. So I've spent some time in Oak Creek, but I didn't know Jenna then. You're right, though, I'm sure she has her reasons for never leaving her house."

Outlaw didn't say anything else, and neither did he. They both knew what it was like to not share reasons publicly. Jenna could tell hers if she wanted to.

Twenty minutes went by without any sign of Bronwyn

"Where is she?" he muttered. "She's going to lose her window."

He couldn't stand the thought that she'd aborted her mission and he'd lost the opportunity to get this tracker on her.

"Yeah, it won't be long before Kerpar is back to the hotel. Maybe she couldn't find a way to get another room key—oh shit."

"What?"

"We've got a potential problem down in the garage. I've picked up Kerpar and his men coming in down there, and Bronwyn is there too. It looks like she's moving in for some sort of attack."

Shit. She wasn't trying to steal something from Kerpar's room; she was going to rob him in person.

There were so many problems with this plan he couldn't think of them all as he bolted out of the room and ran down the same stairway he and Bronwyn had fought in yesterday.

Kerpar had armed guards—four of them. They wouldn't hesitate to kill her. Plus, she wasn't trying to keep her identity a secret at all.

"Shit," Outlaw confirmed. "I think she is going to try to take them out herself. She's lying in wait."

Sarge sped down the stairwell, taking the steps two at a time, ignoring the pain from his fight with Bronwyn. "I need you to kill the cameras down there. Whatever's about to happen, I don't want there to be any record of it."

He didn't want Kerpar's counterparts or law enforcement to be able to find her. Both would be looking.

"Roger that, boss."

"And don't let any 9-1-1 calls out of the garage either. Nothing unless you hear from me."

"You better be careful, Virgo," Outlaw said. "This has ugly written all over it."

"I know it does. It has from the beginning."

Sarge didn't slow down until he hit the door for the garage. That he took quietly and was careful not to let it slam behind him. He ducked behind cars and made his way down to the VIP parking lot.

Kerpar, that cheap bastard, should've coughed up the fifty dollars to pay for valet. He could've avoided this.

He heard the noise before he actually saw them, but it didn't take long before he caught a glimpse of what was going on.

Bronwyn was fighting, once again not pulling any punches, and this time, she had a knife.

Sarge stayed low but moved quickly. He could hear faint moans as she got in blow after blow. He didn't know if she took any hits. He heard the sound of something metal hitting the ground and saw a gun skid across the pavement.

One man was lying unconscious or dead near a parked car. Bronwyn was fighting two others. It looked like the guards had stashed Kerpar in his own vehicle. Where was the fourth man? In with Kerpar?

Sarge was about to intervene when Bronwyn used her knife to take down one of the guards with a stab to the neck. He wouldn't be getting back up.

She was fighting with the remaining bodyguard when he saw the fourth start to crawl out of the car, gun raised. He ran and dove for him just as he got his shot off. He didn't look to see if it had hit Bronwyn.

He ignored the pain in his ribs, landing against the man, throwing him the rest of the way out of the vehicle and onto the ground. Sarge grabbed the gun from his hand and swung it around, clocking him in the head. He wasn't dead, but he wouldn't be waking up for a while.

Kerpar was huddled in the back seat as he climbed in. "You don't know who you're messing with. I have money. I can give you whatever you want. But if you kill me, I have people who are going to come after you."

"Shut the fuck up." Sarge looked away from him to see if Bronwyn was still standing.

It wasn't him he needed to worry about. It was the five-foot-three brunette weighing hardly a hundred pounds currently kicking the ass of all his men who should be scaring him.

"You need to stay down," Sarge told him. He didn't have any lost love for this man whatsoever, but Sarge wasn't going to let Bronwyn take his life if he could stop it.

Before he could get another word out, the door on the other side jerked open.

Bronwyn. Once again not looking anything like the woman Sarge knew.

"Room key." She held out her hand, voice dead. Completely emotionless.

"I'm going to fucking kill you, bitch. Do you know who I am?" Kerpar sputtered.

Faster than either of them could think she would move, she was inside the car and had slit Kerpar on his face with her knife.

"Room key now." She didn't even look at Sarge.

Kerpar put a hand up to his bleeding face. "You cut me."

"I will continue to cut you every five seconds until you give me your room key."

Kerpar was at least smart enough to realize she meant what she said. He got the room key out of his pocket and held it out toward her. "Hey, you're the bitch from the bar, the one with the eyes."

She was going to kill him. Sarge didn't know how he

couldn't see it, but he sure as hell could. He dove across the car to stop her, catching her wrist midair, the knife pointing down at Kerpar's chest.

"I can't let you do that, Pony Girl. You're going to regret it someday."

Her eyes stayed glued on Kerpar. "I must complete my mission."

She still wasn't looking at Sarge, but at least she wasn't fighting. Not the way he knew she could.

He didn't want to fight her while she had hold of that knife. The only way for him to stop that before it got out of hand would be to break her wrist—and at this angle, it would cause damage for the rest of her life.

They held their position with the knife over Kerpar, who thankfully remained quiet. "Don't do this, Pony Girl. Stop now."

She bit her lip until it bled, but she still didn't look at him and didn't ease up. "I must complete my mission."

This was an internal struggle. She was fighting it as best she could.

If Sarge wanted to get that knife out of her hand without hurting her, he needed to fight this battle within the parameters as they'd been set up.

"Does your mission require that you kill him?"

"No," she said without hesitation.

"Then let him go. Go complete your mission."

Her face contorted, and he knew she was fighting whatever was controlling her. Sarge wanted to help her, to get her out now. But he had to play the long game with the tracker. It was the best way to keep her safe even if it meant letting her go now.

Increasing pressure on the knife to keep it out of Kerpar's chest, he grabbed the tiny tracker with his other hand. He reached up and cupped her neck, above that damned choker necklace, forcing her to look at him. "Complete the mission without killing him."

She jerked away, but he'd gotten the tracker on her where her neck met her shoulder. It was small and clear; she wouldn't notice it unless she did a full-body check specifically for trackers.

"You're both dead." Kerpar was still trapped beneath us on the seat. "I don't know who you think you are, but..."

Sarge spun, hoping he wasn't making a huge mistake, and clocked him with his elbow, letting go of Bronwyn. He fell back unconscious against the door. She didn't look at him, but she didn't try to kill him again.

Sarge eased back. "You're clear."

She got out of the car, and he climbed out after her. She still wasn't looking at him. But maybe that was better. He needed to let her go. He heard Kerpar groan behind him and turned back to him to give him one more solid punch on the jaw before she could decide killing him was the way to go.

"Virgo, watch your six. You've got—"

Sarge spun, knowing he'd made a rookie mistake by turning his back on his current enemy—Bronwyn. He expected to feel the slice of a blade. He was looking low, ready to defend from the knife, not expecting the jumping roundhouse kick that caught him square on the temple.

He slid back against the car then down on his ass. He could hear Outlaw screeching in his ear.

She crouched down beside him, but she didn't have her knife out. She cupped the back of his neck.

"No trackers," she whispered.

Shit, she'd already found it. He had to get up. He had to stop her. Without the tracker, he wouldn't know where she was going.

"If you follow me now, we both die."

Her sharp chop to the carotid artery at the side of his neck and his entire world turned gray. The last thing Sarge saw was her walking away before black took over.

CHAPTER
TWELVE

SARGE SAT LOOKING out at the view of the Rockies from his back porch. His house was relatively small and plain, but the view of the Front Range had made its high price totally worth it. Way too many times in the Navy, he'd wished he'd had someplace he could be by himself with nothing around him but wide-open spaces.

Today, he was here less to enjoy the view and more because he was otherwise pretty useless thanks to Bronwyn's gifts from three days ago that kept on giving. A cracked rib and broken nose from their fight in the stairwell, a concussion from that roundhouse kick to the head. Dozens of bruises from head to toe.

And absolutely nothing to show for getting his ass handed to him by someone barely over five feet tall. She'd put that tracker back on his neck like he'd put it on hers. By the time he'd regained consciousness, Outlaw still screeching in his ear, she'd been gone. She'd gotten what she'd needed from Kerpar and disappeared.

When his phone rang, he wanted to ignore it, but he couldn't. Ian and Landon were still in Wyoming tracking down leads on Erick Huen and the rest of Mosaic. They had somebody they were hoping to send in undercover who could report back on Mosaic's inner workings.

Sarge looked at the unknown number with a Seattle area code on his phone. Seeing that it was a video call made him want to throw the fucking thing across the yard, but he refrained. When the call connected, the screen was still dark. Maybe it wasn't a video call after all.

"This is Harrison McEwan." His voice was gruff, but he didn't give a shit. He didn't have time to play around. He needed to get back to solemnly staring at the mountains and feeling sorry for himself.

More silence, no picture. He heard breathing. Great, just what he needed, somebody butt-dialing him and not hanging up.

"Hey, did you dial the wrong number?" He asked. "Hello?"

He was a second from hanging up when he heard her voice. "Sarge?"

Bronwyn.

Sarge dragged his feet down from the side table where they'd been resting, sat up straight in his rocking chair, and winced at the sharp pain in his ribs.

"Pony Girl?" He brought the phone closer.

She shifted a little so that light partially hit her across her face and he could see those eyes. She looked tired, in pain.

"Where are you?" He asked her.

"West. I don't know."

"Seattle? The number is a Seattle area code."

She looked around like she truly didn't know quite where she was. "Yes, Seattle maybe."

He stood up. "Can you stay there? I'll send someone for you. I'll come and get you myself."

She shook her head, her brown hair falling over her face. It looked unkempt, unwashed. "No, I don't have much time."

Sarge kept the phone close to his face as he walked inside

toward his computer. He needed to get the nerds tracing this number right fucking now. He was sending someone after Bronwyn whether she wanted him to or not.

"I have to go," she whispered. "I have a mission."

"No. Don't you hang up on me. Stay with me, Pony Girl." He didn't know how she was having this clarity now—able to recognize him and be the Bronwyn he knew, but he didn't want to lose it.

Her fingers came to the screen and touched it, as if she were trying to stroke his face. "I hurt you, didn't I? That was real. We fought."

"I'm okay. I can take a beating."

"You could have hurt me, but you didn't," she whispered. "I remember that. But I hurt you. I'm sorry. I should go. You probably don't want to talk to me anyway."

"Bronwyn, I do." Sarge reached up and touched the screen, mirroring what she had done. "I do want to talk to you. Always."

"Why would you after what I did?" Her voice was hoarse, strained.

"You weren't fighting me because you wanted to. You were fighting me because you were somehow compelled to do it. I could tell something was wrong." He sat down at his desk and opened his laptop with one hand, keeping his eyes pinned to her on the phone.

"So you didn't fight back."

"I wanted to see if I could take you out without hurting you." He smiled, even though he knew it was tight. "Spoiler alert: I couldn't. You were too good."

Her smile was so grim it couldn't be called a smile at all. "I'm sorry. Don't come after me anymore."

"I will come after you. Every single time until you're safe."

Sarge shot out an email to Jenna, giving her that phone number, typing with one hand, not looking at the words, so that his eyes remained on Bronwyn. He hoped Jenna would be able to understand.

"Can you tell me what's different now, Pony Girl? Why are you able to talk and be okay?"

Those blue eyes stared at him. "I'm getting stronger, but they don't know. They still think it takes the same amount of time, but I've been easing it back."

"Easing what back?"

"The meds. The injections. I fight the pain."

He had no idea what she was talking about, but he didn't want her to hang up. "Let me help you. Let me get you and help you."

She shook her head. "I don't have enough time."

Shit. He was going to lose her. "We know about Mosaic. We know about Erick Huen. We know—"

"Erick Huen," she interrupted me. "Yes, he's one. But there are more, many more." She rubbed her eyes. "I don't remember. I know one, one is..." She trailed off without saying anything else.

"Pony Girl, stay with me."

"I can't. I can't anymore. I have to go. The mission, the mission."

Damn it. She was rocking back and forth, and Sarge had no idea how to help. She was going to hang up any second and be gone again.

"Listen to me, Bronwyn. I want you to stay alive. Do you understand?" He didn't know why he said that to her, but he knew he had to. "You do whatever you need to do to survive. Be smart."

She stopped rocking and brought the phone closer to her face. "Promise me. Promise me you'll see me again."

"Yes, absolutely, I promise you." Easiest promise he ever made. "I'm not leaving you behind. I'll be coming for you, Pony Girl."

Her face grew paler; sweat broke out on her forehead. She

started rocking back and forth again, coming in and out of the picture on the screen. Whatever was happening to her was getting worse fast.

His hand balled into a fist. She was in so much pain, and there was nothing he could do about it. "Bronwyn— Pony Girl, hang in there. You're so strong. Such a survivor. I know you can do this. I am going to help you."

She stopped rocking and looked straight at him. "Promise me you'll see me again."

"I swear on my life."

"Good. Next time you see me, I want you to kill me."

The line went dead.

Sarge muttered every foul curse he knew and immediately tried to recall the number, but she didn't pick up. He slammed his fist down on his desk, ignoring the pain it sent echoing through the wounds in his body.

He called Jenna. "Did you get my email?"

"Dude, yes," she said. "It took me a minute to translate that many spelling errors. What the heck?"

"I was trying to type while on a video call with Bronwyn."

"What? Holy shit. We traced the call to Seattle, but then it went dead. I did some preliminary research on the number, and it's from a no-contract phone you can pick up at any drugstore or a supercenter."

A burner phone. He ran a hand across his face and sat back in his chair. "Okay. Have someone on your team dig deeper, and see if you find anything useful. I don't think she's going to be in Seattle for long. I know you have your hands full with the Mosaic intel Landon and Ian brought in."

"I'll make sure someone is on it, Sarge. I promise. We'll search every angle."

He knew the nerds would do their best and their best was impressive, but he also knew that they weren't going to find Bronwyn at the end of that phone.

She was gone again.

"Did Bronwyn say anything to you?" Jenna asked. "If she set up a meeting, you should probably be careful. I hate to say this, but it could be a trap."

"No, she didn't say anything about a meetup. She was upset that she had hurt me."

"Okay, that's good. I mean, good that she was remorseful. We'll keep an open trace on your phone. If she calls again, we'll be able to lock onto it immediately."

He hung up with Jenna without providing much more detail about his conversation with Bronwyn so she could get to her job.

He didn't want to let Jenna or anyone know how bad it was getting. That Bronwyn was becoming desperate—like an animal trapped and trying to claw its way out of an impossible situation.

And how dangerous that made her.

———

Bronwyn hung up with Sarge and smashed the phone under her heel. She stumbled forward a few steps, grabbing her head in her hands to keep herself from falling over. Fighting through the pain, she sucked in breaths until she was a little steadier.

Calling him had been a mistake, too risky. If they had caught her buying the phone, they would know they didn't have full control over her. They would figure out there were minutes she had pushed into hours when the pain was manageable and she still knew who she was.

But she'd needed to see his face, hear his voice.

Bronwyn had to know if she had hurt him as badly as her cloudy mind remembered. If her vague recollection of kicking him hard, of trying to kill him, was truth or fiction.

One look at him through the screen, covered in bruises, and she'd had her answer. She'd hurt him. The man who'd done nothing but help her. Been nothing but gentle and supportive.

The man she'd been dreaming of for years. Until lately. Now, there was too much darkness for dreaming. And she didn't want to dream anyway when her waking hours felt like some sort of nightmare. Even life back in Prague had been better than this.

Bronwyn reached back and picked up a tiny plastic piece of the phone, clutching it in her palm. She would keep this piece of Sarge close to her. No one would know what it meant except her.

He would be with her. She would keep him with her.

She stumbled a few more steps, the pain radiating up her skin. She knew where she needed to go, her body pushing her forward toward her mission. Anchorage, a building with some sort of medical files that she needed to steal from the hospital.

She looked down at the piece of plastic in her hand. It was jumping around due to the tremors she couldn't control. This was the longest Dr. Tippens had left her out of the lab, left her out of the dark. They thought they had better control over her than they did.

She had to keep fighting, keep boosting her resistance. It was her only chance…

Bronwyn was serious about what she had told Sarge. If he met her again before she had this under control, he had to kill her. Otherwise, she might kill him. She had almost done it already. It had been with only the narrowest of margins she'd been able to walk away from his unconscious body in that garage rather than kill him.

Right now, she had to complete her mission; she didn't have any choice. The overwhelming need to press the side of her necklace ate at her. Once she did, everything would fall into place, and nothing would be difficult. Nothing would hurt.

She stumbled out of the building, bringing her hand up to her neck as she went. She pressed, not fighting it anymore. She felt the sting of the injection then waited. It would only be a few seconds before the…

It was time. The pain was gone. The mission was all that mattered.

The piece of plastic in her hand fell to the ground.

"I exist only to obey orders. My final mission is to go home."

CHAPTER THIRTEEN

NEXT TIME YOU SEE ME, *I want you to kill me.*

Bronwyn's words echoed in his mind long after she'd hung up. Long after they weren't able to get any trace on that burner phone.

And for every minute of the four days since, he thought it was hyperbole. Something he would tease her about when he saw her again.

Hyperbole would have been something her mother had taught in her university class on literature. Bronwyn telling him to kill her was an epic example of the literary device.

But this latest footage they'd gotten of Bronwyn made him think perhaps her wish wasn't an exaggeration at all, at least not in her mind.

She'd been caught on an ATM camera across from an alley in Anchorage, Alaska.

Sarge watched as she stabbed a man in the chest—a wound meant to kill. He rewound the footage and watched it again.

Bronwyn was lying in the alley, clearly in pain. She vomited more than once and seemed almost too weak to get up. Some shady guy came over and started patting her down, obviously wanting to take advantage of an easy mark.

She grabbed his wrist and broke it. He had no problem with that. He had actually smiled when he saw it for the first time. Good for her.

It pissed the thug off, and he landed a couple of good kicks in her midsection that had Sarge wanting to hunt him down.

He pulled out a knife and bent down closer to her. He didn't try to stab or slice her, just pointed it in her direction. Sarge couldn't tell what he was saying, but probably something along the lines of wanting her to give him her wallet.

Bronwyn didn't respond verbally. Instead, she spun the knife on him and rammed it straight into his chest then back out, the movement efficient, brutal, deadly. The guy fell over in front of her, blood pouring from his wound.

In any court of law, that would hold up as self-defense. The punk obviously had provoked her, and a lawyer would argue that she'd protected herself as anyone would be expected to do. She'd killed him trying to get the knife away.

But Sarge knew the truth. Everyone at Zodiac Tactical would know the truth—that her training would've allowed her to disarm that guy a dozen ways without killing him.

Bronwyn knew the truth too. The camera caught her expression as his body fell over. Devastation clouded her face as she realized what she'd done.

Then her expression fell blank again.

She was going in and out of her own awareness like she had in New York. A few seconds later, she forced herself off the ground and stumbled out of the alley, leaving the guy there, knife in hand.

He watched the footage again. *Still not going to kill you, Pony Girl. We're going to figure this out.*

There was a tap on his office door, and Landon walked in. "I heard you got some footage of Bronwyn."

"Yeah, it's not good."

He sat down across from him. He spun the laptop so he could watch it.

Sarge knew exactly when she shoved the knife into the guy's chest. Landon flinched. Then he watched it again, ready for the violence this time.

He finished and sat back. "Holy shit. This was obviously self-defense, even if…"

Even if they both knew she could have taken that guy out without killing him. He nodded.

"Where and when was this?" he asked.

"Anchorage," Sarge said. "Yesterday."

"She's certainly getting her frequent flyer mile bonus. London. New York. Now Alaska?"

"Yeah. She's being sent wherever Mosaic wants her."

Landon ran a hand through his light brown hair, standing it on edge. "Now that we've got someone on the inside at Mosaic, hopefully we'll get some data and be able to make a move to get Bronwyn back."

"Tell me about this Silas Varela guy." He was the criminal informant Landon and Ian had gotten out of their trip to Wyoming last week.

"Guy beat the shit out of an unarmed civilian and then threatened the life of her daughter. So a real charmer."

"Fucker," Sarge muttered under his breath.

"He's lucky he's still breathing. His options are spending the rest of his life in jail, where Mosaic is certain to get to him at any moment, or providing us some intel. If he does, Ian will make sure he's protected while he's in jail for the rest of his life."

"He doesn't sound particularly trustworthy."

Landon shrugged. "If it gets us information on Mosaic, we'll take it."

Anything on Mosaic was going to get them closer to Bronwyn.

He nodded. "Ian needs to make intel on Bronwyn this guy's first priority."

Landon leaned back in the chair, resting his arms loosely on the rests. His light brown hair and surfer good looks tended to put people at ease—both men and women. He used his charm to his advantage, to Zodiac's advantage, as often as he could. He was endearing, friendly, good with people.

Basically, the opposite of Sarge.

"Ian's goal is to bring Mosaic down as a whole," Landon said. "When we do that, we'll get Bronwyn back too."

He mimicked Landon's stance, leaning back in his own chair. He was trying to manage him, to put him at ease so he didn't demand what he knew was best for Bronwyn.

"Ian is not unbiased when it comes to taking down Mosaic. It's personal, and he'll stop at nothing to do it, even if it means sacrificing others." Bronwyn. "I don't know why that's the case. Ian has never shared the specifics with me. But I know you know the backstory."

Landon didn't get ruffled. His posture remained relaxed. "Yeah, I do. He has his reasons for it being personal. What they did to him, nobody should have to live through."

Sarge thought of how Ian had looked when they'd first gotten the London footage and heard the word Mosaic. He'd been spooked.

He'd known Ian for nearly ten years. The man had held Sarge's life in his hands multiple times. Ian DeRose did not spook easily.

He leaned forward on his desk, catching sight of the Bronwyn footage that was playing again on the laptop. "Look, I love Ian like a brother. You know that. You too, even though you're a pain in my ass. And I get that Mosaic, whatever version we're dealing with, is bad. They're terrorists—people we need to stop before they get out of control."

"I think we're all in agreement."

"But the fact is one of our own is in trouble, and we need to help her first and foremost."

Landon didn't say anything for a long moment. He leaned his head to the side and studied Sarge. "You want to tell me what really happened in New York?" He pointed at the last of his fading bruises.

He hadn't told anybody what had gone down between Bronwyn and him. "I got in a fight."

"So I read in the medical report. Two cracked ribs, a broken nose, and some kidney damage. Doc said in the report that you were noncommittal about exactly how it had all happened."

"I didn't sit around discussing my feelings. So what?"

"Turns out, I decided to see who was able to get the drop on the famous Harrison McEwan. What would it take to do that sort of damage? Four guys? Five guys?"

Sarge didn't provide any info, so he continued. "I went to look up the footage, and lo and behold, it had somehow been turned off in the garage. How exactly did that happen, Sarge?"

"Happy accident," he muttered. "What's your point?"

"My point is, there's only one other time I recall you getting your ass handed to you this way. Back in Prague a few years ago. And just like now, you were pretty mum about those details too."

Landon knew. Sarge could deny it all he wanted, but Landon had put the details together and figured out he knew Bronwyn years ago. He wasn't going to insult either of them by lying to him.

"Fine. I knew Bronwyn back when she was in Prague and she was a kid in trouble. I took that beating because if I hadn't, she was going to be the one to pay the price. I met up with her again after Zodiac opened and told her about the Paris office. She was a pickpocket then; she's a pickpocket now."

"You were involved with her back then?" Landon raised his eyebrow, but his tone remained neutral. He was trying his best not to judge.

"She was a fucking teenager," Sarge said. "No, I wasn't involved with her. I was trying to help her out."

Landon blew out a breath. "Fine. You did the right thing. But she's not a teenager anymore. She's an adult making adult choices."

"She needs our help." He wanted to bang his fist against the desk to emphasize the point. "And we need to be putting our resources into doing that."

"Look at that footage." He pointed at the laptop. "She killed that guy when she could have easily disarmed him and walked away. And New York? There's a suspicious lack of bruising on your knuckles for your ass to have been kicked so hard."

They both knew what lack of bruising on his hands meant. He hadn't fought back, at least not to the degree that he should have.

Sarge said nothing.

"She did this to you in New York."

"I know it looks bad. I know that if you study these pieces separately, it looks like Bronwyn has gone rogue, that she's working for Mosaic. But I'm telling you there's something more to it."

Landon nodded, steepling his fingers once again. He'd always been the peacekeeper of their group even back when they'd been in the SEALs. He had the temperament for it. "Okay, I'm willing to listen. Convince me, and I'll help you convince Ian."

"I don't have the information yet. All I know is that Mosaic is controlling her some way, some sort of drugs and injections that they give her."

"Mind control?" he asked.

Sarge scrubbed a hand down his face, thinking of her blank look when she'd first seen him. "I don't know. Maybe."

They both knew that mind control was sketchy at best and they certainly wouldn't have sent Bronwyn off by herself if they weren't sure that they could control her completely.

"It has something to do with this necklace she has on." He lined up the footage so he could see it. "And there, see how cold her face is when she kills this guy? Almost blank, nothing. But then, look. A few seconds later, she's distraught. It's like she's coming in and out of her own consciousness."

Landon watched two more times. "All right, I'll give you that. Her reaction seems to be on extreme ends of the spectrum."

"She was like that in New York too. Sometimes she didn't recognize me. But then there were times when she called me by name. She's in trouble, Landon."

"I'm going to ask you the same thing Ian would ask you if he were here and if he didn't have a complex relationship with Mosaic. Was she trying to kill you when you fought her in New York?"

Sarge wasn't going to lie to his friend. He may not like the answer, but keeping this truth from him wasn't going to help anybody in the long run.

"Yes. When she had clarity and recognized me, she wasn't trying to, but most of the time, she wasn't clear. She wasn't Bronwyn. In those moments, she wanted to kill me." She almost had.

"Fine. We'll show this footage to Ian. We'll make our case about getting Varela to find out as much as he can about Bronwyn. But I'm going to tell you, Ian is not going to put all his efforts into that. Especially not when she's acting so much like an enemy."

Fuck that. "Bronwyn is one of us."

"Bronwyn is one of us who tried to kill you. Right now,

that makes her a partial enemy at best. Or worse, an unpredictable one."

"Ian's only mission is to stop Mosaic. He doesn't care about her."

"It's not that he doesn't care," Landon responded. "But he knows that, ultimately, Mosaic is the bigger problem. Mosaic is back and more well-funded than ever. We know that there are four heads of the organization now rather than one. We know Erick Huen is one of them. We have a little bit of data on two others, but nothing at all on the fourth one. And unknown variables in situations like this are never good."

"If taking down Mosaic is where Ian needs to focus himself, that's fine with me. But Bronwyn is my priority."

Landon let out a sigh. "The two are not mutually exclusive."

They were to him, and to Ian, but he didn't say that. Landon wanted to believe they could do both at the same time, and he wasn't going to argue.

Landon stood. "All right, let's go talk to Ian. He's up in his penthouse. He'll come around. He's going to want to help you find your woman."

Sarge stood up, following him out. "She's not my woman."

"Yeah, Sarge, keep telling yourself that."

"I'm serious. It's not like that." He forced the thought of the kiss in Paris from his mind. "She's too young. She's been hurt. She's in trouble."

"Yeah. Sounds like she needs somebody who is older, stubborn, impatient, and willing to fight for her. Know anybody like that?"

"You're a fucking pain in my ass."

Landon laughed. "Remind me to say I told you so when you ask me to be one of your groomsmen. Now let's go see what we can dig up on the girl who kicked your ass."

CHAPTER
FOURTEEN

DO *whatever you need to do to survive.*

Bronwyn kept Sarge's voice on repeat in her head when the Mosaic soldiers came and got her in Anchorage and Dr. Tippens had her put back in the dark cell.

Stay alive. Whatever you need to do. Survive.

Sarge had said other things to her too. Things about Mosaic and Erick Huen, but that info was too hard for her battered mind to process and remember.

Instead, she focused on the sound of his deep voice telling her she could do this. That she could survive. That he believed in her.

It made the dark more bearable, knowing that he'd said all those things even after she'd hurt him.

Under Sarge's constant tutelage in her mind, survival took on a different meaning.

Whatever you need to do.

Survival didn't have to mean rebellion. Especially when it started becoming clear that outright rebellion—refusing to give them what they wanted—would make them tighten their fists around her.

So Bronwyn didn't fight Mosaic anymore. When they told

her to say her words, she did it immediately. She started saying them as soon as they opened the slot in the door.

Let them think she was weak. Let them think that they had found the way to control her mind. As long as she was still inside herself, as long as she could remember Sarge and hear his voice, she knew they hadn't won.

She didn't fight her meds. She didn't fight the injections. Instead, she curled inside herself and talked to Sarge. She listened to him as he spoke to her—told her she could do this. She would survive. She'd survived as a child, and she would survive now.

Focusing on him was hard at first, but it became easier. She could hear him more clearly in her mind. She could talk to him more freely in silence. It almost felt like she could reach out and touch his thick, dark hair.

Maybe hallucinating about a man she'd only spent a handful of hours with—many of those encased in violence—shouldn't have made her feel saner. But it did.

Bronwyn realized Dr. Tippens was spacing out her medication more. He and his team didn't know they were losing hold of her. They thought being alone in the dark would break her down further into the tool they wanted.

They didn't know she had someone with her. And as long as Sarge was with her, whatever they were attempting to do to her mind and body wasn't working the way they thought.

Bronwyn wasn't sure how much time had passed in the dark after they'd brought her back from Alaska. Based on her meals and how many times she was taken to the lab, she knew it was weeks.

She hated the lab. She'd rather be left in the dark with Sarge. Under the lab's garish bright lights, holding on to him was harder.

Today especially. Today, instead of being by herself with one or two medical technicians, the lab was full of people.

Dr. Tippens was here with a team of technicians. And

there were dozens of others. Others like her, strapped to chairs and beds.

Some were moaning in pain, fighting the straps that bound them to the gurneys. Some were silent. More than one was completely covered by a sheet.

She knew what that meant.

Sarge always stayed and silently held her hand when she was in the lab. They couldn't talk, she knew that, not there.

But today, he slipped away, fading backward.

"Stay," she whispered, so softly that only he could hear her.

He slid his fingers along her lips, stilling them with a touch she couldn't feel.

You have to listen to what's going on around you without letting them know. Concentrate. You can do this, Pony Girl. I'll be back.

Bronwyn wanted to cry, to beg him to stay, but with a blink of her eyes, he was gone.

Despair threatened to swamp her, but she forced it back. She would do what Sarge said. Listen. Concentrate. Not give herself away.

Dr. Tippens walked around her, looking at a chart. The other man was there too. The one she knew. The one who had come to her hotel room. What was his name?

"She looks like a zombie," the man from her hotel room said. "Like she has that Bell's…whatever disease."

"Bell's palsy." Dr. Tippens didn't look up from his chart. "And it's not a disease, it's a condition. And evidently, it can be a side effect of the genetic modification we're doing."

"We have interested parties who are going to be very upset if her face doesn't work right."

"Her face works fine, Erick. Let me do my job."

Erick Huen. That was his name. She remembered Sarge saying something to her about him. She tried to remember the details but decided to let it go, to focus on now.

"Fine." Erick walked around her, studying her with disdain. She forced herself to remain completely blank, allowing her peripheral vision to fill in details. "It's disappointing to see her this comatose. She was so feisty before. Hard to believe that now."

Dr. Tippens shined a light in her eye. "I agree. She responded much more quickly to the genetic modifications than we expected. We were able to reduce her neuroinhibitors and medication. Sometimes things go right. That's one of the joys of science."

"Glad to hear it after all the funding we've put into your research." Erick moved closer to her again, and she could feel his breath on her face. "And she's ready to kill? We have a very special job for her."

Dr. Tippens let out a sigh and moved his arm to push Erick back from her. "She's killed before, as you know, but it goes against her nature. She was struggling against her programming most when she killed that man in Anchorage. You'd be wiser to use some of our other subjects if you have a murder job in mind."

"Murder job?" Erick snickered. "Stick to the medical jargon, doc."

"I would if you'd get out of my lab and let me do my job," he muttered.

"It needs to be Bronwyn." Erick inched closer to her again. "Evidently, Ian DeRose has found himself a little girlfriend, and we want to send a message to him. Her dead body ought to do that nicely. And then finding out it was done by somebody he hired and trained will make it even sweeter."

It took everything Bronwyn had to keep herself completely still and not show any expression. She didn't want to hurt anybody having to do with Zodiac Tactical. That would hurt Sarge.

She wished he were there. She needed him.

Listen. Concentrate.

She barely avoided a flinch as Erick slid her hair back from her forehead. "You're going to put a bullet right between Wavy Bollinger's eyes."

"Please stop molesting the patients." Dr. Tippens put his arm out to ease Erick back again. "You know what we're doing here is a delicate balance. Your touch could affect the regimen in negative ways."

"Fine." Erick sounded like a pouting child, but he moved away from me. "Make sure she's ready."

———

Bronwyn didn't go back to her cell after that. She went from total darkness to total brightness all the time. The brightness was so much worse.

Sometimes she was in the main lab, but most of her time was in what they called the indoctrination room.

She called it hell.

She was strapped to a chair, her eyes taped so she could do nothing but look at what was in front of her. She couldn't blink much less cry.

She was bombarded with picture after picture of Wavy Bollinger—a kind-looking woman in her early thirties with a big smile and red hair. In some of the photos, Ian DeRose was with her. But never Sarge.

With every picture, she was told Wavy was her enemy as the doctors did something under the skin at the back of her neck. Sharp pricks and slices and burns, always to reinforce the words surrounding her.

"Wavy Bollinger is the enemy." The pinch of a needle prick at the back of her neck.

"Your mission is to kill her for the safety of others." The burn as they injected something. Did something to her body.

"Wavy Bollinger is dangerous, a threat to be eliminated."

The burn spreading as she looked at the woman who'd never done anything to hurt her.

Bronwyn could feel the hatred bubbling through her veins—whether they were her real feelings or what the doctors were doing to her, it didn't matter. The end result was the same. She wanted to kill this woman.

Wavy's not your enemy, Pony Girl. You hold on to that.

She couldn't see Sarge, but she could hear his voice in her ear. He whispered it over and over, combating whatever the doctors were doing to her.

Dr. Tippens was becoming suspicious that something wasn't right. Maybe she was acting too blank. She wasn't sure how she was supposed to act to stop them from strengthening their attempts to control her.

All she knew was that she had to keep Sarge's voice in her head all the time or else she was going to give in to what they were training her to do.

Kill the woman. Kill Wavy Bollinger.

Keeping herself still and curled up around her thoughts of Sarge had been easy in her dark cell. But here, where she was exposed to Dr. Tippens and all his assistants, it was impossibly hard. She was close to cracking, to screaming, to begging them to stop.

But those reactions would show them clearly that their reduced regimen wasn't working. Then they would fix it. They would up the medications and gene editing and neuroinhibitors—all words she didn't understand but knew were her downfall.

Sarge would be gone for good. Once he was out of her head, she wouldn't be able to hold on. They'd turn her into whatever they wanted her to be.

A killer.

"Her blood pressure and heart rate should not be spiking like this," Dr. Tippens said to one of his assistants, "What has changed?"

"Nothing, sir," the woman said. "We've been giving her the prescribed regimen every day as scheduled, applied during the indoctrination."

The doctor stood behind her. She couldn't see him, even with her eyes peeled open.

"Notify Erick Huen that I need to see him. She's not ready. If we send her out like this, she's going to snap. I don't want to waste the data we've gotten from her. Stop all indoctrination for right now."

Bronwyn swallowed her sobs of relief as her bed was lowered to a resting position and her eyes were released from the torturous tape. Wavy's pictures faded from her sight.

She was able to turn her head, and she saw Sarge standing there, arms crossed over his big chest, smiling at her with pride in his eyes. She'd made it. At least for now. Her eyes drifted closed.

When she became conscious of her surroundings again, Erick Huen was there, standing over her where Sarge had been. She had no idea how long he'd been there. Once again, she barely controlled her actions before they gave her away.

"Tippens, you're disappointing me. What happened to sometimes things go right—the joy of science?" Erick flipped a hand around his head in a grand gesture.

"We are working in uncharted territory. It's hard to know what can cause drastic changes. We need more time to see what's happening with Bronwyn. See what can be done to make the process less of a shock for her system."

"I don't care about her system, and you shouldn't either. Mosaic doesn't tolerate failure, not when we're putting out the amount of funding we are to support your research. My partners are starting to question your results. We don't want that, do we, Tippens?"

Dr. Tippens's voice was hoarse. "I need more time."

Erick walked around to her other side. "Fortunately, I don't need sweet Bronwyn here to kill Wavy Bollinger any longer. I've decided to handle that myself. Plans have changed."

"Changed to what?"

"It ends up that we have a mole in our organization. And I'd like your little weapon here to neutralize him. The name is Silas Varela."

Dr. Tippens let out a sigh. "I would strongly suggest one of our other subjects. There are a number who will do a more efficient job than Bronwyn."

"No, I want her."

"You might be doing permanent damage to her psyche not to mention our research."

"I'm pretty sure what's going to happen to her at the end of her usefulness will be damaging enough to her psyche. Maybe I'll be doing her a favor if her brain explodes now." He poked Dr. Tippens in the chest. "Get her prepped and ready for the mission. She leaves in two days."

"Erick, I—"

"Two days. She kills Silas Varela and plants evidence at his house that makes it look like a robbery."

Bronwyn flinched, but neither of them saw her.

"I don't think she's ready."

"Then she will have reached the end of her usefulness, and perhaps you will have too. Get her ready."

CHAPTER FIFTEEN

THE WALLS WERE CLOSING in on her. She drove her nails into her head as she huddled in the closet in Silas Varela's apartment.

For the past three days, Bronwyn had been trying to hold on to the last bit of her sanity. To the last bits of herself that made her who she was. Her mind felt like it had been split open and all the pieces of her were oozing out and fading into nothing.

And now she was there, in this apartment, to kill a man.

She'd vomited half a dozen times already until there was nothing left in her system. Her nose had been bleeding almost nonstop for the hours she'd been there.

The only thing that made any of it go away was to stop fighting the urge to kill Varela.

Even Sarge's voice wasn't helping her.

You're not a killer, Pony Girl.

Survive.

Right now, those two statements were at odds with each other.

The more she tried to fight the indoctrination she'd gone through in the past forty-eight hours, the worse the pain got.

So she gave herself respite by mentally agreeing to kill Varela when he got home.

If she did that, she would survive. But it would prove Mosaic had made her into a killer.

You're not a killer, Pony Girl.

Survive.

Bronwyn had to choose between the two statements Sarge kept saying to her.

To make it worse, it was getting close to time for her to press the button on her necklace that provided her normal regimen. If she didn't do that, the withdrawal pain would start. She didn't know if she had the strength to combat that on top of the agony in her mind. Especially knowing the regimen would help make all the pain go away.

All of it. No more battles, no more worrying about becoming a killer. Just blessed nothingness.

Make killing Varela as easy as it was supposed to be.

But no. If she killed him, then she won't be able to—

A searing pain shot through her head, stealing her breath, doubling her over.

She had to kill Varela.

She had to kill Varela.

She had to kill Varela.

Bronwyn kept that other tiny nugget of a thought buried deep inside. The thing she wouldn't be able to do if she killed Varela. She gave it to Sarge to hold for her. He would give it back to her at the right time.

"Thank you," she whispered.

You can do this, Pony Girl.

"I have to kill Varela."

Then that's what you have to do. Rest now.

She leaned her head against the cool closet wall and waited, not fighting it anymore. Sarge understood. It was enough. Sarge would protect her.

She finally heard Varela inside his apartment. She'd

already planted all the evidence Erick had demanded, not that it was going to fool anyone for long. She got up, less shaky now that she wasn't fighting the urge to complete her mission.

Sarge would help her when the time came.

I'll help you do what you need to do. We'll get through this together.

Bronwyn nodded. She trusted him.

Varela wasn't expecting anything. There were way too many locks on his door for him to think that someone could have gotten in through them.

That wasn't how she'd gotten in. She'd come in through the basement window that should've been too small for any human to fit through. She had bruises along her shoulders and her hips because she'd been too big for it, too, but she'd made it.

Varela was whistling and getting sandwich makings out of his refrigerator. She stepped silently behind him into the kitchen and raised her weapon.

Not yet, Pony Girl. Sarge's whispered voice filled her ears.

Right. Not yet. It had to look like an accident.

Not yet. Not yet.

Bronwyn would kill him, but she was waiting for the right moment. She held her gun in a steady position. She stood there silently until he turned around. He jerked backward.

"What the hell are you doing in here, bitch?"

Still not yet.

What was Sarge waiting for?

Trust me. Not yet.

She didn't say anything to Varela. It was taking everything she had to not pull the trigger.

"You picked the wrong house to rob, lady." He eyed my gun as if he couldn't decide whether to try to take her or not. "Besides, I don't have anything in here worth stealing. I doubt you could carry out a TV on your own."

My gun began to shake. "Please," she whispered. Not to Varela, to Sarge. Her nose started bleeding again. She needed to kill the man in front of her.

Varela's eyes narrowed. "Look, I work for some important people, and if you hurt me, they're going to come after you."

Tell him the truth.

"Those important people are the ones who want you dead," she said. "They know you're betraying them."

The mustard he'd taken out of the refrigerator fell from his fingers to the floor, splattering all over his shoes.

"Oh God." He was taking her a lot more seriously now. "Look, whatever they think they know, it's not the truth."

Tell him more.

Why? Why couldn't she kill Varela? But she did what Sarge said.

"Mosaic knows you're working for Ian DeRose and Zodiac Tactical," she continued. "My job is to come here, kill you, and make it look like a burglary gone wrong."

The other part of that job was to make sure she walked by the security camera that was across the street, knowing that Zodiac Tactical would eventually get the footage and put two and two together.

"Look." Varela held out his hands in supplication. "Whatever they're paying you, I can pay you more. Maybe not right away, but if you're willing to give me a chance..."

"Now?" She asked Sarge. "Please?"

Hold on a few more seconds, Pony Girl. You can do it.

She felt another drop of blood fall from her face onto the floor. Her stomach cramped; the colors faded from the room. She couldn't seem to get enough air.

"Are you all right, lady?" Varela asked.

Take a breath, Bronwyn. Force yourself to get in air. You can't pass out. You're going to need it for what you have to do.

She opened her mouth, forcing oxygen to her starved lungs. The colors came back, and the room stopped spinning.

That's right, gather your strength.

Sarge was helping her. She was going to make it through this.

Take a step closer and get ready. Then say exactly what I tell you, no matter how much it hurts.

Killing Varela wouldn't hurt, didn't Sarge understand? But she nodded.

No matter what, you do what I tell you.

"Okay."

"Okay what?" Varela asked.

It's going to hurt. You gave it to me, but I have to give it back now. Be strong, Pony Girl.

"Are you crazy or something?"

Ask him if Ian DeRose will listen to him.

What? "Why?"

Sarge's voice roared in her ears. *Do it! You don't have much time.*

"Will Ian DeRose listen to you if you have information?"

"Yeah, I mean, I've been working for him, so yeah."

You know the rest. Say it. Hurry, Pony Girl. You're running out of time.

"Go to Ian. Tell him that Wavy Bollinger is in danger. That Mosaic is going to kill her. Tell him he has to protect her. Tell him to hide you, to get you as far away from here as possible. If anyone from Mosaic sees you again, they won't hesitate to kill you."

This was what she'd given to Sarge to hide for her. If she'd allowed herself to consciously think of letting Varela go, she would've collapsed.

This was the only way to help Wavy.

Wavy was in danger. She had to help her. This was the only way.

She felt as if someone was hitting her with a hammer. Blood gushed out of her nose, and the world spun. She had to drop her gun to catch herself on the kitchen counter to stay upright.

"Go now!" Bronwyn screamed at him. If she fell and got her gun while he was still in her sights, she wouldn't have the strength not to finish her mission.

He had the good sense to run out the door. She prayed it would be enough.

Her vision narrowed. If she'd had anything left in her system to vomit, it would've come back up. She felt some sort of sting in her eye as something happened.

Send the report, Pony Girl. You wrote it while you were waiting. Send it now.

Bronwyn hit send on her phone, telling Mosaic Varela was dead. She dropped to her knees, falling against the cabinets. Everything was turning black now.

She was going to die.

You did it, beautiful. Rest. You're not dying.

She wasn't so sure.

When you wake up, you're going to forget a lot. That's okay. It's okay to forget. It's your mind's way of protecting you. But there's something very important you're going to remember.

"What?"

You'll remember when you wake up.

Bronwyn's eyes blinked open slowly. Where was she? She had no idea. She was in some sort of kitchen, but not hers. Her flat in Paris had a kitchen barely half this size.

Paris? No, she hadn't been to Paris in months. She'd been in the dark cell and in the medical chair but...

She couldn't remember.

There was mustard on the floor—and blood. A gun lying next to her.

She'd been here to do something, but she didn't know what.

And she wasn't sure she wanted to know.

You're not going to have much time. If you're going to do this, you're going to have to move quickly.

She looked over and saw Sarge standing in the doorway.

"I don't remember why I'm here," she whispered.

A smile from him. *It's okay to forget that part.*

"But there's something I needed to remember." Her skin started to itch. She had the urge to inject her regimen by touching her necklace. Right now, the compulsion wasn't hard to resist, but that would change.

Does your head hurt anymore?

Had it been hurting before? "No. A little, but not bad."

Good. Then it's time to go, if you're going to do it.

"Going to do what?"

He walked over and crouched down beside her. *I can't get you away from Mosaic for good, Pony Girl, but maybe I can give you a reprieve. You need to figure out where you are.*

Bronwyn looked around. Nothing seemed familiar to her. Not this apartment, not the city.

They underestimated you and overestimated themselves. It will be their downfall.

She slipped her phone out of her pocket. She had no idea where she was. She opened my maps app. "I'm in Pueblo, Colorado."

That's right. If you move fast, you've got enough time. Not much, but enough.

He disappeared right in front of her eyes.

"Wait, come back! Enough time to do what?"

You know, Pony Girl. Sarge's voice came to her. *They didn't take everything from your mind. You know.*

And then it came to her.

Colorado.

She did know.

She jumped up and ran for the door.

CHAPTER
SIXTEEN

THE VIEW of the Rockies Sarge had from his back deck calmed him in a way not much did. But for the past month, even the grandeur of the mountains hadn't done much to help his mind.

He hadn't seen or heard from Bronwyn in almost four weeks. By the time he'd gotten to Anchorage after the footage they'd found of her, she'd been gone. Stopping in Seattle where her video call had originated had led to nothing but a few pieces of crushed phone plastic inside an abandoned building.

He'd made a huge mistake in New York letting Bronwyn go. He wasn't sure if he was ever going to see her again. After the footage from Anchorage, he wasn't sure she was still alive.

And all that kept coming back to him was that if he had just left well enough alone all those years ago—never walked over to stop Nikolai from pushing her around that day she was reading in the windowsill—maybe she would've been better off.

"Sarge."

Sarge had the handgun he kept under his porch banister

in his hand a second later. Because that voice could not be who his brain wanted to think it was.

And if it was, it had to be some sort of a trap.

Bronwyn stayed where he could see her with her hands held out to the sides so he knew she didn't have any weapons. At least not one that she planned to kill him with in the next half second.

She looked like hell, but she was alive.

And she was here.

"I don't have much time," she said.

He brought the Glock up higher as she reached her hand up to her head to hold it as if she was dizzy. Although he didn't know why he did. Would he actually be able to shoot her if she pulled her own gun on him? He honestly didn't know.

"Last time I talked to you, you were trying to get me to promise to kill you if I saw you again."

She flinched. "I—I don't remember that."

He wasn't sure whether to believe her or not. "What are you doing here, Pony Girl?"

Another flinch. "You sent me here."

Sarge raised an eyebrow. "I sent you? I'm pretty sure that's not the case."

If he could've sent her there, she would've been there long before now, and definitely not to get him to kill her.

"No, not you. The other you." She shrugged the slightest bit. "The window is narrow when I have control. I spent a lot of it getting here. I can leave if you want."

Her voice was stilted, the words jarring, as if she was having to focus on each one to figure out what to say.

Was this a trap? Yet another thing he didn't know when it came to her. It could be. But if she had wanted to kill him, she could have done it back in New York. She could've taken him out today without making her presence known.

He kept the Glock in his hand, got up, and walked toward her.

"How did you know where I live?"

She swept her hands up and down her arms as if she was cold and she needed to rub her skin to warm herself. The closer he got, the worse she looked. Dried blood was smeared on her face like she'd wiped it. And there was something wrong with one of her eyes—the blood vessels had burst in it. Not a good sign.

"I remembered it when I woke up. I don't remember the rest, but I remembered that you were nearby." She rubbed her arms harder. "I got your address...before. Because I was going to mail you the money if you wouldn't take it from me."

It took him a second. "You mean that eight hundred dollars you insisted you owed me?"

She nodded. "Then today, once I knew where I was, I remembered."

It was feasible. His address was in the Zodiac computer system. He didn't try to hide it from his fellow employees and friends. He stepped a little closer.

"Why are you here, Bronwyn? What's happening to you?"

The collar of her shirt shifted, and Sarge could see that she still wore that necklace. Her fingers crept up toward it. He pointed to it.

"That necklace, what does it do? It injects you with something."

"I don't have much time," she said. "It hurts."

"What hurts? The injection? What they give you? Tell me what's happening. Tell me how I can help you."

"If I press it, it won't hurt anymore, but then I'll be gone."

She held her hand up toward her head.

"Please help me, Sarge."

A single tear spilled from one of those blue eyes. He tucked his Glock into the back waistband of his jeans. If she were here to kill him, she would have already done it, and he wouldn't have stopped her. She needed my help.

He walked toward her, unsure if she would try to run or not. She didn't—just the opposite. She crumpled toward the ground.

Fuck.

He leaped forward and caught her as she fell. He scooped her up into his arms. "Pony Girl, talk to me."

There was no response. He laid his cheek against her forehead. It was hot as if she had a fever. She moved, groaning, like she was in pain and being unconscious wasn't taking it all away.

She was lighter than she'd been. She'd definitely lost weight since he'd seen her in New York, and she hadn't had much weight to lose then. He hurried back toward the house. She was waking up, rubbing her arms again. Her breath hitched.

"It hurts."

"Should I take you to a doctor? A hospital?"

"No," she responded immediately. "No, I can't. A bath. Water helps."

Her breathing grew more erratic and the rubbing more intense. Something was hurting her skin. There wasn't time to draw a bath, so he decided to go straight to the hot tub next to his back porch. Without setting her down, he threw open the top and then marched them both inside fully clothed, pausing only to take his Glock out and rest it on the edge.

Still in his arms, he brought her down until they were covered up to their necks in water. Almost immediately, she began to relax. Her head fell against his shoulder.

Sarge had so many questions he wanted to ask he could barely keep them all straight in his mind. But for this moment, all he could do was hold her.

"Pressure and movement against my skin make the pain stop for a little while. I discovered it by accident."

He could feel her relaxing more against him. He knew her body's natural state would be to want to rest and sleep now that the pain had stopped, but he needed answers.

"How did you get here, Pony Girl? It's been a month since I saw you in New York. Where have you been?" He didn't want to bring up that he'd seen what had happened in Anchorage.

"My cell. Doctor. Erick. I say the words. I survive. Like you told me to."

Most of this didn't make any sense, but the word Erick definitely did.

"Erick Huen? Do you know where he is? Can you take me to him?"

"No, I can't remember. There were things I had to forget to get here to you."

She shifted in discomfort, so he began rubbing any part of her skin he could reach. She immediately settled back down into his arms. Whatever was going on in her body, touch and stimulation helped control it.

What the hell was going on inside her?

Sarge kept continuous contact with her body, rubbing her back, arms, legs, as he asked her questions. "Tell me about the necklace."

"I press it, and it gives me the regimen. The regimen stops the pain."

"Do you want to press it now?" He couldn't stand the thought of her being in so much pain.

"No." Her head came off his shoulder. "If I do, I go away. The pain stops, but I go away."

Her breathing got choppy, her muscles tightened with tension, her agitation clear.

"Okay. Don't press it. I'll keep rubbing, okay?"

"Take my clothes off, please. I want to touch your skin." She grimaced as her eyes met mine, full clarity there for the first time. "I don't mean… I know you don't want to… I just…"

He kissed her forehead.

"I understand. Let's get your clothes off."

Sarge reached down and pulled the shoes off her feet under the water, setting them on the edge of the hot tub. Her pants weren't as easy in the water, but he rubbed against her legs as he trailed them down and off. He slipped her shirt over her head, careful not to touch the necklace in any way.

He wasn't saint enough to be unaffected by the sight of her naked flesh, but sex was the last thing on his mind. He continued to rub as much of her skin as he could reach.

He caught sight of the scarring along her wrist and held it up. He recognized the markings for what they were. "They restrained you. You fought."

"I can't remember," she said. "I can't remember anything. Not right now."

"You don't have to remember. We're going to help you. All you have to do is survive."

"Yes." Her head fell back against his shoulder once again. "That's what you tell me all the time."

If she'd been hallucinating about him, he was glad he'd said something useful.

The more Sarge rubbed, the more she relaxed. He would sit there and touch her skin for the rest of his fucking life if that would help her.

"I'm sorry I hurt you," she said. "I hurt other people too, I think, but I can't remember."

She didn't need to remember that part. "Tell me more about the necklace. The regimen."

As they talked, her fingers reached for the hem of his T-shirt and pulled it up over his head. "I'm supposed to press the right side every eight hours. But I cheat," she said. "I don't press until I can't stand it anymore."

"How long is that?" He asked her. "Do you know?"

"Almost twenty-four hours. I tricked them. They give me a lower dosage because they think they control me."

Sarge shook his head in wonder. Her body was malnourished and showed signs of abuse, but she'd still had the presence of mind to trick her captors.

He kissed her forehead. "You're amazing, Pony Girl. So strong."

"No. I wanted to kill. I was supposed to—" She sat ramrod straight in my lap. "I can't remember. There was something, I don't know. I can't—"

"Okay." He eased her head back down onto his shoulder and began rubbing her skin again. "Let's keep going. Don't think about it. Tell me more about the necklace."

"I can never touch the left side unless by command. Never."

"A kill switch?" He asked her.

"Yes. It's their way of making sure I don't go offline."

"Are they listening in?"

She shook her head. "No. They know that can be traced."

He bit back a curse. That's exactly what he'd been hoping to do. "Okay, then we'll think of something else."

He needed to get inside, call the office, get some sort of plan working, but he was afraid to leave Bronwyn out here alone. He had to figure out how to help her long-term.

Her pain was ratcheting up again; she pressed herself harder against his hands. Then she rubbed her hands against his chest, both sexual in nature and not. He was thankful wet jeans were pretty damned uncomfortable and kept his body in check.

That wasn't what Bronwyn wanted. She didn't mean for her movements to be sexual. She was trying to find pain relief.

Then she shifted, hooking a leg over his lap so her breasts were crushed up against his chest. "Sarge, I want you."

Maybe that was how she meant it.

CHAPTER
SEVENTEEN

ALL BRONWYN WANTED to do was crawl inside Sarge's body to get as close to him as possible. She knew where she was. She knew who she was. She knew who she was with.

It was more than she'd had at one time in what seemed like forever, and she never wanted it to end.

Everything she couldn't remember, all the pieces that didn't fit together, didn't matter when she was this close to him. She pressed down against him, barely swallowing a groan at how good it felt.

This was Sarge. He was really here with her. Big, strong, protective.

She could still feel the pain under her skin, but she could tamp it down. She had time before she was overwhelmed with the need to press the regimen into her skin to stop the pain. And lose herself.

She knew there were things she needed to remember. Why was she there to begin with? Things she needed to tell Sarge. But if she remembered, it would hurt. Rip her mind apart.

So she wouldn't remember. She would be with Sarge for however long she had before the pain overwhelmed her.

As close to him as possible. She rubbed up against his chest.

"Pony Girl." His voice was so much deeper, sexier than it had been in her head.

It was also tinged with restraint.

"I know," she responded. "I know I hurt you in New York. I know you can't trust me. I know you don't want me."

He cupped her head with his big palms. "It's not that I don't want you. It's about what you need right now, and sex is not it."

Bronwyn didn't know how to form the words to explain it to him. It wasn't so much that she wanted sex, although she wouldn't mind that at all. She wanted to be close to him, closer than they were right then.

She needed him.

She couldn't stop the tears that leaked out of her eyes. "I want to be able to feel you. I want to be able to know that you're with me when the darkness comes back."

She knew it was coming. Worse than before. Whatever it was that she'd forgotten would drag the darkness back with it.

He wiped her tears away with his thumbs. "I want to help you, Pony Girl, so there isn't any more darkness. Let me take you to the Zodiac office."

He rested his forehead against hers, and she breathed him in. She wanted that so bad—to let him take over the fight for her. The burning pain was already starting to ramp back up.

She was running out of time.

"I won't make it. By the time anyone figures out what to do or how to get the necklace off me, it will be too late."

Sarge growled, obviously torn. "Okay. I don't like it, but okay. But let me get my phone so I can record as much detail as possible about that damned necklace. Zodiac's tech team will study it, figure something out for next time."

"Okay," she whispered. But she didn't know if there was

going to be a next time. She rubbed against him more. The pain was getting harder to ignore.

He shifted away from her. "Which will be better for you, for me to leave you alone in the water or for me to take you with me and keep touching you?"

"Please don't leave me alone," she said. The water helped, but without him touching her, she was going to succumb to the pain too quickly.

He nodded. "Hang on to me. I'm going to carry you inside. We'll put you in the shower."

"Okay." She forced the word out. Water wasn't going to help for much longer.

He brushed a strand of her hair back from her face. Somehow, he knew it was getting worse. "You hold on."

Bronwyn didn't know if he meant literally or figuratively, so she did both. She wrapped her arms and legs around him as he got up out of the hot tub and walked toward his house.

She buried her face in his neck, breathing in his scent. This was better. So much better. Her tongue darted out and licked his skin. She heard him groan, but she was so fascinated by the way he tasted that she couldn't stop.

Yes, his taste overwhelmed her senses and helped dull the pain. He had one arm hooked under her hips to carry her weight, his other hand rubbing as much skin as he could reach. She was wrapped around him like an octopus, but she couldn't get enough of how his neck tasted.

Sarge carried her into his bedroom, not caring that they were dripping all over the place, and laid her on the bed. The second she wasn't in contact with him anymore, the pain ratcheted up to an almost unbearable level.

She let out a groan, her fingers inching toward the necklace. That was what she'd been trained to do. When the pain started, she was to press the right side. Now she was fighting the pain and her training—it felt impossibly hard.

He grabbed her hand, gently pulling it back down from

her neck. "No, not yet. You fight for me a few more minutes. Okay?"

She nodded, and he trailed his hand along her arm, rubbing up and down her shoulder as he grabbed his phone off the nightstand and began recording her necklace.

She tried to hold still as he spoke into the recording, noting things about the type of metal the necklace was and the wounds in her neck. But the pain was becoming too much. She needed something to distract her from it.

Bronwyn took his hand that was stroking along her collarbone and pulled it down until it covered her breast. His fingers slid under her bra and began teasing her nipple, squeezing to the point of pain and then letting it go and rubbing gently.

She relaxed into the bed. Yes.

Sarge was still talking into the recording, but she didn't care. The pleasure from his fingers was enough to ease the pain. He never stopped talking as his hand switched to the other breast, and she arched up into him.

She couldn't stop her moan.

He finally set his phone down. "I think I got everything I ne—"

She pulled him to her for a kiss, cutting him off in the middle of his sentence. She needed his mouth.

Bronwyn yanked him on top of her, thankful when he didn't resist and he kissed her back, when he seemed to want her as much as she wanted him. This wasn't only about keeping the pain at bay; this was about Sarge.

His big body covered hers, surrounding her. She pressed up against him and could feel him hard against her. He wanted her, at least on a physical level. Fingers came up and threaded into her hair, holding her still so he could kiss her more deeply.

She groaned into his mouth. Yes, this was what she

needed. She needed Sarge. His tongue invaded her mouth, and she reveled in it, meeting it with her own.

She would've kissed him like that forever. She wanted more of him. She wanted to feel him inside her, to be as close as they possibly could be.

But it was too late.

The pain was gaining strength, radiating out from her core once again. Burning her from the inside out. The compulsion to hit the side of her necklace almost more than she could bear.

She had to leave. It would only get worse from there, and nothing he could do would stop it at this point.

She broke her mouth away from his, breathing heavily, and not just because of his kisses. "I have to go. It's too late. It's too much. If I don't leave now, I'll hurt you again like I did in New York. I can't control it."

Those deep brown eyes looked into hers. "I don't want to let you go. I don't want you to be alone in this anymore."

Bronwyn tried to swallow her terror. She didn't want him to let her go either. "I'll survive."

He slid off her quickly—way too quickly—and she wanted to pull him back. But she couldn't. She arched off the bed as a spike of agony drove down her spine; the room spun. She rubbed her arms again.

Before she could say or do anything, Sarge picked her up and carried her into his office and set her down on his desk. He reached over with both hands and cupped her breasts, teasing her nipples to hardness.

"Stay with me," he said. "A few more minutes."

She moaned, falling back onto her elbows, the pain retreating under the onslaught of his fingers. One hand slipped down her stomach and into the waistband of her panties, not stopping until she felt his finger slide inside her. "Stay with me, Pony Girl. Concentrate on this."

His touch was enough to beat back the pain. She couldn't stop herself from grinding up against his hand. It felt so good.

He grabbed something from one of the drawers. "Bronwyn, this is a micro transmitter." He held some tiny thing in front of her face, but she was too busy focusing on what his fingers were doing inside her body, milking every second of enjoyment to pay much attention.

"It doesn't send your location. It's not a tracker," he continued. "It records your words, activates when you speak, sends it to a voice mailbox. You can talk to me using this. Okay? I won't be able to talk back to you, but you can know that I hear you. You're not alone. I promise."

Another finger slid inside her, and she gasped as he twisted and moved them in a way that tightened something deep inside her. She grabbed his wrist, making sure he wouldn't take his hand away. She needed whatever it was that he was doing.

"I'm putting it in your necklace," he said. "It's tiny, and they're least likely to search for it there. And if I'm right, they make you keep it on all the time."

"Yes," she said. She didn't know if she was answering his statement or responding to the movements of his hand. She felt the necklace shift slightly, but she didn't care. All she cared about was what he was doing to her. He cupped the back of her head as his fingers began moving more quickly.

"Next time I see you, I'm going to be more ready to help you. More ready than this."

"I—I—" She couldn't get a coherent sentence out. Her legs dropped open. All her weight from the upper half of her body fell back onto his hand, but he didn't have any problem carrying her weight.

"Come for me, Pony Girl. If this gives you a reprieve, then it's worth it."

His fingers moved faster, harder, hitting that spot that

wound the coil in her until it finally snapped. His name came out of her lips in a moan while she shattered with pleasure.

She lay limp on his desk for a long moment, eyes closed. When she finally opened them, there was nothing but him and her. Just them, together.

"I didn't know… I didn't know it could be like that."

"It will always be like that between you and me," he said. "We're going to get you out of this, and I'm going to prove it to you."

Bronwyn barely had her breath back before the pain started again. This time, she knew she wouldn't be able to control it. It was already worse than before he'd laid her on the desk.

"I have to go," she whispered. "I can't wait any longer."

"Where are you supposed to be?"

She didn't have to concentrate to know her answer. All she needed to do was not fight it and the answer came to her. "The airport. The final part of the mission was to get myself to the airport."

Sarge nodded. "I'll drive you."

He helped her get back into her still-damp clothes and put her into his car. He used one hand to drive, the other hand rubbing her skin as she rubbed the rest. She only had minutes left now.

"The micro transmitter, don't forget it. You can talk to me anytime. I'll be listening, I promise."

He kept repeating it over and over. He'd be with her. He'd be listening. His words faded away as she fought the pain, fought the compulsion to press the compartment on her necklace.

They were a couple of miles from the airport when she knew she'd reached her breaking point. "Here. Stop now." She barely got the words out.

Sarge stopped without arguing. "I'm with you, Pony Girl. Remember that. I'm with you."

She tried to say thank you. She tried to tell him how much he meant to her, how he'd given her the only good things in her life, but she couldn't say any words. All she could do was open the car door and stumble out.

As soon as Bronwyn closed the door behind her, he drove away. The last feeling she had was thankfulness that he'd understood before her fingers slammed the side of her necklace.

Relief. It was almost instantaneous. The agonizing fires began to be extinguished.

And then there was nothing.

BRONWYN COULD FEEL Sarge's hands on her everywhere.

His lips on her shoulder, her neck. Kissing her with feather-like gentleness then harder as he moved down her chest to her breasts then lower still in between her legs.

All she wanted to do was lie there and feel. Feel him, knowing as long as he was with her she would be okay. Sarge would keep her safe.

He protected her from the pain. Stood guard against it like her own personal warrior.

But the pain was there, lurking below the surface, surrounding her from all sides. She wouldn't be able to ignore it for much longer, even with Sarge.

She wanted to stay with him forever—just the two of them. She wanted to read books with him and talk with him, travel places with him…

But mostly, she wanted to stay in his bed with him. Let him touch her, let him do things to her—with her—she'd never wanted from another man.

"You're beautiful," Sarge whispered, voice clear and deep

in her ear. "You're strong. So much stronger than you give yourself credit for."

Bronwyn couldn't stop her sigh.

"Be strong for me, Pony Girl. Remember, you can talk to me at any time."

Wait. He'd said that to her before, right? When?

"Talk to me. I'll be listening."

She didn't want to talk. She wanted to kiss more. She wanted to feel his hands on her again, but he pulled back. She tried to reach out to grab him and keep him next to her, but her arms wouldn't move.

"She's waking up."

That voice wasn't Sarge's. Sarge wasn't here.

She shook her head. She didn't want anyone else. "No. Sarge."

"Did she say the word sergeant?" That was a different voice.

Where was she? Bronwyn tried to gather her thoughts, but now that Sarge was gone, the pain ate at her. A groan escaped. She needed to be quiet. She pulled at her hands again, but they were restrained.

She cracked her eyes the slightest bit, taking in her surroundings. She was back in the medical chair. She hadn't been restrained in the medical chair since the beginning. They hadn't known there was any reason to restrain her.

They did now.

"Is she awake?" That was Erick Huen, his voice almost in her ear.

Fire burned under her skin, forcing her to swallow a whimper. She couldn't curl into a ball, couldn't do anything to ease the pain.

Bronwyn gritted her teeth and tried to think. She reached for the things she knew she needed to remember, but her mind wouldn't grasp them. All she could remember were Sarge's kisses. But those weren't going to help her now.

"Yes, she's awake. I'm monitoring brain activity now that I know what's going on." Dr. Tippens's voice was tight, cold.

"Her eyes are still closed."

"She's fooled us before, but not this time. Open your eyes, Bronwyn."

She did as he asked. She wasn't going to be able to stay still or silent much longer anyway. The two men loomed over her.

Dr. Tippens shook his head like she'd personally disappointed him. "Your regimen hasn't been working, and you didn't let us know." He pried one of her eyes farther open and shined a small light then did the same with the other.

She didn't say anything. There was nothing she could say that was going to help her out of this situation. What had she done that had given her away? She'd been given a mission.

She'd failed at the mission. She'd failed on purpose. But why?

"Want to know how we know?" Erick moved to the side so she could see him better and clapped his hands in glee. "We found Silas Varela attempting to make personal contact with Ian DeRose right after you reported that he was dead."

Silas Varela. The failed mission.

She hadn't killed him. She'd let him go because of…some important reason. But she couldn't follow along the thread of memory to grasp what that had been.

"I've got to hand it to you." Erick dropped something wrapped in plastic onto her chest. "You helped us make much more of a statement with Varela."

She looked down at the plastic on her chest.

There was a human hand inside it.

Erick laughed. "See what I did there? Hand it to you."

Oh God. Bronwyn began thrashing against her restraints in an attempt to get the dead man's body part off her, but all it did was slide farther down her body.

"Don't worry," Erick continued. "You only get the one

piece. The rest of Varela was chopped up and sent so Ian DeRose and Zodiac Tactical were sure to find them."

He leaned down and whispered in her ear. "Varela died screaming, begging for his life. You would've done him a much bigger favor if you had killed him like you were told."

Varela. She remembered it all and suddenly couldn't get enough air into her lungs. She'd not only failed, she'd made the situation worse. She'd let him go so he could warn Ian DeRose about the danger to Wavy.

If they'd caught Varela on his way to see Ian, nobody knew about the danger to Wavy. The heart rate monitor beeped frantically as she tried to suck in enough oxygen to survive.

"Wavy," she whispered through parched lips. Was she already dead? Why hadn't she fought harder to remember while she was with Sarge? She'd only been thinking about herself.

"Oh, don't worry, I have something very special planned for Miss Bollinger. She'll be joining us soon. You've been ever so helpful in the formulation of my plans."

Bronwyn thrashed against her restraints, wheezing as pain radiated throughout her body. She'd failed on every level. Varela was dead. Wavy would be soon—or worse. And Dr. Tippens now knew his regimen hadn't worked correctly on her.

And Sarge wasn't here. He'd never been here. She wasn't sure that she'd been at his house. If every time he spoke to her, it was only in her mind, how could she trust anything about him was real?

How could she trust anything about her mind at all?

She let the pain take over, not fighting it anymore. She deserved it.

She couldn't hold back her sobs. She knew they'd turn into screams soon. She needed to press the regimen on her necklace, but her hands were restrained.

The necklace. Hadn't Sarge said something about turning it on and talking to him.

Had that been real?

She had no idea. She bit down sobs as Dr. Tippens talked to Erick around her. The fire burning through her skin became stronger. She wouldn't survive.

"Please," she begged. "Please, kill me."

That would be best for everyone. Especially her. Her heart clenched at the thought of never seeing Sarge again. Of never feeling his kisses again.

But had she really felt his kisses at all?

"Oh, I don't think so." Erick got near her ear again so she could hear him over the beeps of the machinery and her own sobs. "You've been promised for something else."

Bronwyn didn't know what he was talking about and didn't care. Her breaths tore in and out of her chest until she was sure her ribs would crack.

"Enough, Erick." Dr. Tippens shot out an arm so Erick had to step back. "She's not a toy. We need to see what data we can get from her to figure out where her programming broke down."

"If she can't do what she is trained to do, we might as well get rid of her now."

"No, we need the data. Plus, she shouldn't be written off yet. We have more extreme methods. She may still be a viable candidate."

"Fine. I have more interesting playthings coming." Erick walked away—tossing Varela's hand up in the air then catching it, like it was a ball—leaving her with Dr. Tippens.

Dr. Tippens looked down at her over his chart, then turned down the monitors so they no longer announced her racing pulse so loudly. "Yes, I think you're still a viable candidate. But I'm afraid this is going to be very painful before it gets any better."

CHAPTER NINETEEN

SARGE PUNCHED THE BAG, ignoring the pain in his knuckles that were already ripped open from the eighteen straight days of the abuse he'd already given them.

Eighteen days since he'd let Bronwyn out of his car and watched in the mirror as she'd touched that fucking device disguised as a necklace, and the woman he knew disappeared in front of his eyes.

Part of him had been happy to see the pain that had racked her body the entire time she'd been at his house finally gone. But she'd walked by his car, looked right at him, and there hadn't been an ounce of recognition in her gaze.

Bronwyn's body had been there, but her mind, her essence, had been totally gone. It was as if the time in the hot tub, in his bed, on his desk, had never existed.

He was going to remember those minutes for the rest of his fucking life, but they were totally gone from hers.

Just like in New York, he never should've let her go. If he had known—

"You need to take that fucking thing out of your ear. Jenna told me what you're doing with it."

Sarge didn't turn from the punching bag at Landon's words. He hadn't expected to see him here, or he wouldn't have come at all. The Zodiac complex, including his current location in the basement gym, was like a ghost town. Every able-bodied person employed by Ian DeRose had been put on one distinct mission.

Recovering Wavy Bollinger from the hands of Mosaic. Specifically, the hands of Erick Huen.

She'd been kidnapped a few days after Bronwyn had stopped by his house, not long after Silas Varela had shown up in pieces.

He punched the bag again, harder this time.

He couldn't deny that it hadn't taken long after Bronwyn's appearance for the shit to well and truly hit the fan. He knew she was connected to it all, although not at fault. Ian had enough on his mind—Sarge recognized the haunted look in his eyes every time he glanced in the mirror—so he hadn't filled him in on the details of Bronwyn's visit.

"Are you going to ignore me?" Landon grabbed the punching bag. "Take the damned receiver out of your ear."

"Fuck off, Libra." Landon was one of his best friends in the world, even though they constantly bickered and couldn't be more different in temperament. He wasn't looking for anyone to cheer him up, and he damned well wasn't taking the receiver out of his ear.

It was his only link to Bronwyn.

So when Landon reached over and pulled it out of his ear himself, Sarge turned around swinging. He ducked and jumped back on the mat.

"You're going to give me that back right fucking now, or we're both going to end up bloody."

He held up the small monitor between two fingers. "What good does this do you?"

"It keeps me motivated."

"I'm not going to let you do this to yourself. Listening to Bronwyn suffer isn't going to motivate you any more than you're already motivated. You're ready to grind the world into dust to get her back. I'd say that's the height of motivation."

"I want to be able to hear if she attempts to communicate."

Landon shook his head. "That, I can understand. But Jenna told me what you're doing. That the nerds modified the device for you so you can replay what's been transmitted over and over."

He had days' worth of recordings of Bronwyn's suffering. Days when she'd gone from weeping to screaming to silent.

The screams had been enough to give Sarge nightmares, but the silence... The silence was going to drive him absolutely insane.

She had been silent for days now. So yeah, he'd forced himself to listen to her suffering.

It reminded him that her pain was his fault. He never should've let her go that day. He should've found another way.

He deserved to break out into a sweat every time he heard her screams. He deserved to have his heart fracture when he heard her whisper his name like she needed to say it to survive.

And he wasn't able to do a damned thing about it.

He narrowed his eyes as Landon. "Give me the receiver right now, or you and I are going to fight."

Landon wasn't deterred. "Then you and I are going to fight because all you're doing is torturing yourself. And it's not helping her for a goddamned second."

Sarge lunged for him, but the bastard was quick. He always had been. They were pretty well matched in the sparring ring. He was stronger, bigger, but Landon was faster. He expected him to take another quick step backward, but instead, his fist flew out and connected with

Sarge's jaw with enough force to send him back a step or two.

Landon wasn't playing.

Neither was Sarge.

He tossed the receiver to the side and put his hands up in a fighting stance. Sarge did the same. They weren't in a sparring ring and didn't have on protective equipment, but the gym at least had a padded floor.

Sarge attacked with a kick-punch combination, pushing him back slightly. But then Landon ducked under his punch and flew at him in a midsection tackle.

They both fell hard onto the mat. He quickly twisted out of Landon's grasp before he found himself in a choke hold. Landon grunted as his elbow caught him in the ribs. He let Sarge go. They both jumped up onto their feet. Sarge barely got his arms up to block a series of kicks Landon threw at him before he attacked with two jabs that Landon dodged.

He caught Sarge with a knee to the midsection, and his breath whooshed out of him. Landon had him doubled over. Sarge waited for another blow.

Wanted another blow.

But it didn't come. He looked up as Landon stepped back.

"We need you, Sarge. Ian is out of his damned mind over Wavy, just like you are over Bronwyn."

"There hasn't been anything from Bronwyn for days," he finally said between breaths. "I know what that probably means. I keep thinking about those two dead bodies we found in the lab."

They'd gotten a lead five days ago that they'd hoped would take them to either Wavy or Bronwyn—a lab distantly connected to Erick Huen. They'd found evidence that Wavy had been held there, but it had been empty by the time they'd arrived.

Except for the two dead female bodies.

Sarge had approached the discarded corpses slowly, his

heart frozen in his chest, sure one of them was Bronwyn's. But neither had been Bronwyn. Or Wavy. Thank God.

Yet now, as the hours had turned into days without a sound from Bronwyn, he felt like he was slowly approaching corpses once again.

And this time, he wouldn't be so lucky.

Landon grabbed him by the collar. "You don't give up hope, you hear me? You or Ian. You be ready so when Bronwyn and Wavy are found, you're there to give them what they need. Torturing yourself by listening to her in pain doesn't do anything but tear you down."

He was right. Sarge nodded. "Yeah. I hear you."

Landon pulled him in for a hug, and Sarge wasn't too macho to know that he needed it.

"She's going to make it, brother," he said near his ear. "Hang on to that."

Sarge wanted to, but he was afraid. Afraid of hope.

They separated, and he grabbed the receiver. He wouldn't listen to the replays, but if Bronwyn said anything else, he wanted to be able to hear it.

"What was the last thing you heard from her?"

He flinched. He couldn't help it. "Them putting her back in the isolation tank. It was…bad."

Sarge would never be able to get her sobs out of his head. She was so close to breaking. Total darkness, soundproofing, floating, unable to see or hear or feel anything. It had been bad enough when she'd gone in the first time. Knowing what was coming when they'd put her back had been more than she could handle.

Landon scrubbed a hand down his face. "Those fuckers. Torture without leaving any physical marks."

They took her out every few days for tests. That was usually when the screams started again. But last time had been silence.

"They should take her out again in a few hours, right?"

Sarge nodded. "If the pattern holds." He rubbed his eyes. He hadn't gotten more than a couple hours sleep at a time in eighteen days. "She's close to breaking. Permanently, Landon."

"She's strong."

"Even the strongest break eventually."

CHAPTER
TWENTY

SARGE HAD PROMISED Landon he wouldn't give up hope, but truth was, he wasn't sure he hadn't.

Silence. Nothing from her but silence.

The transmitter only worked if Bronwyn used her voice, so he couldn't tell if Mosaic had taken her out of the isolation tank as scheduled.

Silence was their enemy.

"Talk to me, Pony Girl," he whispered the next day. At this point, they should be putting her back into the tank. Back into her own personal hell. She should be crying, screaming, like she had before. "Don't you give up. I'm going to find you."

Landon had been right. He'd been wasting his time torturing himself. So he'd spent the rest of yesterday and today going back over the data about her necklace the nerds had dug up based on his video. The types of drugs that might make her body react how it had at his house. Chemical subjugation and genetic manipulation...all the shit Mosaic was into.

It wouldn't help him find her, but it would help him help her when they did.

If they did. Sarge couldn't deny he was giving up more hope every minute.

And then he heard her voice.

"S-Sarge."

He sat ramrod straight in his desk chair, nearly knocking over everything on his desk.

Bronwyn was alive.

"Yes, sweetheart. Talk to me." He knew she couldn't hear him, but it didn't matter.

She sounded so weak, but she was alive.

"W-Wavy. W-Wavy. Wavy." She stuttered the word over and over. That happened when her body first went back into the water of the isolation tank.

"Tip, tip, tip, tip, tip, tip."

What did she mean? Something was tipping over?

"Pens, pens, pens." She repeated over and over.

Then nothing.

Sarge waited for hours, hoping she'd say something else. Praying those nonsensical words weren't the last thing he'd ever hear her say.

Something about Wavy. Something had made her find her voice and talk when she hadn't for days. It couldn't be mindless babbling.

Unless she'd totally cracked. Totally broken beyond repair. And at this point, considering all she'd been through at the hands of Mosaic, and during her short lifetime, he couldn't blame her for that.

It took him nearly all night, and hours of listening to her words on repeat, to figure it out.

It wasn't two separate words: tip and pens.

Tippens.

It didn't take him long after that to discover that there was a Dr. Sheldon Tippens, a genetics research specialist in San Diego. There was something about him Bronwyn was trying to tell him.

Sarge wasn't going to be able to handle this on his own. He needed Ian. He needed the team. He was on his way out the door, planning to call as he drove to the office, and almost ran smack into Ian himself just outside his door.

"I need you, man," Ian said.

There'd been a distance between Ian and Sarge for months. He hadn't focused on Bronwyn the way Sarge thought he should have. Ian had been too focused on taking down Mosaic as a whole. And then on Wavy.

None of that mattered now.

"I've got a lead." They both said it at the same time and then looked at each other, surprised.

"I think Bronwyn was trying to get a message to me." Sarge spoke first.

Ian gave a short laugh that held no humor whatsoever. "Funny. I think Wavy was trying to do the same thing. Tell me Bronwyn's message first."

"She was saying something about a guy named Tippens."

Ian's eyes got wider. "Sheldon Tippens, the genetic specialist?"

"How the hell do you know that?"

"Wavy was trying to get me info about him too. She left a message for me at the lab."

Holy shit. They ran toward Ian's car.

"If you know about Tippens, why aren't you getting the team together, ready to move?" They climbed in, and he pulled out, tires squealing.

"Because I'm willing to cross lines to get whatever information I need from this man. If I bring in the team, then we're going to have Callum Webb and Omega Sector breathing down our necks. They don't want anyone else mailed to them in pieces."

Ian had worked with the law enforcement task force to bring down Mosaic the first time. "Can't blame them for that. And Callum's a good man."

"He is. He won't condone what I'm about to do. But Wavy is out of time."

Bronwyn was too, but Sarge didn't bring that up. He knew what line Ian meant he was willing to cross: torturing Dr. Tippens to find out what they needed.

"So you came to me?"

He kept his eyes on the road. "If you're not willing to do this, I completely understand and respect it."

"I'm willing." There wasn't much Sarge wasn't willing to do when it came to helping Bronwyn.

He drove toward the airfield. "You told me you met Bronwyn Rourke for the first time a few months ago. That can't possibly be true if you're willing to go through these measures."

Sarge grimaced. "That's not technically untrue. I did officially meet Bronwyn Rourke in Paris earlier this year."

"But you knew her before, when she was someone else." Ian was too smart not to figure it out.

"Yes. A teenager with a quick mind and nimble fingers. In trouble. I gave her an out."

"Prague." Ian put more of the puzzle together. "She was the reason you got your ass kicked that one time. I never did understand why you didn't have defensive wounds."

"It was a situation worth taking a beating for."

"I'm sorry I didn't do more for her when we had Varela undercover. I thought it would blow his cover. Ends up it didn't matter."

"You couldn't have known. Monday morning quarterbacks and all that shit."

Ian gripped the steering wheel tighter. "At the time, I had no frame of reference for what it felt like to be willing to do anything—any fucking thing—to get someone back. But I do now. Losing Wavy has taught me that. Losing every bit of color in my world has taught me that."

Sarge nodded. "We're going to get them back. Both of them."

His private jet was waiting at the airfield when they arrived, ready to take them to an airport near San Diego. They were in the air minutes after boarding the plane.

They were both focused on the way, talking only about details of grabbing Tippens outside his house as he left for work. From there, they'd move him to a safe house no one else at Zodiac knew about.

Someplace no one could hear his screams.

Neither of them took this lightly. What they were about to do would leave a mark on their souls neither of them would ever escape.

Sarge didn't care. He would give up his soul to get Bronwyn back. Ian felt the same about Wavy.

When they landed, they made their way to Tippens's suburban, upscale neighborhood and waited as the sun came up.

When Tippens pulled out in his BMW an hour later, they made their move. He wasn't all the way out of his driveway when they rammed their vehicle straight into his. It wasn't subtle, but the neighbors were far enough away from one another that by the time someone called the cops, they would already be gone with him.

Sarge and Ian wore masks, and their vehicle wasn't registered to anyone. Dr. Tippens got out of his car, at first indignant that someone had hit him. But as soon as he saw them with the masks, he recognized the danger and tried to dive back into his car.

Ian grabbed him and pulled him toward their vehicle. "If you tell me where Wavy Bollinger is right now, you might live to finish this day with all your fingers and toes attached to your body."

Tippens blanched at Ian's harsh words, but Sarge knew they were for the best. With someone like Tippens, unaccustomed to violence, being terrified of them from the beginning would help things go more quickly.

"Wavy Bollinger?" His eyes got big. "No. I swear, I didn't want to—"

Ian headbutted him. "Where is she?"

Sarge wanted to ask about Bronwyn too, but he knew there would be time. He would let Ian have his turn first.

Blood poured out of Tippens's nose. "I swear I didn't want to do it. It wasn't me."

Shit. Did that mean Wavy was already dead? He looked at Ian. He didn't want him to lose his temper if that was the case. Even if Wavy was dead—and he hoped to God she wasn't for Ian's sake—Sarge still needed to find out anything he could about Bron—

Then their plans and having time went to shit. The impossible happened. A shot rang out from down the street. Tippens collapsed into Ian's arms, a red hole forming in his chest as blood spread across his shirt.

Sarge turned away from them and returned fire, even though he knew it was too late. That had been a kill shot. Tippens wasn't going to make it.

Ian yelled at the man dying in his arms, begging for info about Wavy. "Look, you asshole. Tell me where your lab is. You're going to die. If you don't want your wife and kid to find your body lying here, you will damn well tell me where Wavy is."

Sarge fired again as Ian continued to talk to him. Finding Wavy was the best chance to find Bronwyn. A few seconds later, Ian touched his shoulder where he was crouched behind the tire.

"He's dead."

Sarge let out a curse. "Tell me you got something."

"Warehouse. Industrial district in City Heights. I don't know if Wavy's alive or dead, but I'm going there to see."

He nodded and they got into the car, both of them praying like they never had before.

CHAPTER
TWENTY-ONE

"THEY KILLED Tippens rather than let us have him. That means he knows something they were desperate for us not to find out," Ian said.

They sped toward the warehouse district Tippens had mentioned. They'd fled the scene of a murder, an action that might come back and bite them with the cops, but neither of them cared. All Sarge and Ian cared about was getting to that building. To Wavy. And if any of his prayers came true, to Bronwyn too.

The Zodiac team was incoming. They weren't keeping anything a secret anymore. They needed backup—people they could trust. They would be there within the hour. Callum Webb and his law enforcement team wouldn't be far behind.

Ian was as frantic as Sarge had ever seen him. Something Tippens had said had shaken him to the core. He didn't need to ask—he was sure it was about Wavy, and it wasn't good.

Sarge remained icy focused. The part of him he'd had to let loose to be willing to torture a civilian was still in control. They were one step closer to Wavy, which meant one step closer to Bronwyn. She'd been alive when he'd heard her voice hours ago, and he was not stopping today until someone told him where the fuck she was.

They pulled up at the warehouse Tippens had mentioned. Ian parked way too close for any sort of stealth. He wasn't thinking strategically. He wasn't thinking at all.

Sarge muttered a curse as Ian opened the car door and started running toward the corner warehouse. He wasn't going to succeed at anything but getting himself killed if he didn't start using his brain. Sarge called after him in a low voice, but he didn't stop.

Damn it. He caught him in a flying tackle about twenty yards from the door. They both went down hard.

"I don't know what the fuck you think you're doing, but you need to use your brain." He wouldn't normally talk to Ian that way, but not only did he not want him to get killed, he was currently Sarge's only tie to Bronwyn.

They both jumped back up to their feet, and Sarge grabbed him by his shirt and slammed him into the wall before he could run again. "What you're about to do is not only going to get you killed, but possibly her too."

Her could mean Wavy or Bronwyn; take your pick.

"I'm going in." The son of a bitch punched him, and he took it on the jaw without moving. Ian wasn't himself, so Sarge let him have that one.

But when Ian swung again, Sarge blocked it, then slammed him against the wall, using his size to his advantage.

"If she's in there and she's alive, the guards will have orders to kill if the building is breached. Now use your fucking brain, and let's see if we can get her out alive."

Ian's fists loosened, and he knew the crisis had passed. "I'm sorry."

He let him go. "Don't be sorry. Be smart. We do recon until backup arrives, and then we go in fast and hard."

They nodded at each other, both fully understanding their

mission. Sarge went around to the south side of the building as Ian went in through a fire escape. It didn't take them long to know they were definitely in the right place—there were nearly a dozen armed guards.

Ian texted him. **Ten armed guards mean something important.**

That was for damned sure. **I concur.**

Sarge got to a vantage point from the side. The guards weren't at high alert, but seemed to be surrounding a crate. They were talking toward it, poking a stick between the slats.

Someone was in there.

Ian realized the same thing. **Guards interested in large crate in the northwest corner. Taunting. Someone's in there.**

Shit. He was going to make a move.

He needed to wait until backup arrived. Landon had let them know they were a few minutes out.

Stay frosty, boss.

Sarge thought he might actually listen to him, but then all hell broke loose. The guards received a call and went on high alert and pulled out their guns. Most of them turned away from the crate, but two kept their guns aimed right on whoever was inside, obviously prepared to shoot.

Guards on the move. I'm heading toward that crate.

Ian was going to get himself killed if he didn't intervene. Waiting for backup wasn't an option.

Ian ran toward the guards, eliminating all sense of stealth, drawing attention toward himself. He took out one guard, and the other fired at him.

Sarge ran in that direction also, firing from his position, even though he was too far to hit anybody. That at least drew some of the attention away from Ian.

But he wasn't going to make it, even with his help. There were too many guards, and too few of them.

Ian was willing to die to keep them from killing whoever was in that crate, or at least buy time. Once he went down,

Sarge would be the only one to stop them. He ran faster, firing as he went.

His friend was willing to die for the chance to save the woman he loved—not knowing for sure it was her. At one time, Sarge would've called that ridiculous.

But everything about his perspective had changed.

Sarge took down one guard, then another as he ran, but it wasn't going to be enough. He was out of ammo, but he kept running. One guard on the far side of the room had his sights trained on Ian, and he couldn't do anything to stop it.

He expected his friend to fall, but instead, the rest of the Zodiac team burst through the other door, providing the suppression fire Ian needed. One by one, the guards dropped as Landon and the rest of the team took them out.

Ian never stopped running toward the crate, trusting them to cover him.

They did.

———

Sarge was happy for Ian. He really was. His instincts—his willingness to die—had been spot-on. Wavy had been the one being held prisoner inside that crate. He'd gotten to her in time.

She was in bad shape, but she was alive.

She had Ian. She had her brother, Finn Bollinger, who was also a part of their small rescue team. They had both taken off with her to the hospital where she could be evaluated and get the treatment she needed. They had hope—the start on the road to recovery, both physically and emotionally.

Which was way more than he had for Bronwyn right now. There was not a damned sign of her anywhere around here.

All that was left was the mess Landon and Sarge needed to clean up. Ian had trusted them to deal with the fallout so he could be with Wavy.

There were two guards still alive, eight dead, and he wanted a chance to talk to one of the still-breathing ones before Callum Webb got there with the rest of his law enforcement team.

And by talk, Sarge meant being willing to do what Ian and he had been willing to do to Dr. Tippens to get the information they needed to take down Mosaic and find Bronwyn.

He walked over to the younger guard, maybe in his mid-twenties, grinning at him and full of himself, despite his hands being bound.

"You'll never take down Mosaic, old man. We're smarter than you, more well-funded than you." He jerked his head toward the crate. "What we did to her is nothing compared to what Mosaic will do to you."

He'd only caught a glimpse of Wavy, but he had seen the hell in Ian's eyes.

Sarge didn't wait for another word. He clocked the guy in the chin. He didn't feel bad about hitting a restrained man. He grabbed him by his arm and hoisted him onto his feet.

Sarge looked over at Xander Voyles, one of the men who worked out of the Zodiac's Los Angeles office. "The official report is going to say that there was one Mosaic guard arrested and eight dead. This punk is not going on the report at all."

Because whatever knowledge he had about Mosaic, besides singing their praises, he was about to share with Sarge, the easy way or the hard way. It didn't make a difference.

Xander nodded without saying a word.

Sarge dragged the punk to a back room far away from everyone else and locked the door behind him. He untied the guy's wrists, and he immediately tried to attack him, as expected. Sarge responded with a double punch to the gut and then another across the chin. He fell back onto a stack of boxes.

He crouched down next to him. "We can do this all day, and I can guarantee you that I'm going to outmaneuver you every single time, old or not."

The guy looked dazed. Sarge shut down all his emotions, grabbed his hand, and with one sharp move, dislocated his thumb. "That should stop you from any more punches."

He let out a howl, but Sarge hardened himself against it. "You're going to tell me everything you know about Mosaic, specifically locations. And I want them right damn now." He reached down and broke the pinkie on his other hand.

There was no swagger left in him now. "Dude, I swear to God. I don't know. They didn't tell us anything. We're trying to get in, you know? Work our way up. That's why we were on guard duty here in the middle of nowhere."

That made sense. "Then I'm afraid this is going to be a very painful next few hours for you. You better think of something you can tell me."

There was a knock on the door, but Sarge ignored it. Nothing was going to stop him from getting the answers he needed, even if he knew he was crossing a line. This guy was probably telling the truth and didn't know anything that was going to help him find Bronwyn. But he'd make damned sure of it before he walked out of this room.

"Open it, or I'm knocking it down." He heard Landon's voice from the other side of the door.

Fuck. Sarge walked over and opened it but kept his arm up so he couldn't enter. "You're not going to stop me, Landon. I'm getting the answers I need."

"I'm not here to stop you."

"Then what do you want?"

"I'm not letting you do this alone. If you're going to put this mark on your soul, we'll do it together."

Sarge hesitated for a second then let Landon in with a nod.

The guy sat up a little straighter on the floor, obviously hoping Landon was going to be the good cop to his bad cop.

Landon crouched down before him and gave him one of his infamous smiles.

"Sarge here isn't much of a people person. That's my job. I've got the friendly grin, charming good looks. People like me." He winked at the kid. "It looks like Sarge here has broken a couple of your fingers."

The guy relaxed a little, thinking the danger had passed.

Until Landon continued.

"But you and your friends were taunting a defenseless woman trapped in a box. So as far as I'm concerned, there are at least two hundred four more bones in your body we can break before we start the legitimate torture."

The guy's eyes grew wide.

"I'm not here to help you, asshole. I'm here to help him." He hooked his thumb back at sarge. "If he can't get the job done, then you damn well better believe I'll be able to get it done."

He knew Landon was fast, but he couldn't believe how quickly he reached out, grabbed the guy's wrist, and broke it with a simple snap. The man started sobbing before Landon stood back up.

Sarge nodded at his friend in appreciation. He honestly didn't know how far he'd be able to take this. Having Landon there meant that if he crossed a line, at least he wouldn't be crossing it alone.

"I don't know how much this guy knows. Probably not enough to be useful."

Landon cracked his knuckles and grinned down at the whimpering guard. "Well, I guess we're about to find out."

The guy scampered away as they moved closer.

"I'm telling you the truth." He held out both injured arms. "I swear to God, I don't know anything. I don't know anything except this building. I was paid to come here every day, and a couple of days ago, they brought that girl in. I don't know anything about her, not even her name. I don't know anything about you. And all I wanted to do was become a soldier for Mosaic."

His bravado was completely gone now.

"Maybe you can think of something to tell us. Once we get to the kneecap-breaking part, ideas usually start popping into someone's head."

There was a sick taste in Sarge's mouth at the thought, but all it took was remembering Bronwyn's whimpers in that fucking isolation tank to shut that down.

Whatever this guy knew, he was going to tell them.

His phone buzzed in his pocket, and he was tempted to ignore it, not wanting to lose any focus. But when Sarge saw that it was Jenna, he answered. "Now is not a good time."

"I know, I know. I heard that you guys found Wavy. But listen, one of the soldiers there got away."

"It doesn't matter," he told her. "They will be too late to send in reinforcements. We've already gotten Wavy out."

"No, Sarge. What I'm saying is that we caught him leaving the building not long after Landon's team infiltrated. We were able to track him via different cameras in town. We think he's heading back toward Mosaic, and we still have a track on him."

"What?"

"Virgo, get your ass in gear!" she yelled in his ear. "We have a viable lead, and we can't lose it!"

Landon and Sarge glanced at each other, then they turned and ran.

CHAPTER
TWENTY-TWO

JENNA LED them nearly an hour outside of town as they followed the vehicle. Sarge gripped the steering wheel until his knuckles turned white, hoping they weren't making a mistake. That guard may not have known much, but they had lost their chance to question him now.

Landon gave him a reassuring nod when Sarge glanced over at him as Jenna barked orders at the rest of the nerds not to lose sight of the vehicle. Every time it made a turn, they had to find new cameras to pick it up. Not an easy feat, even for a team as good as Zodiac's. More than once, they'd had to turn around and go in the opposite direction.

His grip got tighter as silence fell over the phone with no direction from Jenna for a few moments. Had they lost the car?

Then finally, she spoke again. "Sarge, we've got him. He stopped. Keep heading east, and we'll send you the exact address. I'm going to see if I can task some satellites to the building."

Sarge put himself on mute and looked over at Landon. "Does Zodiac have satellites we can task?" He wouldn't put it past Ian.

"Not that I know of. I'm pretty sure this is Jenna putting some not-quite-legal practices into play."

He wasn't going to argue—he'd take any help they could get, legal or otherwise. Sarge stomped down harder on the gas as if they weren't already going at a reckless speed.

Taking a two-man team into what could potentially be a Mosaic stronghold wasn't the best of plans. Their only weapons were what they had in the car—a grand total of three clips each for their handguns. That might get them ten feet into one door. If they were lucky.

The address from Jenna came over in text form. It was only fifteen minutes from where they were. Landon and Sarge rode on in silence.

"All right, you guys." Jenna's voice came back on the line. "Looks like we've got a multilevel compound. Large facility. Evidently, they've gotten word there's trouble brewing because there seems to be a mass exodus."

That was both good news and bad news. Good news because Landon and Sarge couldn't take the entire compound themselves, but bad news because, if they were preparing to exit, they might not leave any prisoners behind.

If Bronwyn was there at all.

"I'm sending the building plans to Landon," Jenna said. "I don't suppose you'd be willing to wait for backup?"

"I can't, Jenna. I can't take that chance. Not if Bronwyn might be in there."

"Okay. But I have to warn you, this building is not pretty when it comes to infiltration. I'll get you as much information as I can—building plans and such." She disconnected the call.

Sarge glanced over at Landon. "You don't need to do this." He was basically leading his friend on a suicide mission.

"Don't fucking start with me." Landon rolled his eyes. "There's no way you're going into that building alone. You won't last a minute."

He didn't try to talk him out of it. He was right. Sarge's chances of succeeding were basically zero without Landon, and not much better than that with him.

But if the roles were reversed, he wouldn't let him go in alone either.

"Holy shit." Landon brought up the plans for the building on his tablet. "This place is huge. Multiple levels, looks like it's almost thirty thousand square feet. And there are—wait, let me do the math…carry the seven—two of us."

Sarge's chuckle held no humor whatsoever. Those were his thoughts exactly.

He let out a sigh. "Please tell me something's funny about this."

"Less than two hours ago, I tackled Ian to the ground because he was about to run inside a building and get himself killed. And now my plan is even worse."

"I'll make sure I'm stretched and ready for tackling before we head in there."

He scrubbed a hand down his face. "They'll kill her. You know they won't leave that facility with loose ends."

"We don't know for sure if she's in there."

He stared straight ahead. "She's in there."

Sarge could feel it in his gut, an instinct he had long since stopped questioning. It was always right.

"Okay." He was thankful Landon didn't argue. "Then we make the most of the chaos. We get in there and stay alive long enough to get her out. I'll try to figure out what our best entrance is."

They were two minutes out from the building when they got another call from Jenna. "I think she's there, Sarge. I think Bronwyn has been in this facility."

"Why?" He would take anything that confirmed what he was already feeling.

"I ran a hunch when I saw that there was an entire

subbasement level. Ends up that there were four different isolation tanks delivered to this address over the past year."

Sarge wrapped his hands tighter around the steering wheel. Bronwyn was there. She had to be.

"Okay, that helps," Landon said. "If she's in the subbasement level, we need to go in the southeast entrance that's closest to that area."

That was at least a plan. "With a compound this size, there's no way everyone knows everybody. Hopefully that works to our advantage. We can act like we belong there."

Landon shot him a grin. "We'll kill them with kindness. Or with a gun, whichever is quickest."

They kept their heads tucked down as far as they could as they sped into the compound. Everyone else was heading in the opposite direction. Nobody stopped their car to ask them what they were doing. But if someone did, they were in trouble.

Landon got back on the phone. "Jenna, call all law enforcement that you can. Local, federal, Boy Scout troops… everybody. Let Callum Webb know where we are right now. Mosaic only thinks we're coming. Make sure they know we're coming."

She agreed and he hung up.

Sarge gritted my teeth. "Law enforcement is looking for Bronwyn too. They'll want to take her in."

"We're not going to let that happen. But right now, we need more people, even if it's to cause more chaos."

Landon was right. Getting Bronwyn out alive was the primary focus. Sarge would worry about law enforcement afterward.

But they damn well weren't going to get her either.

He pulled up as close to the southeast entrance as he could. Dozens of soldiers were running around everywhere, carrying out weapons and equipment. Information they needed to help take Mosaic down.

Sarge walked past them without a second glance. Taking them down would have to wait for another day.

Their luck held until they came down the stairs toward the subbasement level. A guard was posted outside the door.

"Hey, no one is allowed here. I'm waiting for the word to eliminate the prison—"

He didn't finish his sentence. Sarge clocked him in the jaw, and he fell to the floor. He grabbed him by his shirt and hit him again to make sure he stayed unconscious.

It was all Sarge could do not to put two slugs in his chest. Knowing they might need the ammunition stopped him more than any ethical dilemma.

"Let's hurry up," Landon said. "Between avoiding bad guys and good guys, things could get tricky. Law enforcement is going to be right behind us."

Sarge burst into the room and ran farther down the stairs. The place was like a crypt—complete and utter blackness. He had to use the flashlight on his phone to be able to see even a foot in front of him.

The isolation tanks were through another door. He ran up to it, cursing when he saw the padlock. "We're going to have to shoot it off."

Landon let out a low curse. "That's going to draw some unwanted attention. I'll cover the door."

They didn't have any other option. Once Landon was in place, Sarge shot out the lock, the noise deafening. There was no way that wasn't going to bring reinforcements down this way.

Once again, he didn't care. For the first time in his life, he turned his back to the enemy in a firefight. Sarge couldn't leave Bronwyn in her agony a single minute longer.

Trusting Landon with his life, he lifted the heavy lid that kept all light and sound out and then opened the zipper of what looked almost like a body bag.

Bronwyn was inside, her naked body floating just under

the water, arms restrained at her sides. She looked impossibly frail and almost bloodless.

His heart shattered into a million pieces as he let the sight sink in. Her breaths came out in silent sobs; her eyes flinched against the tiny bit of light his phone provided.

"It's me, Pony Girl." Sarge ignored the gunfire behind him as he placed his hand under her head and lifted it so more than her face was out of the water. "Can you hear me, sweetheart? It's Sarge. I'm here."

She didn't respond but kept flinching. He couldn't imagine the stress her body and mind were undergoing—thrust from utter silence and darkness into the deafening noise of gunfire.

"I'm going to release your wrists, okay?"

She was alive; that was the most important thing. Survival was always the most important thing. He knew that, but still…

Seeing her like that made him want to drop to his knees and sob. Made him want to kill every bastard ever associated with Mosaic. Made him understand Ian's single-minded focus.

Sarge unfastened the fetters at her wrists so she could move. She still didn't say a word, didn't open her eyes, didn't try to move away or toward him. He lifted her up into his arms and out of the water. She'd always been on the small side, but now she felt unbearably breakable.

He settled her into his lap then took off his jacket to wrap around her, thankful it was big enough to nearly swallow her.

The shooting behind them stopped. "I got the ones that came down the stairs." Landon turned toward them. "They stopped coming, so I think the cavalry has arrived."

The cavalry was equally dangerous to Bronwyn right now. "I can't let them take her, Landon. She's—"

Sarge wasn't sure what words to use. Broken? Fading?

Damaged? Endured more than any one person should have to?

He carried her over so Landon could see them more clearly in the light from the door.

"Dear Jesus," he whispered. His lips tightened as he met Sarge's eyes. "She's alive. That's the important thing."

He pulled out his phone and dialed. "Jenna, can you give us an update? I'm hoping the good guys have arrived."

"Yeah. Callum and his Omega Sector team are on-site. Damn near every cop in California is on their way."

"Good. Thank you. You saved our asses."

"Did you find Bronwyn?"

"Do you want to be responsible for this information?" Landon replied.

"That sentence tells me everything I need to know."

"Jenna," Sarge said. Landon held the phone toward him. "I need everything you can find on the effects of long-term isolation tanks and how I can best help someone who might have been in that situation. I need to know what can be done without someone going into the hospital, if possible."

"Roger that. I'll send whatever I can find." She hung up.

Bronwyn shuddered in his arms, a low moan falling from her throat. Sarge needed to get her out of there. To get her somewhere safe.

Landon squeezed his shoulder. "I'm going to go run interference upstairs. Keep law enforcement off your tail. You need to get her out of here."

Sarge nodded, looking down at her. More than anything, he wanted those blue eyes to open, to look at him. He wanted to know that Bronwyn was still there inside the shell of the woman he was holding.

"I'm not going to take her to a hospital unless I have no other choice. Law enforcement will check there."

"They'll also be looking at your house. Callum knows how close you two are."

"I'm not letting anybody take her. Not now." Not fucking ever. "What she did, the people she killed…it wasn't her fault. She didn't have control over herself."

"We'll work on clearing her name later. Right now, you get her somewhere safe and out of sight."

"I already know where I'm going."

"Where?"

"You sure you want to be responsible for that information?" Sarge shot Landon's words back at him.

"Touché. But you have somewhere to go?"

"I know a place literally built for her."

CHAPTER
TWENTY-THREE

IAN WAS GOING to have to bill Sarge again for using his jet. But it was the quickest and safest way to get Bronwyn where they needed to go, and he didn't hesitate for a moment to use it.

Landon had done everything short of a full Broadway show to distract law enforcement so Sarge could get her out. He'd made a beeline for the airstrip where he and Ian had landed that morning. Landon would make sure the flight plan was changed so no one—good guys or bad guys—would be able to follow them. As soon as Landon saw they were headed toward the mountains of Montana, he'd know where they were going.

Bronwyn still hadn't spoken a word. She'd spent most of the time since Sarge had gotten her out of that isolation tank curled up in a ball, her head tucked protectively into her own arms.

She'd sat almost completely lifeless as Sarge slipped his shirt over her. Later, she'd been just as sluggish when he'd stopped at a drug store where he could see the car from inside and found a pair of child-size sweat pants that would actually stay up on her hips.

He'd tried everything to get her to eat, but she hadn't done more than take a couple of nibbles of anything he'd offered. She kept water down a little better, thank goodness. She was so scary thin, Sarge wanted to feed her a three-course meal every two hours.

She'd finally opened her eyes like he wanted, still the gorgeous blue that was burned into his memory. But her stare was so blank, so empty, it was hard to count that as anything near a victory.

She hadn't spoken a word. Hadn't looked at him with any recognition. Hadn't done anything to suggest she was capable of actions beyond basic life functions.

Sarge needed to get her somewhere safe. He was beyond relieved when Lucas Everett met them at the airfield in Missoula, Montana as he requested. Sarge shouldn't have been nervous. He'd known the man for more a decade, and he'd never once let Sarge down.

He left Bronwyn in her airplane seat in that state of half-sleep, half-wakefulness she'd been in since they'd gotten her out of the tank, and he walked down the steps to shake Lucas's hand.

"Thank you for meeting me."

He smiled. "After the times you've saved my ass, I would meet you anywhere if you called for help." Lucas had been on a different SEAL team, but they'd crossed paths more than once. "But I have to admit, I was surprised to hear you were coming here in the middle of the night."

"I have a friend." Sarge glanced back toward the doorway of the jet. "She needs a place to heal. To lie low."

"That's what the Resting Warrior Ranch is for."

He nodded. Lucas and a few of his SEAL teammates had started Resting Warrior as a place to help people suffering from PTSD. The ranch itself was open for anyone—former military or not—to come get away from the pressures of life for a while. They also trained service and emotional support animals to help people manage their PTSD. Lucas specialized in horses. And alpacas, of all things.

Lucas knew up close and personal what PTSD was and what it could do to someone. He had nothing but respect for a man who took his personal knowledge and applied it to helping others.

And if there was ever a warrior who needed a place to rest, it was Bronwyn.

"You guys are welcome here as long as you like," he continued. "I think the cabin on the north side of the property will be exactly what you're looking for."

"I have to keep this on the down-low, Luc. There may be people coming after her."

That didn't faze Lucas at all. "I haven't mentioned your arrival to anyone else, so you don't have to worry about anything on our end. Does your friend need medical attention?"

"Probably, but a hospital isn't an option right now. I checked her over her based on my field med training, and there don't seem to be any immediate physical threats. But..."

She wasn't in immediate physical danger, but God, it was so impossibly hard to talk about what had been done to Bronwyn.

He didn't push for details. "I hear you. Resting Warrior isn't set up as a medical facility. We get people dealing with emotional trauma and mental health issues, but usually they're past most physical concerns."

Sarge scrubbed a hand down his face. "Yeah, if I could take her somewhere, I would."

"We have some basics I'll grab for you so you can keep an eye on her vitals. Oral hydration enhancers, oxygen saturation monitors, blood pressure cuff." Lucas reached over and squeezed his shoulder. "If she needs more than that, we'll find a trustworthy nurse at the local hospital who can come out."

Sarge nodded and went back to get Bronwyn. She didn't say a word as he carried her down from the jet and they got into the truck with Lucas. But for the first time, she was actually alert. Her gaze wasn't the sharp awareness she'd always had, but at least it wasn't completely blank.

Something about Lucas made her wake up slightly.

His jaw clenched as he sat in silence next to her. Maybe him taking care of her wasn't right for her. If she was afraid of him or more comfortable being around other people, he needed to honor that. Even if it gutted him.

Dr. Rayne Westerfield was the full-time psychiatrist at the ranch. Sarge had been planning on seeking out her expertise once Bronwyn and he'd had a few days on their own, but maybe he needed to do that right away.

Maybe Bronwyn needed to be with someone else. Not him.

It was only when Sarge realized she was sliding closer to him, away from Lucas, that he finally understood. Her defense mechanisms were kicking in, despite being buried under a wall of blankness. She was attempting to protect herself from a possible threat.

He was glad to see it. She may not want to actively engage in any mental way—and nobody could blame her for that— but her instincts were still firing. And her instincts told her he was a safe place.

Bronwyn was in there.

Sarge couldn't deny his relief in knowing that though she may not be interested in seeing him, she at least didn't consider him a threat.

Lucas didn't try to break into Bronwyn's personal space or engage her in any way. He kept his voice low and calm, talking casually to Sarge about things he knew he didn't consider important—weather, happenings in the nearby town of Garnet Bend. His instincts were correct—Bronwyn relaxed more as they drove.

When they got to the main ranch house, he tossed him a set of keys and gestured to a much older truck parked to the side.

"She's pretty old, but she'll get you out to the cabin. It's fully stocked and should have everything you need for at least two or three weeks. If you need something more, you know how to get in touch with me."

Sarge nodded and shook his hand. "Thanks for your help."

He would've liked to have gone in to say hello to Harlan Young and some of the other guys, but now was not the time. He scooped Bronwyn up and transferred her to the truck. She didn't say anything or look him in the eye, but she didn't make any of those terrified noises like she had when he'd first gotten her out of the isolation tank.

As they drove the fifteen minutes to the far cabin, Sarge tried to tell her as much as he could in case she was interested in knowing.

"We're at a place called the Resting Warrior Ranch. I know the guys who started it—they're former SEALs like me. They do a lot of work with support and emotional service animals now—horses, dogs, and some less traditional ones like alpacas, guinea pigs, and rabbits."

He told her how big and remote RWR was and where they were in Montana. He wasn't sure how much was sinking in with her, but he wanted her to know that this was a safe place, that she had options, that she wasn't alone and helpless anymore.

She didn't say anything or acknowledge his words, but at least she was there, she was awake, and she was alive. And wasn't running from him. Or trying to shoot him.

Sarge didn't get any real reaction from Bronwyn at all until they entered the cabin and he carried her inside and sat her at the table. Lucas had left the lights on. He was afraid they might hurt her eyes, so he turned off the overhead light, leaving only the dim stove light on.

"No."

It was the first word she had said. He spun to look at her.

"You want the lights on?"

She nodded.

Okay, this was something. She was communicating. She was understanding. He turned on every damn light in the cabin. The place wasn't big, two bedrooms, a small living room, and a kitchen with an eat-in dining section. When he came back, she was still sitting at the table where he'd left her.

"Okay, lights are on and will stay that way unless you decide to turn any of them off. Now, how about some soup?"

She didn't respond. Sarge hadn't expected her to. He opened a can of chicken noodle because it was what his mom had always given him when he wasn't feeling well, and he warmed it on top of the stove. It wasn't long until he set the bowl of soup down in front of her.

She blinked at him with those crystal-blue eyes that would always strike him in his gut. He kept his voice as gentle as he could. "Do you want me to feed you, or do you want to feed yourself? Either is perfectly fine with me."

She stared at him and then looked at the bowl.

"Are you real?" she finally whispered. "Or are you just in my mind?"

Sarge covered her hand with his. Hers was so much smaller, so much more fragile. "I'm real, Pony Girl. I'm here."

She didn't pull her hand from his. "I'm afraid I'm going to open my eyes and be back inside the black. Be back in the nothing where I don't exist."

Her fear of that reality was clear by the terror etched in those blue eyes.

He swallowed back the boiling fury. There would be time to make Mosaic pay for what they had done to her. Right now, the most important thing was being here for whatever she needed.

"Never again," He promised her. "No more darkness. No more black. No more nothing."

Sarge knew his words could only do so much. Only time could truly prove that she wasn't trapped anymore.

"Trust your senses, Pony Girl. Eat some of the soup. Feel how warm it is, taste how salty. Keep hold of my hand. I'm here. I'm here, and I'm not going anywhere unless you want me to leave."

She shook her head. "Don't leave me."

"I won't." He'd let her go twice before, and they had been the biggest mistakes he'd ever made. He wasn't sure he was ever going to be able to leave her again, even if she wanted him to.

She stared down at the soup again without picking up the spoon. "I'm broken. I can feel it inside. I won't ever be the same person I was."

His heart cracked wide open at her words. She was so young to have been through so much. He wanted to wrap her in his arms and keep anything from ever hurting her again.

But right now, Sarge would feed her soup. He picked up the spoon and brought it gently to her lips.

"Then I look forward to getting to know the person you'll become."

CHAPTER
TWENTY-FOUR

BRONWYN CAME BACK from the nowhere place to the sound of Sarge reading *The Outsiders* to her. When she blinked at him, he stopped reading and smiled.

"Hi."

That deep voice had become the very center of her existence for the past few… she wasn't sure exactly how long it had been. Sometimes, it felt like hours since he'd gotten her out of that isolation tank, away from the pain and darkness.

But she knew it had been much longer—days. More.

"I slipped," she said.

He knew that meant she had gone to the place where her brain shut off. Usually, it happened when she got scared—something triggered a memory or frightened her in some way.

But sometimes, it happened for no reason at all, like now, and that was the scariest thing. Curled up in her favorite overstuffed chair, wrapped in a blanket looking out into the Montana sky through the window while he read to her—that shouldn't make her mind shut down.

But it had. Bronwyn had no idea how long she'd been

totally unaware of what was going on around her. Sometimes, it was seconds—sometimes, it was hours.

Sarge was always here when she came back out of it.

He set the book next to him on the table. "Remember what Dr. Rayne said? It's your mind's way of protecting itself, and if it needs to go to that place, you have to let it."

She made a face. "Sometimes I think Dr. Rayne says whatever it is I need to hear."

He chuckled. "If I'm not mistaken, that's the point of time with a psychiatrist. Talking through the things you need to hear."

Dr. Rayne Westerfield, the psychiatrist there at Resting Warrior Ranch, had been her other lifeline besides Sarge. She'd seen her three times a week since she'd arrived.

Three times a week. That meant…

Bronwyn sat up straighter. "How long have we been here?"

He leaned back in his chair and crossed his arms over his chest. "You tell me. How long do you think we've been here?"

Grrr. He did that a lot. Made her think about things; made her use her head to figure out the answers.

She stuck out her tongue at him. "It's easier to ask you since I know you know the answer."

He laughed. The sound was beautiful. There was so much wrong in her life, in her head, in her body. But the sound of Sarge's laugh seemed to push it away. Made her feel as if there was a chance everything would be okay.

A chance. A small one.

Bronwyn looked over at the kitchen counter. There were rows of medicines, vitamins, and supplements that she took every day. A few of them she took three or four times a day.

Some of it was to help her body restrengthen after months of being malnourished and without proper sunlight. Most were to combat what Mosaic had done to her to control her mind. To fight the effects of the neuroinhibitors. Gene editing.

Chemical subjugation. A cocktail of drugs developed from Jenna's research with the assistance of the genetics specialist Ian DeRose had hired to help Wavy.

A number of the medications could've been more easily injected into her body, but Sarge had refused unless there was no other way. Her neck still bore the marks of injections—the severely damaged skin and tissue would probably be noticeable for years—and he was adamant about not adding to that process.

So Bronwyn took the pills every day. Some of them she'd probably be taking for the rest of her life.

They didn't always help with the pain. The agony of withdrawal still itched over her skin at times, but she tried not to make it too noticeable when she could.

Although Sarge noticed. He noticed everything.

He saw where she was looking now, and his laughter faded, although his gaze remained gentle on her. He was tired. He didn't think she noticed, and probably a lot of times she didn't, but right now, she could see the exhaustion etching his brown eyes.

How could he not be exhausted after having to put up with her all the time?

She woke up screaming three or four times a night. She sobbed uncontrollably randomly during the day. She had to eat every two hours since her stomach couldn't handle full meals after how she had been starved in the isolation tank. She could barely walk more than twenty yards because her muscles were so weak. She couldn't take a bath without completely freaking out. Even a shower was iffy.

And her hands shook all the time. She looked at them now. She was warm and calm and safe, but the slight tremor was still visible.

Her hands had been why she'd gotten hired at Zodiac Tactical in the first place. Her ability to move quickly, to take things without others noticing. Now she could hardly hold a utensil without it clanging against the plate.

She had to be wrapped in a blanket almost all the damn time because now not only was she cold despite the mild weather, her brain was paranoid from lack of stimulation.

They called it the nothingness.

Dr. Rayne and Bronwyn had talked about it at length. How her body and mind had spent too many hours with no sensory stimulation made worse by the drugs and experiments Dr. Tippens had done.

She was now in a near-constant state of desperation for physical contact. She found herself rubbing her skin like she had before, or wrapping herself tightly in a blanket, but not to stop pain this time. Now it was because she loved the feeling, loved to be surrounded, loved touch.

It was basically the only way she could function. Too long without it, and her mind started to panic.

Bronwyn had been careful not to tell Sarge, and she'd made Dr. Rayne promise not to either. She'd been offended that Bronwyn had felt compelled to ask, but she agreed.

She wasn't going to put that on him. He was already doing so much for her; she wasn't going to make him feel like he had to touch her too.

He studied her now, and she tried to remember what they were talking about. Oh yeah, how long they'd been there in the cabin.

"You've got multiple ways of figuring it out. Pick one," Sarge said as if she hadn't completely zoned out in the middle of their conversation. He must be used to it by now.

She smiled. "The alpacas."

He rolled his eyes. "You and your alpacas. Fine. We've gone twice a week to see them."

Bronwyn loved all the service animals there at Resting Warrior Ranch. The horses, the dogs, the rabbits, but mostly, she loved the alpacas and the one little sheep that thought he was an alpaca. The main alpaca he followed around was named Mac, so everyone called the sheep Cheese. Mac and Cheese were inseparable—mostly because Mac couldn't get any distance from his little stalker.

Each time they'd gone to visit the section of the ranch that held the alpacas, she'd learned the name of a new one. She'd met six, so…

"Three weeks. We've been here three weeks."

He smiled as if she'd solved some complex math equation. "Good. What are some of the other ways you could've figured it out?"

She made another grumpy face at the mental work. "The books you've read to me, the number of times I've gone to see Dr. Rayne, the horses I've ridden."

They kept to a routine, so remembering and counting them gave her structure to pull from.

He grinned. "Exactly. There's your brain working."

She rolled her eyes. "Yeah, I should definitely get a prize for being able to do something the average five-year-old can do."

"You've got to give it more time, Pony Girl. We're barely past measuring your release in days. And healing isn't always a straight line. Give it more time."

"Time," Bronwyn muttered.

How long did they really have? How long could they stay there? How long could she continue to suck the life out of Sarge?

He got up and walked over to her, picked her up out of her chair, and sat down. He resettled her in his lap and wrapped his arms around her.

This. This was what she loved. The feel of him surrounding her. His smell. The sound of his heartbeat under her ear. She'd spent so much time in that tank alone, unable to tether herself to anything, that being in his arms soothed her soul.

Bronwyn wanted more from him, and it had nothing to do with combating what Mosaic had done to her.

She wanted Sarge.

She wanted what he had done to her body at his house. Not because of her mind's need for physical touch, but because it was him. Because he'd been the one constant light through this hell. Because he was the only man she'd ever wanted for herself.

Because he was Sarge—big and protective and sexy as hell.

But holding her in his lap or wrapping her in his arms while she cried was the most he'd ever done. No more kisses. Definitely no more touches on her breasts or between her legs.

Maybe those things had never happened. So much of everything was confused in her mind. Maybe she'd imagined his house and what they'd done. Her mind had given her something she needed—a fantasy.

Bronwyn knew the kiss in Paris had been real, but now the attraction between them, at least on Sarge's part, had passed.

How could she blame him? Who would want to physi-cally connect themselves to someone as broken as her? She let out a small sigh.

"Hey." He tipped her chin up with a finger, forcing her to meet his eyes. "Why so sad?"

Because she wanted him to have sex with her, but she's pretty sure that's never going to happen. "We can't stay here forever," she said instead. "Eventually, we have to get back to real life."

"We can stay here as long as we need to."

She wanted to argue, but she was already so tired. She snuggled back into his platonic arms and tried to convince herself that everything would be all right.

CHAPTER
TWENTY-FIVE

"BRONWYN IS LOOKING BETTER," Lucas said to him.

Sarge leaned up against the fence rail next to him. "Yeah, I guess a month of getting sunshine, regular meals, and not being tortured does a body good."

But his friend was right; Bronwyn did look better. He knew there would be times when recovery would seem to go backward rather than forward. That was how healing worked. It was hardly ever a linear process.

The nightmares that gripped her sometimes were agonizing—so much more than merely fear. Shudders racked her small body until he was afraid they would snap her bones. And all he could do was hold her and help her live through it.

But right now, in this minute, watching the big grin on her face as she trotted along on an old pony, riding for the first time…it was enough.

More than enough.

So much more than he thought he would get a few weeks ago.

Every smile, every word, every grumpy huff Sarge got

from her when progress got hard? Each was a tiny miracle of its own, and he treasured them all.

"She's a natural with animals," Lucas said, "or at least she truly enjoys them."

"Have you seen her with the alpacas yet?" Sarge rolled his eyes.

He grinned. "A lot of people love alpacas. Those things can be contrary as hell but are so freaking adorable to look at. She's welcome to hang with them anytime she wants to."

Sarge chuckled. "Don't tell her that, or I'll never get her back to the cabin."

Which wouldn't bother him at all. The more she wanted to stay outside, the better. It was good for her.

She didn't have any memories at all of the first week they'd been there. No memory of all the blood they'd drawn and tissue samples they'd collected for tests to understand what had been done to her. No recollection of the conversations between Jenna, Dr. Rayne, and Sarge as they attempted to get the chemicals out of her system and figure out what she needed to survive.

She didn't remember him getting that fucking necklace off her and smashing it into pieces. Her throat had been covered with trauma marks from where she'd been injected so many times.

Each mark on her damaged skin was a reminder of exactly how badly he'd failed her. It was a miracle she didn't hate him. A miracle she wanted him around at all.

Bronwyn's laugh rang out as she picked up a little speed on the pony led by Liam Anderson, the ranch's resident jokester and also a former SEAL. Lucas and Sarge smiled. How could anybody not smile at the sound of her laugh?

"You got the message from Landon?" Lucas's smile faded as they trotted by. "Sounds like law enforcement is looking for your girl."

"Well, they can wait. She is not giving any statements to

the press right now. Until we have more on Mosaic and are able to clear her name, I'm not letting anybody near her, good guys or bad guys."

"Fair enough." Neither Lucas nor any of the people who worked there would give out info about then to anyone, including law enforcement, especially not on someone like Bronwyn who wasn't dangerous.

The men who had created Resting Warrior knew what it was like to need privacy. Law enforcement might have good intentions, but they may not understand the nuances needed for dealing with someone suffering from PTSD. They may cause more harm than good. Sarge wasn't taking that chance with Bronwyn.

But Lucas had other responsibilities. "You need us to go?"

"No, but there were a lot of dead bodies involved with Zodiac rescuing Bronwyn and Wavy. Landon says Callum Webb is getting some heavy pressure from his superiors to get answers."

He crossed his arms over his chest and hiked his foot up onto the fence railing behind him. "They won't be getting them from Bronwyn, at least not for the foreseeable future."

Lucas shrugged. "They suspect she's with you, but they don't know where. And now that Ian is stalling all their attempts to talk to Wavy—I'm sure for similar protective reasons—they're going to want to find Bronwyn even more."

"I'm sure they are." It didn't matter. They couldn't have her.

"Landon says it's not quite as cut-and-dried with Bronwyn as it is with Wavy."

"That's true, at least in the eyes of the law." Sarge scrubbed a hand down his face, remembering the footage from Anchorage and what she'd done in that New York parking garage. "But anything she did wasn't her. Or at least wasn't something she could control."

"But it was bad?"

"Yeah. Bad enough."

So far, she hadn't had any recollection of the people she'd killed, and he hadn't brought it up. Dr. Rayne felt reasonably certain Bronwyn would eventually remember what she'd done, but they would cross that bridge when they came to it. Right now, Bronwyn's sole focus needed to be on recovering her strength, both in her body and her mind.

Talking to law enforcement wasn't going to help with that goal, so he had no plans to let them find them. He would hide her forever if he had to, especially right now when she needed as much time as possible to heal.

They watched her ride for another few minutes. Neither of them wanted to stop her when she was having so much fun. Eventually, she got off and wandered over. She walked right up next to him and put her small hand on his arm. "Can we go see Mac and Cheese before we go back to the cabin?"

"Sure. Always."

She squeezed his arm. "Okay. Liam is going to show me how to take the saddle off the pony, and then we can go. I'll be right back." She gave him a smile and turned and walked toward the barn. At one time, she would've run, her natural energy driving her forward at a faster pace. But she was walking and smiling, and for right now, that was enough.

Sarge looked away from her to find Lucas staring at him. "What?"

"How are things going with your and Bronwyn's relationship?"

"There is no relationship. Not in the way you're suggesting."

"I see. Has anybody told her that?"

"What the hell are you talking about, Lucas?" he asked.

"The way she looks at you. The way she touches you."

Sarge shook his head. "It's not like that. This is about her recovery, nothing else."

Lucas leaned back against the railing and narrowed his

eyes at Sarge. "You do know that because someone suffers from PTSD doesn't mean every single other part of their life shuts down."

"I wouldn't do that to her."

"Wouldn't do what to her, Sarge? Consensual sex between two adults is not a bad thing."

"It would be taking advantage of her."

"Would it? Would it be taking advantage of her if that's what she wanted? I've seen the way you look at her." He held out a hand to stop him before he could make an argument. "And it's exactly the way she looks at you."

"Like what, *exactly*?"

"Like she wants more. Like you want more."

He did want more. He wasn't going to deny it, at least not to himself. Under other circumstances, things would be different, but they weren't. So it didn't really matter what he wanted.

Sarge turned to face him. He knew how to shut him down. "I look at Bronwyn kind of the way you at Evelyn, right?"

The pretty, young woman was new to the area and living temporarily at one of the Resting Warrior cabins. She and Bronwyn sometimes talked. Evelyn's eyes had that same terrified look he wanted to keep out of Bronwyn's. Lucas's eyes got soft every time he looked at Evelyn, which was often.

His jaw got hard. "I do not look at Evelyn that way. It's not like that."

"Whatever you say."

Evelyn had demons in her eyes as much as Bronwyn did, although he had no idea what was behind hers. He wasn't sure anyone did.

But if anyone was going to discover Evelyn's demons and help her fight them, it was Lucas.

Lucas crossed his arms over his chest and grinned at him. "How about I agree to stay out of your love life and you agree to stay out of mine?"

"Deal."

It was a deal Sarge was happy to make because he couldn't allow himself to think of Bronwyn in a romantic or sexual way. It had been cringe-worthy enough when he'd "only" been a decade and a half older than her. Now thinking of them that way would be so much worse.

Bronwyn didn't want sex; she wanted comfort. He could provide that—was happy to provide that.

But the rest? No. That was off the table, no matter how much he might want it.

He wasn't sure if they had ever had a window of opportunity for a romantic relationship. But if they had, it was well and truly closed now.

No matter how he might wish otherwise.

CHAPTER
TWENTY-SIX

SARGE AND BRONWYN spent a lot of their evenings reading or watching the small television in the corner by the couch. Most days, she was tired after the physical exertion of merely living and didn't make it very long past sunset before she crawled into bed.

She never knew when Sarge came into bed after her. A lot of times, she would fall asleep to the sound of him doing a workout at the other side of the cabin. Push-ups, sit-ups, and other exercises to keep his body in fighting shape.

He was always in bed with her when she woke up with a nightmare. She could reach for him, and he would be there. But besides that, he was careful to stay on his half of the big bed.

She peered at him now over the top of her paperback, the second of the *Twilight* series, and wondered what he would do if she slid over to his side of the bed tonight.

Wondered what he would do if she kissed him.

Wondered if he knew how much she wanted to.

Wondered if the memories she had of him touching her body at his house were real or a fantasy.

As embarrassing as it was to talk about, she'd mentioned

it to Dr. Rayne earlier today during their session. She'd asked her if there was any way to know if a memory was real or not.

She'd felt like a perv telling her what she thought she remembered, but she hadn't batted an eye. True to form, after listening to everything she had to say, Rayne tapped her pen against her lips and made a simple statement.

"I think the real question isn't whether it really happened but whether you wanted it to have really happened. Can you answer that question easily?"

Yes, she could.

And, yes, she did want it to be real. Desperately.

But… "If it did happen, I don't think Sarge feels the same way anymore. He makes sure his touch is never more than friendly, platonic. He always gives me comfort, helps me, is willing to do anything I need. But beyond that…nothing."

Rayne tilted her head to the side. "And why do you think that is?"

"Because I'm broken. Because why would he want to get involved with someone as damaged as I am? I can't force myself to turn off the lights at night."

"I agree Sarge probably won't ever make an advance toward you. But not because he thinks you're broken, Bronwyn, but because he is."

"What?" That didn't make any sense. "Sarge is the strongest person I've ever known."

She tapped the pen against her lips again. "Sarge is the one who got you the job that eventually led to your captivity and torture. Sarge was the one who stood by helpless, knowing what was happening to you."

"But it wasn't his fault," she whispered.

"I don't think he sees it that way. And for a warrior, watching someone he cares about—someone he would die to protect—suffer is basically the definition of hell. So I don't know that this is about Sarge not being attracted to you. It's more about forgiveness."

"There's nothing I need to forgive him for. I don't blame him for anything!"

Rayne gave her a gentle smile. "Not you. He has to forgive himself. And, like your healing and recovery, that's going to take time."

"So you think I should leave it alone. Not push for a physical relationship at all."

She broke out into a grin. "Actually, the opposite. You're going to have to be the one to take the lead this time."

"How's your book?"

His question pulled her out of the conversation playing in her head. "I've always loved this series. Have you read it?"

He shrugged. "Yeah, a few years ago to see what all the hysteria was about. I liked it okay."

She had to respect a man who could admit he'd read a sparkly vampire series without embarrassment.

She put the book to the side then scooted a little closer to him on the couch. He gave her a tight smile then stood.

"I think I'm going to do my work out a little early tonight. Are you tired after the horse riding excitement?"

Before today's conversation with Rayne, she would've taken his actions as yet another sign he wasn't interested in being near her. But maybe she was right, and this wasn't about her at all.

"Not too tired. Can I ask you a question before you start? I have a memory that I'm not sure is true or not."

It was the first time she'd asked about something like this. Except for this one memory, she'd been pretty happy to let the missing ones stay missing.

He sat back down next to her. "Of course. If I can help, I'm happy to. Ask me."

It was now or never. She decided to jump straight into the deep end.

"Did I have an orgasm on your desk at your house?"

She'd caught him off guard. He hid it well, only a slight

muscle twitching in his cheek giving away that her statement had surprised him. "Pony Girl…"

"I did, right? That's not a fantasy I made up in my mind? You kissed me on your bed, and then we did…more on your desk."

"I…" He shrugged, face tight. "You were in pain. Your skin was…"

"You were helping me combat the effects of the regimen."

"Yes." He rubbed his eyes. "I should've found another way. I shouldn't have—"

"No. I liked it. I wanted it." She reached over and touched his arm. "I want it again. I want that and more."

He closed his eyes, his jaw tight. "Bronwyn…"

It took all her courage to keep going. "I know the situation between us is complicated. I know you must look at me and see someone too broken for repair."

His eyes popped open. "No. Not at all. I think you're strong and resilient."

"But you're not attracted to me? Not interested in me in that way?"

"No. I mean, yes, I am. But I don't want to take advantage of you." He rubbed his hand over his face.

Bronwyn leaned away from him. "Then we're back to you thinking I'm broken. Or at the very least, you thinking I'm not like other women—normal women."

He shook his head almost frantically. "No, that's not what I mean at all. You're amazing. But you've been through so much…"

Dr. Rayne had been both right and wrong. Right that Sarge blamed himself but wrong in that Bronwyn wasn't sure he was aware of it.

This was so hard. The biggest part of her wanted to leave it alone, to go back to her little bubble that was full of alpacas and books and nothing that forced her to move forward.

But if she wanted Sarge, if she wanted their relationship to ever be more than mentor and mentee, she had to make a stand here. She had to move them both forward.

"What happened to me was not your fault."

He shot up from the couch and began pacing, not looking at her. When he didn't speak after a long minute, she stood and stopped his movements with a touch of her hand on his arm. But he still refused to meet her eyes.

"Harrison, look at me." When he still didn't do it, she cupped his cheek with her hand. "I'm here, alive, because of you."

Finally, those brown eyes met hers, and it broke her heart to see them brimming with tears. "What you went through…"

"Was not your fault. None of it. You made the best choices you could based on the intel you had. It wasn't your fault."

"But…"

Bronwyn brought her other hand up so she was cupping both cheeks. "Even more important, it can't be changed. What happened, happened, and all we can do is move forward from here. Both of us."

He turned his head to the side and kissed one of her palms. "You're right."

"You told me you looked forward to getting to know the person I've become." When he nodded against my hand, she continued. "That person wants you. If you want her too."

His eyes closed again. "I do. But I don't want to take advantage of the situation. Or of her. Of you, Bronwyn."

This conversation would become circular if she didn't move it forward. She took her hands from his cheeks and pushed one finger against his chest until he took a step backward, then another, until the backs of his knees hit the couch.

She pressed harder with that finger until he lowered himself to sit and she was standing between his legs. "You're the most honorable and courageous man I've ever known. You won't be taking advantage of me."

Bronwyn moved closer, setting her knees on the couch so she straddled him. She'd sat in his lap untold number of times, but never like that.

Moving them forward.

She lowered herself until she was fully on top of him, wrapped her arms around his neck, and put her face right next to his. "How about if I take advantage of you?"

A soft growl left his throat as she pressed her lips to his. "Yes, please."

And just like that, all Bronwyn's concerns about if Sarge really wanted her melted away. He did. She smiled against him as he wrapped his arms around her hips and pulled her closer.

She used her teeth to gently bite his bottom lip and slipped her tongue inside to play with his when his lips opened. She pressed down against him and was left with no doubt that he definitely wanted her.

Heat swamped her when he trailed his hands up her back to cup her shoulders and push her harder down against him. They both groaned. He traced her lips with his tongue.

"I have only one thing to ask of you," he whispered.

She drew back so she could see his face. "Tell me."

"We take this minute by minute together. If something doesn't feel right to you, if you need to slow down or stop completely, you tell me. For any reason. Not just now, but always."

It had not occurred to her to ask for reassurances that he would stop.

It was Sarge; he would stop in a heartbeat if Bronwyn asked. She knew that throughout her very soul.

But he needed to know she knew it. Needed to know that he wasn't ever going to be one of the people who had taken her choices away from her. "I promise. But I need you to trust me too."

"How so?"

She cupped those granite cheeks with her hands again. "Trust that I will do what I've promised. Trust that you don't have to stand guard and hold back. Because I promise I will tell you if I'm not okay. Trust that I'm strong enough to know what I want or don't want."

His rugged face lit up into the most genuine of smiles; it was beautiful to behold. "I can definitely do that."

His lips met hers again, his arms wrapped around her hips, and as if she weighed nothing at all, he stood with her in his arms. She locked her legs around his hips as he walked them to the bed.

He lowered her onto it then slid off his clothes before slowly peeling away hers, studying her with sheer appreciation in his eyes. "I'm glad to have the lights on at the moment, that's for sure."

Bronwyn was too. She wanted to spend hours getting to know his body.

But he had other plans for right now.

His lips met hers again then moved over his jaw and down her neck to her shoulders. Kissing down and up her torso and arms.

All she could do was take it all in.

She loved the way his body felt over hers, loved all the sensations—not just his lips, but his weight on her, the hair on his legs slightly prickly against hers.

She loved the way he smelled—the scent from his shower gel mixed with a male who spent his time outdoors. A mix uniquely Sarge's.

She loved the few freckles on his shoulders that she could see now that they were this close and naked, and the feel of his scalp against her fingers when she cupped the back of his head to pull his lips to her breast.

All the things that made up Sarge surrounded her, sensation after sensation crashing over her in beautiful symphony —chasing away the nothingness until it disappeared into her mind. She wanted to melt into the sensations. Melt into him.

When his lips became too softly against her skin, she kept her promise and asked for what she needed.

"Harder," she moaned as he took her nipple into his mouth. "Please."

He gave a growl of approval before sucking hard on the flesh. She arched into him as he pinched the other nipple not quite hard enough to hurt, but hard enough to drive her crazy.

Bronwyn wanted him inside her. She shifted her legs, opening herself so they were lined up perfectly against each other. She slid her hand between their bodies and wrapped her fingers around his hard length.

She loved that he let out a shuddery breath as his head came up from her breast and his eyes met hers. "I wanted to make this last a long time for you, Pony Girl. But I don't think I'll be able to at this rate."

"Longer next time. Right now, I want you inside me." She needed it. She didn't know how to explain that she needed to feel him from the inside out.

"We need protection."

She shook her head. "No. I had an IUD placed before I went on active duty. So as long as that's enough for you…"

He broke out into a grin. "More than enough."

He trailed his hand down and worked his fingers inside her like he had on his desk, slowly at first then faster and deeper when she demanded more.

Then that wasn't enough.

She wanted Sarge over her, surrounding her, inside her. She couldn't get the words out, so she clutched at him. He understood and shifted his weight, his big hands holding her thighs open as he buried himself inside her.

He moved slowly at first, allowing her to adjust to him, but then his movements became hard, long thrusts that brought his body fully up against hers. She wrapped her arms and legs around him, burrowing her face into his chest, breathing in his scent.

Bronwyn sobbed his name as pleasure crashed over her. He kept her clutched to him as he continued thrusting, then called her name almost as a prayer when he found his release.

He slowed then gathered her closer, still inside her. They held each other, neither of them wanting to move.

The nothingness had never been further away.

CHAPTER
TWENTY-SEVEN

A WEEK LATER, Sarge and Bronwyn were lying in bed. Long gone were the days when he stuck to his side. His big body was wrapped around hers, one arm hooked over her waist, the other snaked under her neck and back up around her shoulders, his leg thrown over both of hers.

They discovered that they both slept better that way. With him fully touching her, surrounding her, pressed together almost completely.

At first, she'd been embarrassed about it. They already spent almost all their time together—more so now that they could hardly manage to get out of bed. It seemed selfish to want him so close even when they were sleeping.

But whenever she tried to scoot away to give him his space, he immediately pulled her body back to his.

"Stay."

Even when he wasn't fully awake, he would say the words and tuck her back under him. Since that was where she wanted to be, she wouldn't get offended that it sounded as if he were training one of the Resting Warrior's service dogs.

His body surrounding hers helped chase away the nightmares.

That, and being so completely exhausted from their lovemaking.

"Evelyn and I are going to go into town to have coffee. It's her day off."

"I think that's a great idea." His voice was a low, sleepy rumble in her ear. She burrowed back into him, which, in turn, produced a little growl from his throat.

She loved that sound, loved that he seemed to want her as much as she wanted him.

She brought his hand up from her belly and kissed his palm. "I like Evelyn, and I like Lena at the coffee shop too."

"Yeah, Lena is something else," he murmured. "Definitely different from you and Evelyn."

Lena was loud and fun, laughed a lot, and had fire-engine–red streaks through her hair. Definitely different from Evelyn or Bronwyn. "That's why I like her."

"I think coffee with your friends is a good idea."

Bronwyn relaxed a little. She hadn't been asking his permission exactly, but if he hadn't wanted her to go, she probably wouldn't.

Hell, knowing he wanted her to, it was still going to be hard. But she knew she needed to.

They had to establish some sort of new normal if she was ever going leave this place and get back to real life. And despite what he'd said about not being in any hurry, she knew they couldn't stay there forever.

Over the past week, Sarge had been getting more phone calls. Or maybe he'd always been getting a lot of phone calls and she'd finally started paying attention. Mostly, they'd been Landon and Jenna. She'd actually talked to Jenna a couple times—it had been good to hear her voice. To thank her and let her know she was doing better.

But whatever phone conversations Sarge was having made his lips pull down and brows furrow. Especially when he didn't think that she was watching.

He never told her what they said, but she knew it wasn't good. What she didn't know was if it was about her. And Bronwyn was too much of a coward to ask.

She did ask about Wavy. Dr. Rayne had gone to Denver to work with her, and she was glad to hear Wavy was doing better than she had been. But the other… Unless Sarge brought it up, she wasn't going to ask.

"There's some money on the table you can use while you're in town."

She stiffened in his arms. She didn't want to take his money, but what choice did she have?

"What?" he whispered before gently biting her ear.

"I don't like to take money from you." He'd already given her way too much of everything. Money felt over the top. "And don't distract me."

She could feel his lips move into a smile against her skin. "It's not my money. That's your bonus money as a Zodiac Tactical employee who was injured while on a mission. It's a stipend provided to any employee during their recovery."

She turned to face him, mostly to get away from those lips that kept nibbling on her ear and his hand that was rubbing soft circles on her stomach that would distract her way too easily. "Are you making that up?"

"No." He kissed her nose. "It's in your contract."

"Even though I'm probably never going to be an active agent for Zodiac again?"

He pulled her closer. "You haven't given yourself enough time to know whether that's the case or not, but yes, it doesn't matter if you aren't an active agent, it still applies."

Even if Bronwyn could somehow get her hands to stop shaking and her nightmares under control, she wasn't sure that she ever wanted to go back to what she'd been doing for Zodiac. But what were her other options? She didn't have any other real skills, and she definitely didn't have any schooling. She wasn't a United States citizen, so she couldn't stay there. She would have to go back to the Czech Republic.

Everything in her rebelled at the thought of being back in the same country as Nikolai. He hadn't forgotten what she'd done—every time he looked in the mirror would be a reminder. If he caught so much of a whisper that she'd come back, he would find her and kill her. She wasn't going back there ever, even if it meant finding a way to be an active Zodiac agent again.

Sarge dipped a finger under her chin to force her to look at him. "What? What are you thinking about right now?"

Now it was her turn to try to distract him. She didn't want to talk to him about her past. The vision of Nikolai's men beating Sarge so badly still haunted her dreams. Sarge wouldn't have forgotten it either.

"I'm a little nervous about my first trip out on my own." She slid her hand between their bodies, down his stomach, and wrapped it around his length. She loved the hiss that escaped his lips. "I'll miss being in bed with you."

He tangled his fingers into her hair and pulled her lips to his. "Then I'll have to give you plenty of reasons to make sure you want to come back as soon as possible."

―――――

Bronwyn was almost late for her coffee date.

Sarge had very thoroughly reminded her of what she would be missing and why she should come back to him as soon as possible. She was a little bit sore as he drove her to the main Resting Warrior Ranch house.

And she loved every bit of it.

She loved it when he wasn't gentle and didn't worry about whether she was breakable. Loved to feel him lose control just a little bit. Loved he knew she could handle it.

She waved to Evelyn and got into her car. She kept her

distance from Sarge and, as always, pretended she wasn't looking at Lucas. Bronwyn wanted to ask her about them. Whether they had ever been a couple or whether she wanted them to be a couple, but she wasn't sure if those types of questions were appropriate. She'd never had much experience with girl talk.

But she would try. Because that was why she was doing this, right? Trying to work her way into some sort of normal. "Do you like the ranch? I do. I like the animals, especially the alpacas. Mac and Cheese are my favorites."

Great, now she was rambling.

Evelyn nodded. "Yes, I like it."

"Have you lived here a long time?"

"No, not long. Lucas offered me one of the guest cabins, and I took him up on it when I first arrived in the area."

"Oh. I hadn't realized. Where were you before here?"

Her hands tightened on the steering wheel. "Around."

Bronwyn stopped asking questions. She understood not wanting to talk about the past. They spent the rest of the ride into town talking about the animals. Saying goodbye to them was going to be the hardest part of eventually leaving.

That and having to share Sarge with the rest of the world.

They made it to Deja Brew, the coffee house where Evelyn worked, timing it so that they would hit between rushes and the owner, Lena, could join them rather than be working.

"There they are!" Lena rushed by them over to the window as they came in. "Did you guys drive yourself, or did Bronwyn's sexy man drive?"

"We drove ourselves." Evelyn hugged her boss as she turned from the window. "So no need to start drooling."

Lena turned to her, fanning herself. "Speaking of drooling, look at that smile Bronwyn has. That is the smile of a woman who has gotten something good. And very recently too."

She could feel the heat crawl up her cheeks, but she couldn't deny it. She didn't want to deny it.

Sarge was her man. She didn't know for how long or what it would ultimately mean. But right now, yes, he most definitely was. And hell yeah, she had gotten something good.

Evelyn smacked her friend lightly. "Stop. You're making her blush."

Lena turned to Evelyn. "When are you and that Lucas going to do something worthy of me teasing you into blushing?"

Evelyn looked away. "It's not like that between him and me."

Lena patted her on the shoulder. "You keep telling yourself that, sweetheart. I've seen the way he looks at you."

Lena kept talking, thankfully moving on from blush-worthy topics, as she grabbed them all some coffee. She'd never known a woman like her, so boisterous and funny, so sure of herself. She'd been out to the ranch a few times, and everyone liked her.

As she put the coffee on the counter, Bronwyn pulled out her money. "How much?"

She shooed her away. "This is on the house. That's the benefit of owning your own coffee shop."

"Oh." She put her money back in her pocket.

"You look disappointed."

"Not really. I actually have more money than I expected."

She winked at her. "That's a good problem to have."

When Sarge had said there was money for her on the table, she hadn't expected it to be more than a thousand dollars. He'd dragged her over to his computer before she could freak out and showed Bronwyn her contract. The money really was hers.

She didn't bring it all with her for coffee, of course, but it felt weird knowing she had so much. Enough to take care of herself for a while. At least until she figured out a plan.

Her hands weren't quite as shaky as she reached for the mug Lena handed her.

She was thoroughly enjoying hanging out with these women, even if she wasn't talking very much, as one cup of coffee turned into two. She was mid-sip when a cat jumped across the couch out of nowhere. More surprised than afraid, she jerked out of its path and dumped the remains of her cup onto her shirt.

"Holy hell, Bronwyn, are you okay?" Lena jumped off and shooed the cat away. "That thing is a stray, and I haven't been able to get rid of it. Did you burn yourself?"

"No, it wasn't very hot." She wiped at her shirt with a napkin. It didn't hurt, but her cream-colored shirt wasn't hiding the stain very well.

"Are you sure you're not hurt?" Evelyn had lost all color in her cheeks.

"Yeah, fine, promise." She rubbed at her shirt some more, but it wasn't helping.

"Hey, Evie, look at her. She's all right." Lena put an arm around Evelyn.

Something about the hot drink spilling had triggered Evelyn. Bronwyn didn't ask for details. Triggers were vicious beasts and often struck without warning.

"Yeah, I promise, I'm fine. Just a mess."

"Let me see if I have something in the back you can change into," Lena said.

"Actually." She dropped the napkin onto the coffee table next to her empty mug. "If it's okay with you guys, I'm going to run into the clothing store across the street and buy something for myself."

Lena looked relieved. She obviously wanted to make sure Evelyn was okay. "There you go. Spend some of that money burning a hole in your pocket. I'll bet that's what Sarge would want you to do."

Lena was still soothing Evelyn as she dashed to the small boutique. The teenage girl working the counter barely looked up from her phone when she came in. There was no one else around, so she wandered. She'd never been shopping in the United States before. It was new. And weird.

And wonderful.

She wasn't sure her exact size. The teenager decided to get off her phone and help her, gathering a few items Bronwyn never would have chosen, and guiding her toward the dressing room in the back.

"You should start with this sweater crop top. It shows off the midriff. It doesn't work on a lot of people." She hung multiple shirts on a hook by the door. "But you've got a tiny little figure, so you can pull it off."

Probably would be best not to explain that she got her tiny little figure from being imprisoned and starved for months.

"Okay, thanks."

"I'll go see if there's anything else. You don't need cream or white. That washes you out. You need color…" She was still muttering to herself as she walked back into the main section of the store.

She tried on the crop top first, but it was way too short, whether she had the figure for it or not. She grabbed the next one, a pink sweater. She brought it up to her cheek and rubbed against its softness.

Yes, this one. Bronwyn was already in love with it. She pulled it over her head and looked in the mirror.

She looked different.

There were a couple small mirrors in the cabin, but she hadn't really paid much attention to them except when brushing her teeth. But here, with the full-length mirror taking up half the dressing room wall, she couldn't escape herself.

She was definitely skinnier than she'd ever been in her life. But there was a color to her cheeks, a smile pulling at my lips that a few weeks ago she hadn't been sure she'd ever see again.

The pink sweater was soft and feminine with her jeans.

And all she wanted to do was show it to Sarge. He would understand why she liked it so much.

Right before he took it off her and threw it on the floor.

She didn't need the teenager to bring her anything else. This was the one. She ran her hand down the soft material again then turned and opened the changing room door.

A man she didn't recognize standing stood there. "Hello, Bronwyn."

Before she could say anything, she felt a prick on the side of my neck. She turned and found a second man standing silently by the door that led out the back of the shop.

Then everything faded to black.

SARGE HOISTED the bag of feed off his shoulder and into the barn with more force than necessary. They were going to have to leave Resting Warrior Ranch. There didn't seem to be any way around it.

He looked over at Lucas. "I can't bring law enforcement down on you guys. What will happen if you get arrested for obstruction of justice? The work you do here is too important."

While Bronwyn was gone on her coffee date, he was helping Lucas in the barn. He'd been interrupted by yet another message on his phone from Landon. Law enforcement from multiple agencies—particularly Callum Webb with Omega Sector—were starting to get very hard up to talk to Bronwyn.

"We can always tell them we didn't know you were around." Lucas poured feed into a trough. "That you took up residence in the cabin, and we didn't know you were there."

"That's not going to hold much water since they know our military connection."

Callum didn't know Bronwyn and Sarge were there, but it wouldn't be long before he sent someone to ask Lucas what he knew. He didn't want to put his friend in a position where the ranch would be at risk.

Lucas finished pouring the bag and looked over at him. "Do you have somewhere else to go? A safe house?"

Sarge hefted another bag onto his shoulder. The physical work felt good, but it wasn't enough to eliminate the frustration clawing at him. "Yeah, but a safe house isn't what Bronwyn needs."

She needed space where she could be outside. She was starting to turn corners for the better. He didn't want to put her somewhere that limited her activities and forced her to stay inside and hide, slowing her progress or maybe halting it altogether.

But what was the alternative?

"I'll find something," he continued. "She wouldn't want to take a chance on anything happening here because of her."

Lucas nodded. "Why don't we have a meeting and come up with the various safe houses and potential hideout locations among all of us? I know some of the guys have places no one has ever used, even cabins more remote than—"

He cut off as Evelyn walked into the barn. His face all but lit up. Normally, a smile didn't come naturally for Lucas, but it did for Evelyn. "Hey, you. How was coffee?"

She didn't smile back. Didn't move from the doorway. Her hands were clenched together, thumbs rubbing over her fingers nervously. Sarge looked over her shoulder for Bronwyn, but he didn't see her.

"Everything okay?" Lucas asked.

"Where's Bronwyn?" he asked. "Is she here?"

Evelyn bit her lip. "I was hoping maybe she came back here or you knew where she was."

Sarge dropped the feed bag where he stood. "Why would she be back here? You were her ride. What happened?"

"She spilled some coffee on her shirt then went to the store across the street to replace it. She never came back."

Every instinct in his body went on high alert. "How long ago did this happen?"

Evelyn shrank back. Sarge knew he was scaring her, but damn it, he was scared. "How long, Evelyn?"

"I don't know. An hour? It took us a while to realize there was a problem, and finally I came back, hoping she was here. She doesn't have a cell phone."

She looked over at Lucas, hands still wringing. "I should have called you. I don't know what I was thinking."

"It's fine. Bronwyn is fine. We're going to find her. Don't worry." Lucas kept his voice soothing, a lot like how he sounded when he was gentling a horse. Evelyn obviously needed it, but I couldn't worry about her right now.

Where the hell was Bronwyn?

"I need to get into town." The thought of her being back at Mosiac's mercy was like acid pooling in my gut. "I shouldn't have let her go alone."

Lucas nodded. "Let's not assume the worst. Maybe she had a panic attack and wandered off. I'll grab a couple of the guys who are good at tracking, and we'll meet you there."

Sarge ran for the truck.

"I'm sorry." He heard Evelyn whisper as he passed by.

Sarge stopped and turned to her. Time was of the essence, but he knew Bronwyn would want him to reassure Evelyn. "This is not your fault. She was happy to go with you. Happy to have some friends. Thank you for letting us know."

She nodded, and he turned again and sprinted away.

He kept his eyes along the side of the road as he drove, hoping maybe Bronwyn had gotten overwhelmed and decided to walk back to the ranch. A couple of times, he stopped and got out to shout her name. If she was scared, hiding somewhere, maybe his voice would help her.

But nothing.

Sarge drove the rest of the way to town and parked in front of the coffee shop. Lena immediately ran up to him from behind the counter. "Did you find her? Was she back at the ranch?"

"No. Have you seen anything or heard anything else? Tell me what happened."

"She spilled some coffee then decided to go buy a new shirt across the street. Evelyn was upset, and I wanted a chance to talk to her, so I encouraged Bronwyn to go. She said it was what you would want her to do." Tears welled up in her brown eyes. "I'm so sorry, Sarge."

He scrubbed a hand down his face. "No, it's not your fault. That is what I would want her to do. Was she okay when she left? Any signs of panic or anything?"

"No, she was actually a little excited about it, I think. About having money."

That's why he'd given it to her all at once, right? Because he wanted her to have a sense of independence, even if it was small.

Sarge ran across the street to the clothing store, once again looking for anywhere Bronwyn might be hiding. Although it didn't sound as if she had been stressed or panicked.

He never thought that news would make him feel worse instead of better.

There was a teenage girl working the register in the store. She barely looked up from her phone when he entered. "Hey, did you see a lady come in here? Blue eyes, brown hair?"

"Did I see her?" She slammed her phone on the counter. "She's going to get me in so much trouble with my mom. After all, I did to help her pick out an outfit, and then she ran off without paying."

"Slow down. What are you talking about?"

"She wanted to buy something, and I was giving her some suggestions, steering her away from the old-lady shirts she wanted. She's too young and hot to be wearing that sort of stuff." The kid let out a dramatic sigh. "Then, as thanks, she shoplifted."

"So she stole a bunch of shirts and walked out the door?" Sarge was trying to wrap his mind around what the girl was saying. Bronwyn had a history with theft, but he had no idea why she'd do something like that when she had plenty of money.

"No, she walked back to the dressing room, and I brought her some stuff. And next thing I knew, she was gone, along with one of the sweaters."

"The dressing room. Where is it?"

The girl rolled her eyes, not budging. "Man, I'm going to be in so much trouble when my mom finds out that somebody shoplifted."

He fought to keep his temper. "How much was it? I'll pay for it."

"$39.99."

He grabbed two twenties out of my wallet and handed them to her. "Show me where the dressing room is."

Now that the kid wasn't going to be in trouble with her mom, she was more helpful. She showed Sarge the dressing room, and he immediately froze.

He pointed to the door next to the dressing room. "Where does that lead?"

"Out back. That's why I was going to get in trouble. I'm supposed to have the alarm on, but I didn't because my boyfriend was going to come by later."

"So anybody could have come in or out of the door without you knowing."

She gave a one-shouldered shrug. "Yeah."

"Do you have any security cameras or things like that?"

The girl looked down at the floor.

He knew what that meant. "You turned it off because your boyfriend was coming."

"Look, all I wanted was a chance to make out with him. My mom is super strict. She doesn't like Derek."

Now Sarge had no way of knowing if Bronwyn had run

out the back or if someone had taken her. Either way, he headed out the door.

"Don't tell my mom, okay?" The girl called as he left. He threw up a hand to show he had heard her. He didn't know who her mom was, and he didn't care what the kid had done. All he wanted was to find Bronwyn.

The alley at the back of the store didn't show much sign of a struggle, but Sarge wasn't sure Bronwyn would put up much of a fight if she was taken.

Physically, she was getting stronger. But mentally, emotionally… Someone taking her against her will might make her shut down completely. Every bit of progress she'd made in the past weeks could be lost in an instant.

"Where are you, Pony Girl?"

———

They searched for Bronwyn the rest of the day and into the night. Lucas had all the Resting Warrior guys helping them. There was no sign of foul play, which led Sarge to believe that something had triggered Bronwyn.

He talked over everything with Lucas, and they'd come to the conclusion that maybe giving her all that money at once had been a bad idea. Maybe she'd decided she'd be better off on her own.

And while he couldn't deny that was a possibility, it didn't feel right to Sarge. Bronwyn wouldn't run like that. Not unless she had reason to.

There were a lot of other options. Residual brainwashing or something having triggered her. Or someone taking her.

But before they started searching farther out, he wanted to eliminate the possibilities closer in. It was her first time away from the ranch since she'd gotten there. Maybe she'd panicked, got scared, and went off by herself.

They concentrated their efforts in town then on the properties surrounding it. Half of Garnet Bend came along to help in the search though they didn't know Bronwyn. They only knew there was a woman who might be in trouble.

But nothing. No sign of foul play, no sign of stolen vehicles she might have used if she'd run, and no sight of Bronwyn.

It was nearly dawn when he headed back to their cabin, praying he'd find her there tucked up in bed. Maybe she'd have no recollection of what happened, and that would be fine. As long as she was safe.

But again, nothing.

And when he saw she had left some of the money in the cabin, Sarge knew it was time to call in the big guns. There may have been no signs of foul play, but that didn't mean someone hadn't taken her. He'd wanted to believe she was making her way back to him, but with each passing hour, it became clearer that wasn't the case.

He needed Zodiac Tactical. He knew Ian hadn't been in the office much—he'd been spending all his time with Wavy, nursing her mental health. He and Sarge hadn't talked to each other at all since that day they'd been prepared to torture information out of Dr. Tippens. Sarge wasn't sure if Ian knew Bronwyn was with him.

Or that she had been with him. His stomach dropped like a lead anchor. He hadn't let himself think that she was truly gone again.

Sarge needed his team.

As he grabbed his phone to call Ian, it buzzed in his hand. Landon.

"I've got a problem—" Sarge said with no preamble.

Landon cut him off. "Bronwyn's gone."

His grip tightened around the phone. "How do you know that?"

Another video from Mosaic? He couldn't live through that again.

Or, Jesus…pieces of Bronwyn mailed to law enforcement like Silas Varela had been?

Bile burned up his throat. He felt like all the oxygen had been sucked out of the room.

"It's not the worst, Sarge. I swear to you. It's not Mosaic."

He had to repeat it again before Sarge could hear him through the roaring in his ears. "Then what the fuck is going on?"

"It's Callum Webb. Omega Sector has her."

Shit. That was better than Mosaic but still bad. "They arrested her?"

"Not exactly. It's not her Webb wants. He needs to talk to Wavy, but Ian has been completely stonewalling him. Webb wants you to convince Ian to let him question Wavy."

Sarge slammed his fist against the wall. "Webb thinks Ian is going to say yes to me if he's saying no to him?"

"Webb thinks Ian might allow it if it means keeping Bronwyn from being arrested. But Ian won't talk to him at all. That's where you come in."

"How?"

"Ian has taken Wavy out on a yacht for some R and R. Webb wants to land his helicopter there, but there's no way in hell Ian is going to allow that. You, on the other hand, Ian will allow on that ship. Webb will just be with you."

He rubbed his fingers over his eyes. It had been a long fucking night. "Ian'll be pissed."

"But he'll forgive you. Especially because Bronwyn's involved. Webb has given his word he'll take you directly to her as soon as he gets to talk to Ian and Wavy."

Callum Webb wasn't a bad guy. Omega Sector as a whole was one of the top law enforcement units he'd ever worked with.

But that didn't mean Sarge wasn't about to kick some serious ass.

"No charges filed against Bronwyn? We're all agreed to

work toward taking down Mosaic, not in pinning blame where it doesn't belong?"

"Yes, Webb gives his word."

"Okay." He didn't like the thought of lying to his boss—his friend—and potentially causing some sort of emotional setback for Wavy. But Sarge would do it to get Bronwyn out. "I'll do it."

"I've already sent the plane for you."

CHAPTER
TWENTY-NINE

WITH EVERY BREATH, Bronwyn fought back the panic.

She was okay, she reminded herself over and over. She hadn't been harmed. And most importantly, she hadn't been put back in any sort of isolation pod.

She could breathe.

She could breathe, and she wasn't restrained. There was a window in the room she was in, along with a table with two chairs on either side and a couch where she'd gotten a couple hours of sleep before the sun had come up.

The room was almost like a much plainer version of Dr. Rayne's office. She had more comfortable furniture and paintings on the walls and a set of clocks that showed the time on three different continents.

All in all, this place wasn't terrible. Not like the cell Mosaic had held her in. There was a bottle of water on the table and some snacks. And a clear view to the outside—although there wasn't much to see besides an empty parking lot.

But the door was locked.

She sucked in a long breath again, doing her best to swallow past her fear.

When she'd awoken from whatever they'd injected her with, she'd been in a car, the two men from the boutique in front of her. She'd immediately reached for the door handle, ready to throw herself out of the speeding vehicle.

Those doors had been locked too.

One of the men was talking on the phone and turned to her. "Yes, sir, she's waking up now." Pause. "Yes, sir."

He handed the phone back to her, which was the last thing she expected. An image of a handsome man with dark skin and light gray eyes appeared on the screen.

"Bronwyn, I'm sorry for all the drama. My name is Callum Webb. I work for a law enforcement task force known as Omega Sector. I want to assure you that we don't mean you any harm."

She'd heard Sarge talk about Omega Sector, so she knew it was a real thing. She vaguely remembered someone named Callum too.

"Where am I? What do you want from me?"

"We're taking you to a holding facility. Not in Montana."

Bronwyn vaguely remembered a plane, but she didn't know if that had really happened. Her pulse skyrocketed. Holding facility sounded an awful lot like cell. She bit her tongue to keep from curling into a ball and wailing.

"Am I under arrest?" She finally got out.

Callum's brows furrowed. "No. That isn't my intent. As a matter of fact, we took you from Garnet Bend to keep you from being arrested. We were not the only law enforcement agency looking for you."

That still didn't tell her if they were friend or foe. "So you kidnapped me."

"I'd prefer not to look at it that way either." He rubbed his hand over the top of his head. "Agents Monboit and Palgrave have strict instructions to make sure your needs are met and keep you out of law enforcement's hands. Hopefully, this will work out well for everyone."

"I don't understand."

"We need intel from Ian DeRose, and I'm hoping you're going to be key to my getting that."

"I hardly know Ian." Why was everyone always trying to use her to get to Ian DeRose?

Callum let out a sigh. "I know. But he doesn't want you to go to jail."

"Why would I go to jail?"

He was silent for a long minute. "How much do you remember of what happened while you were held by Mosaic?"

Bronwyn shrank back against the seat. "Bits and pieces. I'm not sure which memories are real and which are made up in my mind."

Those piercing gray eyes pinned her. "I believe you. And it's what I keep trying to convince my bosses. But I've got to give them something, and you're my best chance for that."

"I still don't understand."

He smiled, but it was more sad than anything else. "No, I'm sure you don't. Once again, I'm afraid you're a pawn, Bronwyn. In a chess game I hope doesn't blow up in my face."

He'd ended the call not long after that—with her still as confused as she'd been when it had started—and she'd ridden on with agents Monboit and Palgrave in silence.

They'd ended up there in the holding facility that wasn't a cell but definitely had a locked door.

She took another deep breath.

Was Sarge worried? How would he know what had happened? Did he think she'd run off with the money? It wasn't an unreasonable line of thought. She didn't know how long she'd been there or how long she'd been unconscious before she'd woken up in that car. There'd been no mountains around, so she definitely wasn't close to the Resting Warrior any longer.

Bronwyn was back to counting meals to figure out how long she'd been there. Four so far. Monboit or Palgrave had come in and taken her to a small bathroom a few times.

She did okay unless she thought about the fact that she was trapped in that room. That, despite it being larger and nicer and having more furniture than where Mosaic had kept her, she was still at the mercy of others.

Others who could decide at any point to take her out of this room and throw her into a box. Make her lose herself again.

Bronwyn wouldn't survive this time.

When it started to get dark outside, things got worse.

There was plenty of light in the room, but the walls felt as if they were closing in on her. She sat in one of the corners and wrapped her arms around her head, fighting for each breath.

Hey, Pony Girl.

It wasn't Sarge. She knew it wasn't him. But the sound of his voice helped her throat ease enough to allow air into her lungs.

When she looked over to the side, she saw him smiling at her.

"You're not here," she whispered. "I'm crazy."

You're trapped in a room that reminds you of your captivity. It's getting dark outside. You're struggling to handle it. That doesn't make you crazy.

She shook her head. "No, I'm crazy because I'm talking to you and you're not really here."

You've got to do what you've got to do. Survival is always the most important thing.

Bronwyn let his words sink in. He was right. And he'd said that to her more than once. Survive. She took a moment and focused. The lights were dimmer in the room, but it wasn't dark. And the nearly full moon out the window would provide illumination even if the lights went out. She was okay.

Her pulse lowered, her breathing evened, the room opened back up again.

And maybe I'm here because I like your company.

Sarge winked and gave her his rusty smile, looking so exactly like he did in real life that she would've sworn he was sitting there.

"You're not here."

Are you sure? Feels like I am to me.

It did to her too.

She was so tired. She lay out on the floor and could feel Sarge wrap around her like he did when they slept—one arm around her midriff, one around her shoulder, a leg thrown over hers.

She fell asleep in his embrace there on the floor.

———

"I see you prefer the floor to the comfort of a couch."

Bronwyn sat straight up from where she'd been sleeping at the sound of a voice inside the room.

It was morning. She'd somehow managed to sleep through the night.

There was no sign of Sarge anywhere around, but that didn't surprise her. She got to her feet.

"Who are you?" This wasn't either Monboit or Palgrave. He was shorter, a little stocky, and had a European accent.

"I'm Agent Theodore Wilson. I'm not with Omega Sector." He said it almost with disdain. "I'm with Europol. The European Union Agency for Law Enforcement Cooperat—"

"I know what Europol is."

He raised his eyebrow and crossed his arms over his chest as he walked closer to her. She forced herself not to move.

"Good. Since they've brought you to Europe, I thought I would take a moment to meet you in person."

Europe. She definitely hadn't known that.

But she would have to freak out about that later. Right now, she needed to handle the threat in front of her. Agent Wilson wasn't like Monboit and Palgrave. Not that she had any abiding love for the other agents, but they'd never looked at her the way this guy did. Like she was a criminal.

This was someone who would like to throw her in a cage. A different one than Mosaic, but a cage nonetheless.

"Where are the other agents?"

Agent Wilson gave her a smile that was closer to a sneer. "Palgrave and Monboit received an important summons and had to go handle some things. Seems like Callum Webb didn't have official clearance to keep you here. Working rogue again."

"So you're here to arrest me."

"I'm here to ask you some questions."

"And if I don't want to answer your questions?"

He pulled out a pair of handcuffs and had them snapped on her wrists before she could move. With a jerk, he had her pulled toward the table and seated in one of the chairs. He attached the handcuffs to a bracket locked on the top of the table so she couldn't get back up.

Now his sneer didn't even attempt to be a smile. "People underestimate me all the time. They assume I'm slow since I'm not as tall or fit as your average agent. As you can see, that's not the case. And I know what you can do, so I'm not going to leave you unrestrained."

She was barely listening to his diatribe. The feel of the metal around her wrists threw her right back into her Mosaic captivity. She began to pull, trying to free herself.

Bronwyn couldn't let him lock her in a cage. She couldn't go back into the dark. She wouldn't survive. She would—

A slamming noise in front of her jerked her back into the

present. "Focus, Bronwyn. I have questions for you. If you want your hands unlocked, then you're going to have to answer them."

She blinked at him, trying to get her terror under control. She wasn't back in the isolation tank or the cell or the lab.

Focus. Breathe.

She wasn't sure if it was Sarge's voice in her head or her own.

Wilson slid some pictures across the desk so she could see them. They were grainy, but they were obviously of her.

"These were taken off a window reflection in a garage in a New York hotel from a few months ago. The cameras in the garage amazingly became disabled during this event, so there's no actual footage, just a few shots from a vehicle security device."

The images were blurry, but she could still make out the dead guys lying on the ground. "So?"

He slid another picture across. This one of a woman standing over a dead body. It caught her from the side, so her features weren't clear.

But Bronwyn knew. That was her.

"Look familiar?" he asked.

She stared at the images. A memory tugged at the back of her mind. A fight in a garage. A mission that had to be completed.

"Sarge?" she whispered. He had been there, right?

"That's right. Harrison 'Sarge' McEwan was in that garage too." He slid over another picture.

The quality of this one was worse. You could barely see Sarge lying on the ground. She still couldn't identify the woman standing over him, but you could definitely see that she was hurting him. She was mid-blow—attacking a man who was already down.

Her. Attacking Sarge.

Wilson made a face and shook his head. "I'll bet that hurt."

She wanted to cover her ears. She didn't want to hear his words or his stupid accent. She didn't want to think about her hurting Sarge. She closed her eyes.

"You're fortunate that there are no clear images of you. Otherwise, you wouldn't be in this comfortable holding room. You'd be in a cell."

Bronwyn could feel her breathing become harsher at the thought. The walls were closing in on her again. She pulled at her restrained hands. "Let me go."

Wilson sat back in his chair and stared at her, one eyebrow raised. "I don't think so."

Getting enough oxygen was becoming harder. She could see the gray on the edges of her vision.

Bronwyn, stop. Breathe.

She could swear she felt a hand on her shoulder. She looked over to find Sarge standing there.

She was losing her damned mind. Sarge was not there.

Breathe right now, Pony Girl. Figure out the crazy part later.

She shook her head back and forth. She was insane. He squatted down next to her.

Breathe. Damn it, Bronwyn. Breathe!

His roar inside her head startled her into breathing. The gray that had been taking over her vision receded. And with it the full memory of the fight in that garage returned.

"I remember," she whispered.

She remembered it all. The mission to steal from Peter Kerpar. Sarge trying to stop her, trying to place a tracker on her, trying to help her. Her hurting him.

"I'm sorry." Tears dripped down her cheek as she stared at the imaginary Sarge next to her.

"Sorry that you killed these men? Sorry that's you in the photos?"

Quiet now. Sarge's brown eyes stayed locked on hers. *Focus on breathing.*

Wilson kept asking her questions, but she ignored him. She kept her gaze on Sarge. "I'm sorry."

No permanent harm done. Stay gold.

Wilson slammed his hand down on the table, and she looked up. Sarge disappeared. "I won't be ignored, Bronwyn. Answer the question."

She didn't know what the question was. She stared at him without talking.

"Fine," he eventually said when it became obvious she wasn't going to say anything else. She didn't owe him any of the story. She only owed Sarge an apology. The real Sarge, not the one her broken mind had made up.

"Then how about this." This time, Wilson slid a computer tablet in front of her, then pressed play on a video.

There was no doubt the woman in the alley was her this time. She watched as a man tried to take her wallet, kicked her, then she killed him.

The memory of that pressed on her brain also. The man had hurt her, made an aggressive move with a knife, and she'd killed him without hesitation.

She still didn't say anything. She didn't need Sarge there to tell her to be quiet.

"Nothing to say about that?" Wilson played the footage again. "I suppose someone could argue it was self-defense. And granted, the guy did have a violent record. But you still should've been brought in for questioning."

Bronwyn blinked at Wilson. She didn't know what he wanted. She didn't know why he didn't arrest her right now if that's what he wanted. There was no one to stop him.

She could breathe right now, and that was all she cared about. She was keeping it together. The walls weren't closing in.

Her job was to keep herself alive, not answer any of

Wilson's questions. Dealing with the fact that she was a killer would have to come later.

"Okay, so you don't want to talk about this. Fair enough. Can't say I blame you." Wilson pulled the tablet back from her side of the table. "I'll be honest, the people you've hurt—that's no great loss to society. Kerpar's men were criminals, the guy you stabbed was obviously not an upstanding member of society."

Bronwyn continued to stare without talking.

Wilson picked up his chair and brought it around to sit next to her. He was too close, but she couldn't escape him with her hands shackled.

Breathe, Pony Girl. It's going to be all right.

She couldn't see Sarge anywhere. She continued to stare ahead, ignoring Wilson next to her.

"I don't care about the others. A few thugs being killed is America's problem." He touched her chin to force her eyes over to his. "Do you know why I'm here, Bronwyn?"

She didn't respond. Didn't want him touching her.

"I'm here because of Mosaic. I'm here because, unlike those thugs, Mosaic is not just America's problem—that terrorist group has branched out into Europe, and I'm going to be the one to put them into the ground."

"Good." She didn't like him touching her, but if ending Mosaic was his mission, she was all for it.

"If that's how you really feel, then why don't you help me?"

"How? I don't remember anything."

She tried to look away, but his fingers got firmer on her chin, keeping her face pointed at him. "You don't remember, or you don't want to remember?"

For the near month they'd been at Resting Warrior, she hadn't tried to remember. Even with Dr. Rayne. She wasn't sure what was real and what was in her head. She hadn't wanted to think about it—hadn't wanted to know what truths made up the nightmares that woke her almost every night.

"Both," she whispered. "And what I do remember can't be trusted."

Because ultimately, her mind was broken. That was obvious in so many ways. Sarge standing in the corner, arms crossed over his chest, watching all of this right now being the main one.

Wilson let go of her chin and went back around to the other side of the table, leaning his weight on his arms, looking down at her.

"Ultimately, that's not the root of my questions anyway. What Mosaic did to you while they had you or what you did while under their control is not what I need to know."

Once more, she didn't say anything. He would get to his point. She looked over at Sarge in the corner.

"The real question is why you?"

Now her eyes found Agent Wilson's. "What?"

"I've looked over all the data pertaining to you and Mosaic. Looked over all the ties between Mosaic in its original form a few years ago and the version of it now. Erick Huen is the main tie between both versions, and his intent is to get revenge on Ian DeRose."

"I know Erick Huen." She could still remember him dropping Silas Varela's hand on her torso when she'd been strapped to that medical chair. She couldn't stop the shudder that racked her body at the memory.

"The question is, why did Erick Huen know you?"

"What?" She said again.

Wilson pushed himself up from the table. "No offense, but you're nobody in Zodiac's ranks. Erick kidnapped you to use against Ian DeRose, but you'd hardly met the man. He cared about you distantly, as an employee, but had no true ties. If Erick Huen wanted to send a message to Ian using one of his employees, why choose one Ian had no ties to?"

"I don't know."

She didn't know anything.

"That's the thing, Bronwyn. I don't believe you. I think the answer is inside your brain, and what we need in this situation is someone not afraid of asking you the hard questions. So, I'm going to ask you again."

He leaned down on the table once more, getting closer to her face this time. "Why you?

CHAPTER
THIRTY

"YOU'RE FUCKING lucky Ian isn't having me bury your body where no one will ever find it." Sarge looked over at Webb in the car taking them to the building where he was holding Bronwyn.

He'd dragged him halfway across the damned planet and used him as his ticket to get his helicopter onto Ian's yacht. And had eventually gotten what he wanted—a chance to talk to Wavy.

Webb shrugged. "It was a chance I had to take. You and Ian were hiding the only two people who can give us any info on Mosaic. We've got a body count that has to be reconciled."

"Pull something like this again, and I won't wait for Ian's permission to make you disappear, Webb. Leave Bronwyn alone."

They weren't far from where Bronwyn was being held. Webb was lucky she was on their side of the Atlantic. If not, he would've been pummeling him the entire flight home.

Was she okay? Scared? Panicked? She had so many triggers. What if the men holding her left her in the dark?

Hang on, Pony Girl. I'm coming.

Webb looked over at him. "I know what Mosaic did to

Bronwyn. I know that it's worse than what Wavy went through, and that was bad enough. I don't want to hurt her any further. All I want is your word that if she does remember anything or is willing to talk to law enforcement, that you will let us know. We've got to make progress on shutting Mosaic down. You heard about the bombing in Warsaw last week?"

Sarge shrugged. "Vaguely."

"That was Mosaic. So now we've got two wiped-out buildings we know they're responsible for. One in the US, one in Europe. And a lot of dead bodies. We need intel."

"Bronwyn can't give it to you. Use what you got from Wavy."

"But if Bronwyn's willing to talk—"

"I promise you'll be the first person I call. As long as you're not planning to arrest her. The things she did…"

"We're not. We couldn't make a positive ID of her in New York, and that guy she killed in Anchorage was clearly self-defense. Not to mention, we never found a body."

Mosaic had cleaned it up. At least they were good for something.

"Don't ever try to take her like this again, Webb. If she's hurt…"

"She's not. She's with two of my best men. Monboit and Palgrave are trustworthy and see the overall big picture. Their instructions were to make sure she was comfortable. She's not restrained, not in a small room, not in the dark. Like I said, I'm not trying to—"

He cut off when his phone buzzed. "Speak of the devil." He brought the phone to his ear. "Palgrave, we're about eight minutes out."

He couldn't hear what was being said, but Webb's face got tight at whatever was being relayed to him.

Sarge drove faster.

"Get back to the building. We'll already be there." Webb disconnected the call with those words.

"Problem?"

"My men were summoned by Europol. Or at least they thought they were. Ends up a Europol agent by the name of Theodore Wilson wanted a chance to talk to Bronwyn. He's our European counterpart."

"Is he a problem?"

"He wanted to come with us to talk to Ian, but I said no. He's a good agent but definitely an end-justifies-the-means sort of guy. Not great bedside manner."

"Smart not to bring him, then."

"Agreed." Webb glanced over at him. "But turns out that he drew my men out on a false call, and now he's with Bronwyn."

Sarge didn't say anything but drove much faster than was safe in the French Riviera. He didn't ease up until they pulled up to the building where Bronwyn was being held. He rushed inside behind Webb.

Wilson stood over Bronwyn at some desk—his fucking face way too close to hers—asking why Mosaic had chosen her when Webb and Sarge burst into the room.

Sarge might have been able to get himself under control if he hadn't seen that she was handcuffed to the table. She wasn't pulling at them now, but she had. He could see the red marks on her soft skin.

Over the scars of where she'd fought Mosaic's restraints.

He flew across the table and caught Wilson in a tackle. The guy was a shit-ton smaller than him, but he didn't care. Sarge got three good punches into his face, definitely breaking the bastard's nose, before Webb pulled Sarge off him.

He got in a couple punches on Webb for good measure.

"Damn it, Sarge. Stop." Webb spat blood. "Bronwyn needs you."

No other words would've gotten his head out of his ass so quickly. He dropped Webb and turned to Bronwyn.

"Pony Girl?"

Sarge was expecting the worst. Tears. Demons in her eyes. But she was steady, looking more like the woman he'd kissed in Paris than she had in weeks.

She jerked at her handcuffs. "Want to get me out of these things?"

Webb slipped a key into his hand, and he released her. The metal dropped to the table as he swept her off her feet and jerked her against his chest. Cursing himself, he was about to put her down. This wasn't about what he needed; it was about what she needed. And she may not want to be touched right now.

But her arms and legs wrapped around him, keeping him close.

"Are you okay?" He threaded his fingers in her hair, holding her head so he could see her face.

"I'm okay. I've only been restrained the past hour or so while Agent Jackass was here. Otherwise, a little spooked, but...okay."

"Did he hurt you?" Maybe he'd get to hide a body today after all.

"No. He's not my favorite person in the world, but he didn't hurt me. I promise." She tucked her face in his neck. "He showed me some pictures of things I did. People I killed. People I hurt. You."

Sarge needed to go punch that bastard another dozen times. The things Bronwyn had done while under Mosaic's influence would have to be dealt with eventually, but not while she was still recovering. He couldn't stand the thought of her suffering more. "What he told you might have been worse than what really hap—"

She put a finger over his lips. "I remember. I think the

memories have always been in my head, but his actions jarred them out. I remember New York. Anchorage."

"And you're okay?"

She let out a sigh, arms and legs still wrapped around him. "No. I have to process that I'm a killer. But I think I'd rather know and face it than have it sneak up on me unawares."

Maybe he should've told her. Given her a chance to face it head on. "I'm sorry."

She cupped his cheek. "Just take me out of here."

"My pleasure. And I like your sweater."

————

Sarge took her to Èze. If they had both been dragged against their will to the French Riviera, they might as well enjoy the best parts of it.

Their small bed-and-breakfast offered breathtaking views of the Mediterranean from the medieval village perched high on the mountain cliffs that were only accessible by foot.

"I've never seen anything like it," Bronwyn whispered, face pressed against the window. "But I guess that's not saying much given how little I've traveled."

He walked over and stood behind her, looking at the blue of the water that reminded him so much of her eyes. "It's truly one of the most beautiful places I've ever been, and the Navy took me all over the world."

They'd been there for two days. He would've liked to have spent the time in bed or enjoying the sea so close to them. But instead, they'd spent it looking through all the footage and pictures from New York and Anchorage.

They'd dragged the table over to the window so they could at least enjoy the view while they dug through hell.

She studied the computer screen playing the footage of

her stabbing the thug. "Am I a coward for not facing this sooner?"

"No." His answer was immediate and unwavering. As it had been the other times she'd asked a version of the question.

"If I had sorted through these memories earlier, maybe I'd already be remembering something useful about Mosaic."

Sarge reached over and threaded her fingers with his. "You were healing. You still are. It takes time. Just like with physical recovery, pushing too hard with emotional recovery can cause setbacks."

He wasn't sure if she believed him, but she'd let it go. They'd probed as much as they could into what she did remember. People—Dr. Tippens, who was dead. Erick Huen, for whom Zodiac was actively searching. They also knew there were three other unidentified partners in Mosaic. Nothing she remembered was helping with that. He hated to see her beat herself up over it.

"Agent Wilson was right," she said in front of him at the window.

"I doubt that." He gently circled her wrist with his hand, bringing it up so he could kiss the bruised skin. "Damn near everything he did was wrong."

"But his question was right. Why me? Why did Erick Huen choose me to get Ian's attention? How did I get on Erick's radar to begin with?"

He wrapped an arm around her torso and pulled her back against his chest. "There could be a lot of reasons. You're young and new. You're part of Zodiac, so Ian would care if something happened to you, but weren't so embedded in the team that it would be hard for Erick to get to you."

"Maybe."

"It might not be that complicated. It could've been nothing more than bad luck. You were the lowest-hanging fruit—a Zodiac employee who spent a lot of time alone. He saw an opportunity and went for it."

Bronwyn lowered her forehead against the glass. "There's something I'm not remembering."

He kissed the top of her head. "You've got to give it more time. The pieces will continue to come together."

"Will they? I'm not sure. I don't know if I can trust my mind."

He turned her to face him. "Why do you say that? For two days, you've been facing what happened to you head on. You haven't flinched from it, haven't shut down."

Her lips pressed together, and she looked away from him. "But I haven't told you everything. I haven't told you the worst."

His stomach clenched at the thought that there could be more she had gone through that he didn't know about. He wasn't sure either of them could handle it. He hadn't told her about the recordings he had of her from the transmitter. There wasn't any point.

But whatever it was she needed to disclose, he would shoulder for her if he could. If she would let him. He pressed a finger under her chin. "Tell me."

She let out a small sigh. "I see things. People. Who aren't there."

That hadn't been what he was expecting at all. He relaxed slightly. "All the time?"

"No. Mostly when I'm freaking out. Panicking. I talk to them, and they talk to me, but they're not really there."

He yanked her against his chest, wrapping his arms around her. "You scared me, Pony Girl. When you said you hadn't told me the worst, I thought…"

He screwed his eyes closed. He couldn't put into words the worst he could think about, but her conversing with imaginary friends wasn't in the top one hundred.

She pushed back from him. "But don't you get it? This

means my mind is broken. It happened all the time when Mosaic had me. Then it happened again while I was in that holding room with Agent Wilson."

Sarge's relief was so tangible it was hard to take this seriously, but it was important to her so he needed to try. "Tell me details. Walk me through it."

"When things got bad, I would see…you. You would talk to me."

"What would I say?"

She shrugged. "Mostly to survive. That I could make it. To be quiet if I needed to. To focus. Breathe."

He cupped her face. "If I had been there when you needed me most—and I would give everything I own if I could've been—I would've said those exact things to you. That you're strong. Capable. That you can do anything you set your mind to. That survival, no matter how you do it, is always the most important thing."

Those blue eyes blinked up at her. "I know you would've. You've always done whatever you could to protect me. But still, it's a splinter in my psyche I can feel now. I'm crazy. Broken."

This woman.

She was a dichotomy in every way a person could be one.

Fragile but strong. Capable but unsure. Broken but beautiful.

And he was in love with her. He had been since she was a fucking teenager, although he hadn't felt it in the same way he did now.

Now she was a woman, he wanted to worship her in every way one person could worship another.

Sarge slid his hands down her body and slowly lifted her slight weight into his arms. "I am honored and humbled that your mind chose me as the vessel to talk to you."

She shook her head. "You helped me."

"No, you helped you. Whatever you saw when you were

at your lowest may have looked and sounded like me, but it was your mind providing you what you needed." He walked them toward the bed. "I don't call that broken, I call it resourceful. Intelligent. Amazing."

"But why couldn't I say those things to myself? Why did I have to imagine you saying them?"

He put his forehead against hers. "Because you trust me. And that is the most profound gift you could ever offer me. I cherish it."

"You don't think I'm weird?"

He laid her on the bed and slowly peeled off her clothes. "I think you are a survivor. I believe you have gone through what would have crushed most people but have come out the other side—if not whole, then with at least with big enough pieces to keep glued together. And I believe being here with you is the greatest honor of my life."

"Sarge—"

He loved the heat in her eyes. He stood at the foot of the bed and pulled his clothes off. He didn't want anything between them. He wanted her skin against his. Her soul against his.

He crawled back onto the bed, running his lips up her legs. "You're a warrior. A survivor. Beautiful and giving."

He covered her body in kisses as he spoke. Knees, thighs, hips. He wanted to taste every part of her.

She let out a moan as he covered one breast then the other with his mouth before he worked gentle kisses back down and settled between her legs. All the rest of the things he wanted to say would have to wait.

Right now, he would give her what he could: pleasure.

CHAPTER
THIRTY-ONE

WAVY HAD REMEMBERED something about Mosaic. Something important. Something that was going to help law enforcement put Erick Huen away for good.

Which was more than Bronwyn had been able to do.

Sun-soaked days in the French Riviera hadn't helped. Going back to the familiarity of the Resting Warrior Ranch hadn't helped. Knowing there was information inside her head that she couldn't get out definitely hadn't helped.

She hid it all from Sarge. He was so excited that she'd been making forward progress—remembering and dealing with some of what had happened—that she didn't have the heart to tell him she'd hit a wall.

As she sat in the kitchen of their tiny cabin and heard him on the phone with Landon, she knew she couldn't continue down the same path they'd been on since he'd carried her out of the Mosaic compound.

Ian and his team were heading to some island where Wavy had been held. That's what she had remembered. They were going to take Mosaic down. Ian wanted Sarge on the team, but he wouldn't go.

Because of her.

Because, if anything, she'd taken steps backward since first remembering some of her captivity with Mosaic. Her hands were shaking again. The nightmares were worse. The need to do something was tugging at her all the time.

But she wasn't sure what.

When Sarge had been out, she'd called the genetics specialist who'd been treating her, the same one who'd been helping Wavy, and told Dr. Han she needed to up her medication.

The doctor wasn't surprised and said that was to be expected. The genetic modification and chemical subjugation experimentation that had been performed on her would have long-term effects. She explained her body might be fighting what they did to her for the rest of her life.

Bronwyn was prepared for that. Even okay with it. But if her life was going to fall apart forever, she wasn't going to take Sarge down with her. She refused to.

The same way he had refused to help his boss—his friend —because of her.

Always for her.

It was time for her to do something for him.

When he came back to their little cabin from helping Lucas with a new horse, she'd been frank with him. "I'm ready to go back to work. It's time for us to go home."

Home. The word tasted weird in her mouth, as if she wasn't pronouncing it correctly. Maybe because she didn't actually have a home.

Sarge kept his poker face, merely raising a single eyebrow. "There's no need for us to leave here yet. No hurry."

"I'm ready. Staying here doing nothing isn't helping me. Coddling me doesn't get me any further along in the recovery process."

He crossed his arms over his chest. "Pushing yourself doesn't get you any further along either. At least here you're happy."

She had been when she'd been blissfully unaware of what she'd done, of what was still trapped in her brain. But not now. Now she had a responsibility to help clean up the mess she'd made. And to stop dragging Sarge into that mess with her.

"I need to work." Lies. He needed to work, and she wasn't sure she ever wanted to go back to active missions. But she would say whatever was necessary to get him to believe her. "We both need to work."

"Pony Girl…"

He was going to deny her request. He was going to, once again, go against what was best for him in order to do what was best for her.

But this time, unlike all the other times, she wasn't going to allow it.

"You've got to stop treating me like I'm breakable, like I'm going to crumble at the first hard thing that comes my way."

The words felt like acid in her mouth.

Sarge had never treated her that way. He'd gone out of his way to always make her feel stronger and more capable than she probably was.

Hurt burned in those brown eyes before he blinked it away. "That was never my intent."

Bronwyn wanted to go to him and wrap her arms around him, tell him she knew that. That he'd never made her feel weaker, only stronger. But if she didn't make a stand now, she was going to keep letting Sarge protect her to his own detriment.

She blew out a silent breath and gathered her strength. "It's time for both of us to get back to work. We can't keep hiding here. We're needed."

That, he couldn't argue with. He studied her for a long minute then nodded. "Let's pack our things."

———

"I love Montana, but it's good to be home."

She forced a smile as she walked past the door Sarge opened for her at his house in Colorado. Home. The word, whether he said it or she did, still felt weird to her.

This was familiar, but it wasn't home.

Sarge carried both their bags. They hadn't had much with them at Resting Warrior. They'd stopped by the main ranch house to drop off the vehicle and let Lucas know they were leaving. They hadn't gotten to say goodbye to anyone else.

It was probably better that way. Except...

"Hey, you okay?" He cupped the side of her head and ran his thumb down her cheek.

"I'm going to miss my Resting Warrior friends. Evelyn, Lena..."

"Mac and Cheese?"

He knew her so well. She would keep in touch with the human friends she'd made. But the alpaca and sheep that hung with the alpacas all the time thinking he was one? Her heart hurt at the thought of not seeing them again.

"Yeah. Stupid, right?"

Sarge kissed her forehead. "You're talking to a man who's well-known for not having any people skills. I grew up on a farm. I know what it's like to love an animal like it's your friend."

Bronwyn hugged him. "Maybe Evelyn will send me videos. It'll force her to see Lucas more." She leaned back and waggled her eyebrows at him.

"You little matchmaker. Although I've never known people who could use it more than those two."

"Evelyn has been hurt." She hadn't told her that, but she could recognize it in her.

"I know." Sarge pulled her close again. "That's why she and Lucas are perfect for each other. They'll help heal each other."

At least Evelyn could be healed. Bronwyn wasn't sure she

ever could. She pulled away from Sarge and looked around. "Even with what you told me, I wasn't sure my memories of this place were real."

"You were here." He grimaced. "I should've never let you go. I should've whisked you into Zodiac and figured out a way to get that damned necklace off you and combat everything they'd put in your system."

"You did what you thought was best." Her memories of this place were so unclear, as if they were surrounded by a dense fog. She only remembered his hands on her body, chasing away the pain.

He wiped a hand down his face, suddenly looking exhausted. "I gave you that transmitter, thinking it would be enough."

"I don't remember a transmitter."

"No, you were trying to fight off the effects of the regimen. Trying not to press the injector on that necklace."

"But you gave me a transmitter?"

"Yes. It was voice activated. I could hear anything you said after that." He stepped away from her, big shoulders hunched.

"What did I say?"

"Not much. Mosaic must have discovered they didn't have as much control over you as they thought. You didn't say very much in the days after you left here."

She walked farther inside the house. "Are you sure the transmitter worked?"

"Yes. Very sure."

"How do you know?"

He shook his head. "It doesn't matter. Let's just get settled in."

She turned back to him. "Sarge, tell me. I want to put the pieces together."

He crossed his arms over his chest. "Maybe some things are better not remembering."

Bronwyn's hands started shaking, but she had to know. She used her faithful emotional club. "Don't treat me like I'm weak."

But she was weak, and he knew it. He knew she was getting worse and not better. But she'd put him in an impossible place, making him think that protecting her was hurting her.

His arms dropped to his sides, defeat evident. "I know the transmitter worked because I could hear you scream, sob, beg for mercy. I could hear your terror when they trapped you in that isolation tank for days at a time. I could hear you call for me, but there wasn't a damned thing I could do to help you."

Each sentence hit her like a blow. She didn't have clear memories of any of those things, but she knew they were true. She knew they were the roots of her nightmares and the reason why her hands shook. She knew they were the explanation for why, more than a month later, she was still physically weak and underweight.

Those were the days that had torn apart her very psyche, and Sarge had been there as a witness.

"How can you even look at me knowing how broken I am?"

"Because against all odds, and with a strength not known to many, you knit those pieces back together. You continue to do it every single day."

"No. I have to tell—"

His phone rang in his pocket, preventing Bronwyn from telling him the truth. That she was getting worse. That she needed help. That she wanted to do what was right for him, but that she was afraid her pieces were coming unglued.

He looked at the phone, then set it down on the counter without answering. It continued to buzz.

"Who is it?" she asked.

"Mark Outlawson from work. It can wait."

No, for God's sake, she—and the Greek tragedy that was

her life—could wait. "Go ahead and get it. I want to look around, see what I remember."

Sarge picked up the phone quickly enough to let her know that's what he'd really wanted to do, although once again, he'd been willing to forgo that desire to protect her.

"Outlaw, talk to me."

She was turning away when Sarge's low curse had her spinning back around.

"I'm putting you on speaker so Bronwyn can hear you too."

"Hey, Bronwyn," Mark said. "We don't know what happened. I'm piecing it together myself. Wavy shot Landon."

"What?" She yelled.

"Evidently, it was some sort of mind control or something, and Mosaic used her as a weapon. The location Ian and the team went to was a trap. It's fucking chaos. Ian is on his way back."

"And Landon?" Sarge asked, knuckles white around his phone.

"Alive. That's all I know. We've got at least two dead on Ian's team. Callum Webb was with them and got injured. Ian's also injured but not too bad."

"Where's Wavy?" she asked.

"We don't know. She shot Landon then walked out of the building and disappeared. We're working on it." Mark let out a sigh. "Sarge, we need you."

He looked over at her. Bronwyn could tell that, once again, he was about to decline. She shook her head.

"He'll be right in," she answered before Sarge could say anything.

"Good." Mark hung up without another word.

"I don't have to go." Sarge dropped the phone on the counter again. "Zodiac is bigger than any one person, even Ian."

"Yeah, but Ian and Landon both being out? You're needed. Go." She hardened herself. "I don't need a babysitter."

He rubbed his hand down his face. "You know I don't feel that way."

She was such a bitch. She stepped up to him and cupped his cheek. "I know. I'm sorry. There's a list of people who need you right now, and I'm pretty low for once. So go."

His lips pursed, but he nodded. "I'm going to lock this place down. I've got security measures in place—no one will be able to get in. I'll give you the emergency codes in case you need to get out."

She nodded. She wasn't going anywhere, but she wanted him away from her as soon as possible.

In the chaos of the news, Sarge hadn't put together some pretty simple facts.

Wavy had shot Landon.

Mosaic had used her as a human weapon, and they had only held her captive for two weeks.

If she could shoot someone she knew after only being held that short of a time, then how much more of a weapon could Bronwyn be when they'd had her for months?

CHAPTER
THIRTY-TWO

SARGE LEFT Bronwyn in his house, more torn than he'd ever been.

He knew she'd been getting worse since France. She'd been trying to hide it, but he'd seen it anyway. He didn't want to leave her now, but what was happening at Zodiac affected her too.

He called and got an update on Landon on his way into the office. He was critical but stable. Given that he'd taken a point-blank shot to the chest from a .22, critical but stable was the best that could be expected.

He immediately made sure they had Zodiac security at the hospital. They weren't giving Mosaic another shot at him.

Ian was barely keeping it together when Sarge saw him. Not only was he injured, his best friend had been shot by the woman he loved, and now she was missing again.

They worked side by side to put the pieces together. To figure out where Wavy was and what their next move would be.

There was hell burning in Ian's eyes as he turned to Sarge from watching the footage of Wavy leaving the building for the twentieth time.

"She didn't do this of her own accord. They did something to her."

He squeezed his friend's shoulder. "I know, Aries. We all know that."

He did know Wavy wasn't responsible for what had happened, just like Bronwyn hadn't been responsible for the people she'd killed while under Mosaic's control.

As they dug deeper and realized Erick Huen had planted false memories and trigger words in Wavy's psyche, his gut clenched. Those were things Bronwyn was going to have to deal with too. As if she didn't have enough weighing on her already.

Landon was conscious and going to survive, thank God, but everything about this was ugly.

Thirty-six hours after he'd gotten the call that everything had gone to hell, they had figured out where Erick was holding Wavy. Ian was prepping to leave for a compound in the Sierra Nevadas, the same place where he had died—multiple times—fighting the original Mosaic.

If he wasn't careful, he was going to die there again. It was Sarge's job to make sure he didn't. Ian was moving in under cover of night to get Wavy out of the compound that was guarded by dozens of Mosaic soldiers.

Sarge and his team were going to provide a big enough distraction to allow them to make it.

Outlaw and him were prepping the gear they needed. They were wheels up in two hours.

"You okay, man?" Outlaw asked him as Sarge placed the explosives they'd be using into a backpack with a little less finesse than was probably wise. "I know this mission is a little slack on the actual planning, details, and probable success rate."

That was putting it lightly. They had zero time, very little intel, and stakes that were way too high. Under any other circumstances, Zodiac would never have considered a mission like this.

But Ian was going after Wavy whether they helped him or not, so they were going to do everything they could to get them out alive.

But that wasn't why Sarge was barely keeping his shit together.

"We'll make it work." He rubbed the back of his neck. "I'm worried about Bronwyn."

He hadn't seen her in thirty-six hours, and it was eating at him. They'd texted, but it wasn't enough. If he had known he'd be leaving her alone less than an hour after arriving back in Colorado, he would've left her at Resting Warrior. At least there, she would've had Mac and Cheese nearby, not to mention a group of former SEALs who could protect her.

He was needed for this mission. But she needed him, and he needed her. Sarge wasn't going to be able to function without knowing she was safe.

The people he trusted most to protect her were either out of the state, in the hospital, or going on this mission. He didn't want to put a random security detail on her that might do more harm than good.

"Do you think she's in danger?" Outlaw grimaced and gave an apologetic look. "Or…a danger to others?"

"I don't think she's either. But I don't like leaving her alone right now, and there are not a lot of people I trust with her."

"Do you need someone who can physically protect Bronwyn? Is that what you're worried about?"

I don't need a babysitter.

Her words rang in his ears. She'd said it more than once. He knew he was borderline overprotective, but it wasn't because he thought she was weak.

Sarge couldn't stand the thought of her having to face her

nightmares alone. That was something he was going to have to work on.

He wiped a hand down his face. Jesus, he was tired. "No. She'll be fine, but I wish I had someone who could stay with her while I'm not there. PTSD is such a tricky bastard. It can throat punch you when you least expect it."

"If you need someone who has up close and personal experience with PTSD, who definitely won't mind spending time with Bronwyn, I have the perfect person."

"Who? I don't want a stranger."

"You've got to think a little outside the box. Or, as it may be, deep inside the box."

"I'm not tracking."

"Jenna."

———

"It's important to me that you don't think of this as babysitting. I swear to you that's not how I mean it."

Bronwyn grabbed Sarge's hand as they walked up to Jenna's door. "I know. I never should've said that. You've never treated me that way."

He hooked a hand behind her neck and pulled her lips to his. "We're not sure what's happening, and I have to know you're safe. I can't function otherwise."

She kissed him then leaned her forehead against his. "I know. Jenna is a good choice. And I don't want you worrying about me either—you need to focus on keeping yourself safe and coming back to me." She raised an eyebrow at him. "I can't function otherwise."

His lips found hers again. "Deal."

She wanted to kiss him more, but they couldn't. He was out of time, and every second he stayed, the more likely he was to realize how terrified she was of him going. Bronwyn liked Jenna, but being without Sarge gnawed at her. She'd barely made it through the past forty hours without him.

Knowing he was about to put himself in danger on a mission that had a lot of potential pitfalls...

They knocked on Jenna's door and could hear the sound of multiple locks being released on the other side. Neither of them said anything as they waited for the door to open. Those locks would be keeping her safe in a few minutes.

Once they were in, Jenna immediately closed the door behind them, her lips tight. Obviously, opening the door wasn't something she liked doing.

"Hi," she said. She'd seen her before on the screen but never in person. She looked different, but still the same.

She gave Bronwyn a tight smile. "Hi. Welcome."

Sarge put his hand on her shoulder. "Thank you. This means a lot to both of us."

"It's been...a while since I had a girls' weekend. I'm happy for the company. We'll have fun." She was relaxing more now that the door was closed.

"You're not running the mission comms?" She knew Jenna had all the equipment to do that from here since she never left her house.

"No. We've got a team at the office coordinating with the on-site team. There are others better at this sort of thing." She glanced over at Sarge then back at her.

She let out a sigh. "And because I'm here and could possibly be a liability."

He slipped an arm around her. "Pony Girl..."

"It's okay. It's the right thing to do. I want you to be safe." Even from her.

Jenna nodded. "The current configuration gives the mission the greatest chance of success for a lot of reasons."

"Then I'll take it." She pushed at Sarge's chest. "You go. Come back to me soon."

He kissed her hard then ran out the door without another

word. Jenna shut it behind him, visibly relaxing as soon as the locks were once again engaged.

Bronwyn hefted her overnight bag over her shoulder and followed Jenna farther inside. The front of the house seemed pretty normal—kitchen, living room, even the guest bedroom where she had her put her bag. Best of all, windows with lots of light. If she had to stay inside, she was grateful for that.

She wasn't sure what she'd expected for someone who didn't like to go outside, but it wasn't this.

She caught Bronwyn staring at her surroundings. "Expecting coffins or something?"

She gave a low chuckle. "More like grenade launchers and barred windows."

"The windows are made of bullet-resistant glass. No need to worry about break-ins."

"Good."

She shrugged and walked toward the kitchen. "I don't go out. Everybody knows it. In this day and age, you don't have to anyway. Everything I need I can get delivered here— groceries, medicine, clothes, toilet paper. I like the safety of my house."

She was defensive, but Bronwyn wasn't about to point that out, especially not when she was so intimately familiar with avoiding the real world.

Jenna wasn't avoiding it; she'd just built her real world in a fashion that worked for her.

She should probably take a few notes from her playbook.

"I like the safety of your house too. I'm not going to try to talk you into a picnic or to go pick flowers. I'm good here." She shrugged. "Although I'm not exactly sure how good I will be at the girls' weekend stuff."

Jenna leaned back against the counter. "That works out well because I've got a much better plan than us painting our nails."

CHAPTER
THIRTY-THREE

"I'VE BEEN GOING through everything we have on you, especially after what happened to Wavy," Jenna said. "When Sarge asked if we could hang out, I was going to put it all away, but…"

Bronwyn's eyes flew to hers. "You have it?"

"Got a whole room of it. Want to see?"

"Hell yes, I do."

She followed Jenna into what should have been another bedroom, but instead looked like some sort of shrine. There were photos everywhere. Printouts, timelines, all dealing with Mosaic—specifically Wavy and Bronwyn. There were pictures of her, Wavy, Erick Huen, Dr. Tippens. She didn't like looking at those, so she turned to the printouts of buildings and locations she didn't recognize.

She walked around, staring in silence for a long time. This was way more information than she knew about the past few months of her own life.

She stopped in front of a picture of a large building. "What's this?"

"That's where you were being held when Sarge and Landon got you out."

Bronwyn nodded as she turned from the photo and caught Jenna sliding something out of sight.

"What was that?" She asked her.

"Nothing."

"Hey, we're in this now. Don't start pulling your punches."

She slid the paper out so she could see it. It was the specs of the isolation tank she'd been held in. She stared at it for a long moment. Make, model number, size...including a picture.

Her throat tightened as she studied the information, making it hard to breathe. Her hands shook so hard she stuffed them under her armpits.

She didn't have clear memories of her time in that tank, but they were pressing at the edges of her mind.

That was the problem, wasn't it? If she was going to remember it all—enough to be helpful in taking Mosaic down—then she was going to have to remember it all.

Bronwyn had told Jenna not to pull her punches. Was she sure she could handle the blows?

"Are you okay?" Jenna whispered.

Her nod was jerky. "Trust me, I like looking at it much better from the outside than I did from the inside."

She turned away from the information, anxious to see anything else. There were all sorts of medical charts every-where, from both Wavy and her. "Do you understand this stuff?"

She gave an awkward shrug of one shoulder. "Actually, yes. I had a double major in computer science and biomedical engineering. I didn't actually start using the computer science part of my degree until much more recently."

"I had no idea," Bronwyn said.

"Yeah, most people don't," she said. "It's part of a past I don't talk about."

Bronwyn walked around the room more, thumbing

through images and looking over reports. The data she had was more than complex.

"Did Ian ask you to do this?" She turned to face her. "Or Sarge?"

Jenna shook her head. "No, both of them have been busy." She tucked a strand of her black hair behind her ear. "I've been providing them information if it would help your recovery, but looking at all of this holistically is a little much."

"Then why do you do it?"

She gave another awkward shrug. "I get a little obsessed with things. Maybe it's a by-product of being alone. Most of the time, I get obsessed with stupid stuff like painting a room until it is the exact color I saw in my mind. Or writing a computer program for something nobody needs. In this case, my mind got stuck on figuring out the details of what happened to you and Wavy."

Bronwyn's stomach tightened, and she flinched. Hearing Wavy's name triggered an unpleasant sensation like seeing the pictures of her had.

Jenna noticed it. "What just happened?"

"I don't know. Something about seeing the pictures of Wavy and hearing her name. It makes me angry. That's so unreasonable, but ever since I've been getting my memories back, I have this distinct dislike for her. I didn't realize it until now."

She pulled out a computer tablet and started typing faster than Bronwyn had ever seen anyone type. "What do you mean dislike? As in, you don't want to hang out with her? As in, she shot Landon and you're pissed?"

"No." She rubbed a shaky hand down her face. "As in, I feel the need to hurt her."

"That's pretty extreme."

"I don't know. I've never felt like this toward anyone."

Jenna nodded, then showed her another picture. "And Silas Varela? How do you feel about him?"

She studied the picture. That same ugly feeling in her gut. She wanted to rip up the photo. Punch him in the face.

Bronwyn wanted to kill him.

"The same. Looking at his picture makes me angry. I want to hurt him, or worse, even though I know he is dead." Her mouth went dry as she shook my head. "That makes me a pretty shitty person, doesn't it? I know that Erick Huen killed Varela and chopped him into little pieces."

"Not in that order, but yeah, he did," she responded. "Based on what you're telling me and how Erick manipulated Wavy, I think you were probably programmed to kill both of them. You have all the residual signs."

"How do you know that?"

"Because in my other life, when I was a biomedical engineer, I was forced against my will to develop some of the biomedical methods that Dr. Tippens would've used to help foster those behaviors. I assisted in their design of the programming."

"Oh," Bronwyn whispered. "Will these feelings ever go away?"

She nodded. "Probably, with time, since you're no longer being given the drugs or being subjected to their programming on a daily basis. You and Wavy may never be besties, but you won't want to hurt her."

"That's good." She looked around a little more, dread pooling in her stomach. "But I'm probably a walking time bomb like her, aren't I?"

Jenna ran a hand down her dark hair. "Based on the medications we found in your body, what Mosaic did to you is not the same as what they did to Wavy."

"But I could still be used as a weapon, couldn't I? I could have some sort of trigger word."

"It's unlikely," she replied. "Yours was more of a chemical subjugation rather than genetic."

"But it's possible?" She asked.

"Yes, it's possible."

"Then I want you to tie me up."

"Why?"

Bronwyn sat down in the chair in front of the desk. "Because it's time for us to figure out what information is still inside my head that I'm suppressing. I have intel that we need to get to. You have both the knowledge and the skills to get it out."

"Are you sure you want to do this?"

"Yes."

Jenna rubbed her eyes. "Tying you up is probably overkill. And is probably going to be a bitch on your psyche."

"I don't care. If there's something in this that's going to trigger me, I want to make sure that I don't hurt you. We both know that with your computers here, if something triggered me, I could take you out and do all sorts of damage to the mission that Sarge is on. I won't take that chance."

Jenna nodded. "Okay, tie you up it is."

———

They went through everything.

Sarge had walked her through a lot of it already, but it didn't take her long to realize he'd been protecting her, sheltering her from a lot of the details.

Or, after listening to the recordings of herself trapped in that isolation pod, maybe he'd been sheltering himself. The sound of her on the recording—the screaming, the sobs, the deafening silence—was hard to bear, but she did it without flinching.

Because as hard as it was to listen to, it had been much harder living through it.

Bronwyn remembered. With each piece of intel Jenna fed her, her mind cracked a little more and let the memories through.

For the first time since she'd been taken, she could piece together a true timeline of what had happened to her. How she'd been taken. Exactly how long she'd been gone. People she'd hurt or killed. Things she'd stolen.

None of it had been of her own free will, but she'd still done it. And it was time to face it, no matter how shaky it made her hands or how many more nightmares she might have.

And she knew there would be many. There was no going back to the cotton wool of selective amnesia.

Jenna and Bronwyn were both tired. They'd been at it all night, confronting painful detail after painful detail. But neither of them wanted to stop. They were both desperately aware there was something they were missing. But they could see it was coming.

She'd untied her after twelve hours of nothing triggering her, and they'd gotten word that Sarge's mission had been a success. Thanks to the work of Sarge and the team, Ian had rescued Wavy relatively unharmed. Erick had been arrested in the process of fleeing.

Sarge had to debrief but then would be coming home. She wanted him there with her. It was as if a piece of her was missing every time they weren't near each other. She was tired, cranky, frustrated, and she wanted him home.

Home.

"That phrase." Bronwyn studied a picture of Peter Kerpar. "I keep coming back to the words they made me say."

I exist only to obey orders. My final mission is to go home.

She didn't like to say it out loud. She could more clearly remember the early days of captivity now—the dark, the cold, those words repeated over and over until she'd finally said them.

Jenna crossed her arms over her chest and leaned back against the desk. "You didn't have any reaction from either saying them or hearing me say them."

They'd tested for all sorts of physiological responses to those words—change in blood pressure, pupil dilation, adrenaline spike—but she hadn't had any.

"I know. But there's something about the word home that keeps scratching at my mind."

"All right." Jenna grabbed her computer tablet and jotted down some notes. She was nothing if not thorough. "That's something to consider. But it's possible that you feel displaced. You're an uprooted orphan. That's why the word home bugs you."

She winced at her almost brutal honesty but couldn't argue with what she said. "That's true. I guess my question is, why would Mosaic have put that in my programming? What is home?"

"For their purposes, it was probably a fail-safe put into your programming so you would always return there."

"So why am I not there now?"

Jenna set her tablet aside. "Genetic reengineering and chemical subjugation aren't exact sciences when it comes to controlling human beings. Maybe something went wrong. Or maybe they didn't get to finish that part of your programming before Sarge got you out. Maybe you were resistant to it, or only triggered by Dr. Tippens saying it. It could be one of a hundred things."

Bronwyn walked around, looking at all the images and printouts on the walls without really seeing them. What Jenna said made sense, but...

"I feel like this is key to something, but I don't know what, and I don't know why."

She grabbed her tablet again. "Okay. If there's one thing I learned during my captiv..." She trailed off and restarted. "If there's one thing I've learned, it's to not fight your gut. So let's discuss home for you."

"Like you said, I don't really have one."

"Where did you live growing up?"

"I was born in Ukraine, but honestly, I don't have much memory of that. We had to relocate to the Czech Republic, and then my parents died, so not much of a home there either."

"Okay, no house that you think of when you say home. It must be code for something, we just don't know what."

She rubbed her eyes. She was tired and trying to force a lead that was going nowhere. "You're probably right. I never really used the word much. The only time I ever heard it used growing up was by Gregory. He was the leader of the family"—I rolled my eyes at the term—"when I lived in Prague."

"I assume that means it wasn't much of a family."

"Not unless you consider stealing, prostitution, and regular beatings as part of being a family."

"Damn," she whispered. "How did you make it out of there at all?"

"Sarge. He met Bronya Roch before she ever became Bronwyn Rourke. He helped me get out."

"Doesn't surprise me at all."

"But no, Prague is not the place I would call home. The only person who would want to call that home for me would be—"

She came to a picture of Erick Huen on the wall, and suddenly everything clicked into place.

"Oh my God."

Jenna rushed over to me. "What?"

"I remember something Erick said to me when he came to my hotel room in Marrakesh. *I was informed you were feisty.*" Bronwyn shook her head. Everything was now making a sick kind of sense. "That asshole Agent Wilson was right."

"I'm not following. Agent Wilson, the Europol agent?"

"Yes. He said there had to be a reason Erick Huen picked me. It wasn't only because I was part of Zodiac Tactical—it was more personal than that."

"Okay, that would make sense."

"Mosaic has a partner in Europe. And I have a sick feeling I know who that is."

"Who?"

"The only person who would want me to come home. So he could destroy me."

CHAPTER
THIRTY-FOUR

AS FAR AS MISSIONS WENT—ESPECIALLY ones where they were shorthanded and going into the situation practically blind—this one had had the best possible outcome.

It almost hadn't ended that way. Ian had nearly died at Erick's hand and was only still alive because Wavy had risked her own life to save his.

Now those two were at the hospital getting their wounds tended to, and that bastard Erick Huen had been arrested.

Sarge would like ten minutes alone in a room with him. He wouldn't waste time asking him any questions, but he'd damn well make sure he understood what it felt like to be helpless and in agony. Give him a tiny taste—one that would involve multiple broken bones—of what he and Tippens had done to Bronwyn.

Unfortunately, he'd have to settle for him spending the rest of his life in prison. Sarge almost hoped he would cut a deal and provide info about Mosaic in exchange for his freedom. He was sure it wouldn't take much for him to convince Ian that the world would be a better place without Erick in it.

And if it meant his soul burned in hell for it, he'd consider that a fair trade.

But right now, he had to face his own temporary kind of hell: debriefing. Ian had needed medical attention and refused to leave Wavy's side, and Landon was still in the hospital, although thankfully out of the woods.

That left him as the highest-ranking member of Zodiac who needed to answer for the number of Mosaic bodies littering the wilderness camp in the Sierra Nevadas. Law enforcement was pissed. They'd been left out of the loop again.

There hadn't been time to do this by committee.

Sarge wished he could give a written report and be done with it. Callum Webb owed him after that stunt in the French Riviera. But somehow, he didn't think bad guys shouldn't mess with them or they'll fuck them up—which would basically be his report—would fly anyway.

So he was sitting there in this holding room waiting to answer whatever questions he could when all he really wanted to do was get back to Bronwyn. Talking to her on the phone to let her know the mission was over and everyone was safe wasn't enough.

Sarge needed to hold her. He needed to let her know that they were going to make it through this. That if what had happened to Wavy happened to her, they would figure it out.

That he wasn't going to let anything hurt her.

If they needed to move back to Resting Warrior to keep her away from other people for the rest of her life, he was willing to do that. More than willing. He'd happily do it. He was raised on a farm; he knew animals. And what he didn't know, he would learn. Lucas and the guys would give him a job.

He'd miss active missions; he wasn't going to lie. He may be in his forties, but he still had a lot of good years left to fight bad guys. He'd miss his Zodiac team, his friends.

But Sarge would walk away from it all if it got Bronwyn what she needed. She'd paid way too high a price for someone so young. Now it was her turn to live a life free of fear and pain. He was damned well going to give it to her.

He would if Callum Webb would get his ass in there so they could get the debrief over with. It had been twenty-four hours since they'd finished the fighting. More than half of that time, he'd spent on site overseeing the damage and walking the law enforcement agents through what had happened. Then he'd been brought there.

He needed a damned shower. But more, he needed to get to Bronwyn.

But it wasn't Webb who walked into the room a few minutes later. It was Theodore Wilson. Every hackle Sarge had rose at the sight of that asshole.

"Where's Webb?"

Wilson gave him a tight smile. He still had the strip of white medical tape over the bridge of his nose where he'd punched him last week. Good. He hoped it fucking hurt. "Callum Webb has been relieved of duty. He is no longer an active agent for Omega Sector."

"Why?"

Wilson shrugged. "One too many renegade choices, I would assume. Allowing Zodiac Tactical to make move after move unchecked. He's lucky he's not facing criminal charges."

"What are you doing here rather than in Europe?"

Wilson took the seat at the table across from him. "I've been placed in charge of the interagency task force charged with taking down Mosaic. Believe me, I will not be as lenient as Webb was when it comes to your cowboy shenanigans."

Cowboy shenanigans. Sarge barely refrained from rolling his eyes. He didn't have time for this pissing contest.

"Look, Mosaic brought the fight to us, not the other way around. Zodiac wants to keep its people safe. Erick Huen decided to seek revenge on Ian DeRose and bit off more than he could chew."

"Zodiac can't go around playing vigilantes without repercussions."

He crossed his arms over his chest, more to make sure he didn't punch Wilson in the face again than a show of machismo. "That's bullshit and you know it. Ian DeRose worked for you guys taking down Mosaic the first time. He almost died multiple times doing it. Scratch that, he *did* die when his own brother and Erick buried him and revived him multiple times."

"That was then. Now Mosaic is back and committing acts of terror all over the globe—much worse than their original version. Allow me to show you what happened yesterday in Hamburg, Germany while you were running around the mountains with your friends."

Running around stopping fucking terrorists. Sarge swallowed the comeback. Barely.

And the comeback was completely forgotten as he watched a pretty young woman not much older than Bronwyn walk up to the front of a government building, then proceed to blow it and herself up.

Her face was completely blank as she did it. A blankness he recognized from Bronwyn in New York when she'd had no idea who he was. "Oh shit."

"That was Tenisha Day, American graduate student. No known ties to any terrorist organizations. She had two loving parents and three younger brothers. She killed twenty-two people yesterday."

He paused for dramatic effect, but Sarge knew there was more.

"Before yesterday, her family hadn't seen her in four months. But we found this." He spun a picture around so Sarge could see it. It was Tenisha Day and Dr. Tippens. "She was one of Mosaic's zombie soldiers. Like Bronwyn was."

He scrubbed a hand down his face. "This is tragic, Wilson, I agree. And hell yeah, it needs to be stopped. But we're all on the same side. Quit acting like you don't know that. All I want to do is give my statement and go home."

"To Bronwyn Rourke."

Sarge sat up straighter in his seat. "You'll leave her out of this if you're wise."

He had to give it to the man; he wasn't intimidated even though I had probably six inches and fifty pounds of muscle on him.

"Bronwyn Rourke knows more than she's telling."

"No, she doesn't. Believe me, she's not hiding things."

Wilson studied him with narrowed eyes. "Maybe that's true. But at the very least, she knows more than she thinks she does. The key to finding out the truth behind Mosaic—and who's in charge—is with her."

"No. Bronwyn has done her part, and she's out of this. You've got Erick Huen in custody. Go question him to get your answers."

Wilson crossed his arms over his chest. "You and I both know Erick Huen isn't going to say a thing that doesn't help him directly. Plus, any information is going to take too much time to get. Bronwyn will be quicker."

He could feel his fists itching for his jaw again. "Bronwyn is not an option. She doesn't remember anything valuable."

"We can try nontraditional methods. Hypnosis. Chemical assistance. Medical scans. They might be a little invasive, but in the end, if it saves lives, it will be worth it."

Sarge gritted his teeth until his jaw ached. "So you want a woman who has already been subjected to physical and mental torture to waltz in here and let you poke around her brain a little more?"

"It might be uncomfortable for her, but I think we'd all agree it would be worth it if we got any information."

He leaned forward, putting his weight on his elbows on the desk. "Did my fist feel uncomfortable when I broke your nose, Wilson? I can break it again if you need a refresher."

He was wise enough to lean back in his chair. "No need for melodrama, Mr. McEwan."

"You are not going to poke around in Bronwyn's head, further torturing a woman who has damned well been tortured enough, to try to get info that may or may not be there."

"That's not your decision to make."

"I tell you what, if Bronwyn comes to me and asks to use any known methods to retrieve her memories, you'll be the first person I call. Until then, you will not demand anything from her."

Wilson and Sarge stared each other down, but his brain was already jumping into full gear.

He and Bronwyn might have to run for a while. Hide out. That wouldn't be any great hardship. He'd keep her in bed and feed her. That sounded like a perfect way to spend a year. Or a lifetime.

They'd get the hell out of Dodge and let law enforcement work its magic to figure out how to get intel about Mosaic from Erick. Bronwyn wasn't a pawn for their use.

The sooner the bastard sitting across from him figured that out the better.

"I'm done here, Wilson. I'll write up my statement, but the questioning is done. Stay away from Bronwyn. You want to threaten someone, go have a power play with Erick Huen. Get intel from him."

Wilson left without another word. Sarge got to work writing out his statement about the events of the past forty-eight hours. He gave them only the details law enforcement needed. In this case, brevity was best for multiple reasons— reducing Zodiac Tactical's liability and because he wanted to get the hell out of there as soon as possible.

Less than an hour later, they let him out of the holding room, and he was heading toward the door. With every step

Sarge took, he felt more relief because each step was taking him closer to Bronwyn.

He was almost to the front door when he heard Agent Wilson's voice.

"Mr. McEwan, hold a moment."

Sarge turned. He had a man on either side of him. He shook his head. "I'm done, Wilson. I'm leaving."

"Actually, you're not."

Do not break his nose again. Witnesses present.

"Yeah, I think I am. You have my statement."

He gestured to the two men with him. "No, you're not going to be leaving. You're under arrest."

He knew instantly what the little fucker was doing. "Don't do this, Wilson. Don't use me to get to her. You have Erick; he's your best bet."

"Actually, Erick Huen was killed an hour ago before we could get any information from him. Evidently assassinated by his own lawyer—Mosaic doesn't like to leave loose ends."

"Shit." Sarge scrubbed a hand down his face.

"And now the only loose end we have available is Bronwyn."

CHAPTER
THIRTY-FIVE

BRONWYN NEEDED SARGE.

She was almost numb to what she'd figured out. Although she tried to comprehend, she couldn't explain the full scope of it to Jenna. But Sarge would get it. He'd known her then. Known her situation.

Known the person who had reason to hate her enough to sell her out to Erick Huen.

Nikolai.

Nikolai Novotný was Mosiac's European leader. He was the reason she'd been taken to use against Ian DeRose—not because she was such a great candidate, but because Nikolai wanted revenge for what she'd done to him when she'd escaped Prague.

"Are you okay?" Jenna had sat Bronwyn down at her kitchen island and started pushing food in front of her. Cheese cubes, chicken salad, chocolate chip cookies… evidently Jenna wasn't much of a cook. "You look worse than you did before we dove headfirst down the rabbit hole."

She nibbled on a cube of cheese. "The thought of seeing Nikolai again, being anywhere near him at all…" She set the cheese back on her plate. "I can't stomach it. You probably think I'm a coward."

She let out a short bark of humorless laughter. "Honey, you're talking to someone who doesn't leave her house anymore because of her past. Trust me, I don't think you're a coward."

"Jenna, I—"

The loud knock on the door startled them. Every bit of color bled from Jenna's face.

Her phone beeped. She looked down to read the text.

"It's Outlaw. Mark Outlawson. He says he's outside."

A fist slammed against the door again. "Jenna, let me in. Hurry."

Some of the color came back into her face, and they rushed to the door. She looked through the control panel to confirm it was really Mark then unlocked and opened the door. He stepped inside, and she closed it quickly.

"What's going on?"

Mark looked over at Bronwyn. "I'm here to get you out."

She couldn't stop the terror that climbed up her spine. "Where's Sarge?"

His mouth had a grim twist to it. "There's been a complication."

The terror enveloped her further. "What happened? Is he hurt? Taken by Mosaic?" She looked over at Jenna. "What if—"

Mark shook his head. "No. He's not hurt. But he has been arrested. Law enforcement wants you, Bronwyn. They think you're the key to finding out more about Mosaic. Sarge got word to me, and I'm supposed to get you out. He doesn't want—"

Another fist slammed on the door; she and Jenna jumped, and Mark muttered a curse under his breath.

"Jenna Franklin, this is the police. Open the door. We have

a warrant for the arrest of Bronwyn Rourke, and we know she's in there."

She recognized that voice. Agent Wilson. She turned to Mark. "Wilson is the one who arrested Sarge?"

Mark nodded. "Maybe I can get you out the back."

"Open the door now, Ms. Franklin, and I won't have to arrest you too. I'm only here for Bronwyn. This is your choice."

Jenna's eyes darted around her house, her breaths coming in and out so rapidly it wouldn't be long before she passed out.

Bronwyn grabbed her by both upper arms. "Breathe, Jenna. I'm going to go out there to surrender myself."

"No," Mark interrupted. "I can get you both out."

"You can't get us both out, Mark." Jenna would be comatose within seconds if he tried. "It's okay. I'll go with Wilson. You stay here with Jenna."

Mark shook his head. "Sarge went to a lot of trouble to get a message to me and—"

Something slammed against the door, and they all jumped back. Jenna hadn't reengaged the locks after Mark had come in. Wilson was using some sort of battering ram. Another slam and the door burst open.

Jenna whimpered, huddling against the wall, arms wrapping around her head protectively. A uniformed officer stepped to the side, and Wilson walked in.

"We meet again, Ms. Rourke. I've gone to a great deal of trouble to find you, including letting Mr. McEwan think he was getting an encoded message to Mr. Outlawson here. Then it was a simple matter of following him straight to you."

She rolled her eyes. "I'm beginning to think you missed your calling in theater with all the melodrama, Wilson."

He gave her a patronizing smile. "You can come with me now and I'll leave your friends, or all three of you will be cuffed and taken in for interrogation. I don't think Ms. Franklin finds that thought very appealing."

Jenna had crouched down, curled into a ball, arms still around her head. She couldn't stand it.

"Leave them. I'll come with you willingly."

He raised an eyebrow. "And submit to whatever testing we need to do to get the information about Mosaic out of your mind?"

"Bronwyn, Sarge specifically tried to keep this asshole from getting his hands on you." Mark stepped toward her, and the uniformed officer drew his weapon.

She held out an arm to stop him. "Take care of Jenna. Sarge was trying to rescue me like he always does. But this time, I'm going to rescue him."

Outlaw nodded slowly, although he obviously didn't like it. Maybe he realized Jenna needed someone by her side right now more than Bronwyn did. Either way, she walked away with Wilson and heard the door close behind them.

"So we're clear," Wilson said, "by coming with me, you are agreeing to the utilization of whatever methods are necessary in order to get the information out of your head."

She didn't look at him as she walked to his car. "You won't need to use any of your nefarious tactics. I already have the information you need. I know who the Mosaic leader is in Europe."

"Who?"

Now she looked at him. "I'm not telling you a damned thing until you release Sarge and I see him myself."

———

Bronwyn got half of what she asked for.

"There he is." Wilson pointed to Sarge on the other side of a two-way mirror. He sat ramrod straight in a chair with his hands cuffed behind his back.

"Let him go." She wanted to go in there, kiss him, make sure he was really all right. He looked exhausted.

"Not going to happen. You said you have a name for me."

Her hands shook again, so she clasped them behind her back. She had to stand her ground. Once she told Wilson about Nikolai, she'd lose all leverage.

"You move Sarge to a more comfortable holding room, and you take those cuffs off him. And they stay off. And then you let me in the room with him."

Wilson's eyes narrowed. He didn't like giving up any of his power. "I have you here now. I can run the tests."

She forced herself not to show how much the thought of someone digging around her brain without permission terrified her. She wouldn't survive intact. She already knew it. "You can. But you'd be wasting time fighting against me, especially since I'm willing to give you what you want right now."

"Fine."

Bronwyn had to give him credit; once Wilson made up his mind to do something, he was quite efficient with his actions. Within fifteen minutes, Sarge was uncuffed and being taken to another room. She had to watch in silence from the other side of the glass as he demanded to know about her—if she was there, if she was okay.

He lunged for Wilson when the man walked through the door, but he was stopped and re-cuffed by two other agents.

"Don't you touch her, Wilson. I will fucking end you."

"Now, now, Mr. McEwan, threatening a law enforcement officer is a crime."

If Sarge could've gotten his hands on Wilson right that second, it would not have ended well for the smaller man. The other agents began leading Sarge out the door.

"Where are you taking me?" Sarge demanded.

"Somewhere more comfortable. Somewhere you don't have to be restrained, if you'll cooperate. Thankfully, some people are more reasonable than you. We're all on the same side, remember?"

"Bronwyn is here, isn't she?" Sarge struggled against the men holding his arms, but there wasn't much he could do. He realized that and stopped walking. "Wilson, listen to me. Don't do this. Bronwyn, she… Don't do this to her. Please. You don't know what she's been through. I'm begging you. I swear I'll quit Zodiac and go full time helping you take down the rest of Mosaic. Just don't do this to her."

She put her hand up against the glass, wishing she could get closer to him.

"Interesting," Wilson murmured. "But I think she's stronger than you know."

"She's stronger than anyone I've ever known, but even the strongest break." Sarge bowed his head. "If you need a fall guy for shit that has gone down with Mosaic so far, I'll take the blame. I'll do time if that's what has to happen. Please, don't do anything to Bronwyn. She's been through too much. Please."

Her heart shattered as Sarge's voice cracked on the last plea. He was willing to give up everything for her. To put his pride aside and beg.

Wilson shook his head. "You two are quite a pair. She came with me willingly if I agreed to release you based on intel she provides."

Sarge closed his eyes and let out a shaky breath. "If you're going to do this, let me stay with her. She'll need me. All the rest of my offer still applies. Just please don't make her do this alone."

Wilson tilted his head to the side. "You broke my nose."

Sarge didn't hesitate. "You can return the favor right now."

Bronwyn was about to start slamming her hand against the mirror. She didn't know if Sarge could hear her, but she wasn't about to let him take another beating for her.

"That won't be necessary. Follow me." He led Sarge out of the room, and she couldn't see them anymore.

By the time Wilson came back to get her a few minutes later, she was ready to break his nose herself. "Was that really necessary? Why didn't you tell him I'd remembered on my own and your invasive methods weren't needed?"

"We'll see if your intel truly provides anything useful. The tests aren't off the table yet." He shrugged. "And besides, he broke my nose."

They walked down the hallway, and he stopped in front of the door. "This gives you both a little bit a comfort, but believe me, it's temporary if what you provide isn't use—"

"Nikolai Novotný." Bronwyn cut him off. She didn't need more threats. "He's who you're looking for."

Wilson raised one eyebrow. "In Prague. He's been on our active watch list for a while. You're sure?"

"Yes. It's how I got on Mosaic's radar in the first place."

"How do I know you're telling the truth?"

"How long has he been on your watch list?"

"Since his father died and he took over and started quickly growing the family terrorist and racketeering busi-ness. Almost three years."

She crossed her arms over her chest, once again to stop her hands from shaking. "Two and a half years ago, Nikolai was attacked and his face was scarred."

"Yeah. I've seen the photos. So?"

"I'm the one who did that to him, to get out from under his power. He sold me out to Mosaic as part of his revenge. Find Nikolai. He's the one you're trying to stop."

Wilson nodded and opened the door. She stepped inside, not caring that the lock clicked behind her as the door closed.

She flew into Sarge's arms.

SARGE CAUGHT Bronwyn as she crashed into him. He clutched her against his chest, breathing in her scent. "I'm so sorry, Pony Girl. I didn't want you here. I was hoping Outlaw could get you out."

She shook her head against his chest, arms wrapped around him tight. "No. I wasn't going to leave you here."

"But the things Wilson wants to do to you to get the information…" He closed his eyes. He couldn't bear to think about it. He would give anything if he could go through the anguish rather than her.

All that stuff he'd offered Wilson had been nothing less than the truth. He would do anything to keep Bronwyn out of this situation.

Sarge opened his eyes when her head left his chest.

"None of that will be necessary. Jenna and I worked together while you were gone, and I remembered some things. I know who the European leader of Mosaic is. It's Nikolai. You remember him, right?"

"What?"

She reached up and cupped his face. "Are you okay? You look tired. Let's sit down."

He wasn't going to take his arms from around her even to walk the few steps to the couch. He lowered them to her hips and lifted her up and walked them over there, sitting her in his lap.

"I'm fine. It's been a long few days. But tell me more about Nikolai."

She cuddled into him, and between having her there and knowing she wasn't about to get mentally tortured by the good guys, he could almost relax. He could at least breathe, which was more than he'd been able to do since Wilson had threatened to use Bronwyn to get the info he wanted.

"I remembered something Erick said the night he took me in Marrakesh—that he'd heard I was feisty."

"Shit. Nikolai called you that the day I met you."

She nodded. "He called me that all the time. And it ends up Wilson was right. There was a specific reason why I'd been targeted to be used against Ian DeRose. It wasn't luck or chance—Nikolai pointed me out to Erick. He wanted me to suffer."

"Why? Because you got away from him?"

Her hands shook in her lap, and she gripped his arm to control the movement. "When you came back the second time and told me about the job in Paris, I knew I wanted to go. Almost right away, I went to Gregory, Nikolai's father, to see if I could work out a deal with him. I knew I'd have to pay money to make up for what it would cost him to lose me, but he'd always been reasonable."

"He wouldn't let you go?"

"I think he would've. I hid and heard him and Nikolai fighting about it. But a few weeks later, Gregory had a heart attack and died. There was no way Nikolai was going to let me go."

"So you lost your way out and your protection against Nikolai all at one time."

"Yes," she whispered.

He held her tighter. "God, Pony Girl. I'm so sorry."

Once again, she'd been alone to face her horrors. Once again, something he could've prevented if he hadn't let her go. He should've taken her with him from day one. Gotten her out of the situation for good.

She burrowed in closer to him. "I didn't fight him. I knew that would make it worse."

Sarge closed his eyes. Fury ran up and down his spine, but that would have to wait. He kept his voice even. "That was smart. You did what you had to do to survive."

"Nikolai got tired of me after a few months. Then he decided to offer me to his men. That's when I knew I had to leave."

"Good."

"He caught me. Hurt me. To escape, I burned him with some boiling soup that was on the stove. He has scars all over his face."

"Good," he said again. "I wish you'd killed him."

"He was already growing in power after his father died. He wanted to do more, control more. I was hoping he would forget about me, but I knew I'd be looking over my shoulder for the rest of my life."

"Instead, he sold you out to Erick Huen."

"He wouldn't want me to have a quick death. He would want me to suffer. I know Erick was reporting back to him, telling him what they were doing to me. My agony probably entertained Nikolai to no end. Everything that was done to me makes more sense now."

There were so many people Sarge wanted to kill for this woman. Everyone who had ever hurt her. He couldn't do that, but he would damn well stand between her and anyone else who would ever try.

"I'm glad you remembered and Wilson didn't have to do whatever god-awful experiments he had planned."

"Me too." She moved, shifting until she straddled his hips

rather than lying draped across his legs. Those blue eyes looked more clear and focused than they had since France. "I heard you a few minutes ago. The deals you were prepared to make with Wilson to stop him from performing the tests on me."

He shrugged. "There isn't anything I wouldn't have given him to keep him from hurting you."

"You have to stop rescuing me, Harrison McEwan."

He kissed her nose. "That's Sarge to you, Pony Girl. And I think you were the one who did the rescuing this time. I'm sure Outlaw could've gotten you out, but you came back for me."

"I wasn't going to leave you to pay the price for my freedom."

He cupped her cheeks. "It would've been worth it. Knowing you were safe? Not being hurt? That would be worth any price. And if doing whatever I can to keep you safe is synonymous with rescue, then you can be expecting me to do that for a very, very long time."

Her eyes filled with tears. "I'm still broken. My hands shake all the time. And I'm scared. So scared. Even when I know I'm safe."

He started to interrupt her, but she put a finger over his lips. "I know some of that will get better. But some of it won't. Nobody is ever going to describe me as feisty again."

As if he was ever going to use that particular word to describe her with the connections it had to Nikolai.

Sarge kissed her finger then brought it down from his lips. "You are who you are. I wasn't lying when I told you I was looking forward to getting to know the new person you rebuilt yourself into. You're lying in ash right now, but the phoenix is going to rise from that. And I want to be there to see it."

"You won't mind my shaky hands? I don't think that's ever going away."

It probably would, but only time could prove that to her, so he wasn't going to argue.

"I won't mind that if you won't mind that I'm almost twenty years older than you, generally cranky, and will probably be yelling at people to get off my lawn sooner rather than later."

She laughed, the sound the most beautiful thing he'd ever heard. "I think I can handle that. I'll just wheel you back inside in your wheelchair."

He brought her lips in to his. "I love you, Pony Girl. Who you were, who you are, who you'll be."

Her hands, still a little shaky, came up and threaded into his hair. "You're the only person in the world who will ever know all three."

———

Sarge fell asleep on the couch with Bronwyn in his arms. She hadn't declared her love for him, but he didn't need the words right now. They would come when she was ready.

When he woke up after a couple hours, she was awake next to him, stroking his head with gentle fingers.

"You okay?" He asked her. "Wilson is an asshole, but I'm sure he'll release us soon."

"They're going to have a hard time taking down Nikolai. He's so much more powerful than before. Wilson showed me footage of the woman who blew up that building in Hamburg. He said Mosaic had programmed her the way they'd programmed me."

"Yeah, he calls them Mosaic's zombie soldiers." He pulled her closer. "Wilson and his team will stop them."

"Wilson thinks Nikolai has a lot more of them—more people under Nikolai's control. And he's right. I know it for a fact because I saw them myself."

"Pony Girl…"

"I remembered more while you were sleeping. They were in the lab with me—dozens of them. All young women."

She shot up from the couch and began pacing. "It's going to take Wilson too long to get to Nikolai. How many more people have to die before Wilson takes Nikolai down? Hundreds? Thousands? Nikolai will use the time to escalate because it will bring him more power. He'll use those women as his own personal terrorist squad. And I had totally forgotten they existed until now."

Sarge scooted to the edge of the couch. "None of this is your fault, Bronwyn."

She paused her pacing. "You're right; it's not. Nothing of what has happened up until this point is my fault. There was nothing I could have done to stop it."

He knew what she was going to say and wished there were some way he could erase the thought from her mind.

He knew what she wanted to do.

And he knew he wouldn't stop her even though it was going to damned near kill him not to. She was right that he had to stop rescuing her.

This she needed to do to rescue herself.

"Go on," he whispered.

"You know what I'm going to say, don't you?"

"Yes." Sarge caught one of her hands and brought it to his lips. "But say it anyway."

"I can stop Nikolai. I can be used as bait to draw him out. He's not rational when it comes to me, and he will take chances he might not normally take to get me back under his control."

He let go of her hand and stood. "I want to say up front that I don't want you to do this. You've already paid a high enough price. Let somebody else bring Nikolai down. They'll get him eventually."

"I know. But it will come at a much steeper price."

He scrubbed a hand down his face. "Yes. Strategically, using you to fish him out is the best bet."

They stood staring at each other for a long minute before he yanked her into his arms.

"Knowing everything, I still don't want you to do it." He buried his face in her neck and whispered, "We can walk away from this, Pony Girl. Walk away and never look back. Just the two of us. I can make sure no one will ever find us again."

She stepped back and looked up at him. "No. Every time more people died, I would know I could've stopped it. We have to do this. I have to do this."

He'd never had any doubt that would be her stance. He kissed her on the forehead. "Okay, but it's not going to be easy. The Zodiac team is mostly down. We're going to be stuck with Wilson, and, news flash, he's an asshole."

"But a competent asshole. He wants to stop Mosaic and Nikolai."

"Agreed. Jenna and Outlaw will back us up, if Jenna is okay."

"It would have to be a small team anyway if we want to draw him out." She stepped deeper into his arms, and he tightened them around her. "You and I were a good team before I joined Zodiac, and we'll be a good team together again. I need you to believe I'm strong enough to do this."

"Your strength is not in doubt. And there is no one else I'd rather have on my team than you. Always."

TWELVE HOURS LATER, they were on a plane back to Prague where everything had started for Sarge and Bronwyn.

Not surprising to either of them, Wilson had agreed that using her as bait for Nikolai was the best plan. The specifics for how to do that without getting her killed were a little more unclear.

Of course, he hadn't come right out and said it, but her survival was secondary to making sure Nikolai went down. That's why they were moving so quickly without a true plan in place.

Wilson had been working a plan with his team at the back of the plane. He'd informed them that he'd let them know what it was when they needed to know. As if it wasn't Bronwyn's life on the line.

She'd had to stop Sarge from breaking the man's nose again.

So when Wilson walked up with a laptop and placed it on the table in front of Sarge and her, they were both surprised.

"You've got a video call."

They clicked the open button to find Jenna's face staring at them. As soon as she could see them, she brought her face close to her camera.

"Bronwyn, I'm so sorry. I'm so sorry about what happened at my house. I totally threw you under the bus with this asshole, and it's all my fault you're trapped in this situation now."

She pulled the computer closer to herself. "Jenna, stop. It's not your fault. There was no reason for me to run when I already knew Nikolai was behind all this. I'm glad you're okay."

Although, honestly, she didn't look okay. She had dark circles under her eyes, and her jaw was tight. "Still. What I did was—"

"Understandable. It was understandable given the circumstances and threats involved." She turned to glare at Wilson. His flair for melodrama was what had sent Jenna into her panic attack to begin with.

He reached over and turned the computer in his direction. "How were you able to contact us through this computer?"

She let out a snort. "A determined second grader could hack your task force's communication system. And given the fact that your people are gabbing with two different continents on four different phones at this moment, I happen to know you're over the Atlantic right now. I can give you a specific location if you want me to."

Wilson's face tightened. "This conversation is over. Don't hack our system again, or I'll send someone to show up at your house to take you in."

Bronwyn dug her nails into Sarge's hand. Maybe she was going to break Wilson's nose.

But Jenna took it in stride. "Simmer down there, Special Agent Asshole. I didn't call to chat with my friend. I have information you need if you want to successfully take down Nikolai."

"We don't need your help."

Sarge found it within himself to be reasonable. "Wilson, Jenna is capable of digging up better intel than almost anyone on the planet. Hear her out; we need it."

For a second, she didn't think Wilson would comply, but then he sat down across from them, sliding the computer to the end of the table so they could all see Jenna. "Fine. Go. Although I doubt you've found anything about Nikolai Novotný that's going to prove helpful."

"Nikolai is not where your solution lies, Agent Asshole, so you're right, I won't be providing any intel about him."

Now she had Wilson's full attention. "What are you talking about?"

"Not such a big shot now, are you?"

Sarge twisted the computer so the camera was more focused on them. "Tell us what you discovered, Jenna."

"The key wasn't Nikolai at all—it was in Dr. Tippens's research. I dug into his experiments on you in particular, Bronwyn. It was incomplete data, but I was able to extrapolate his intents. Specifics for what Tippens was programming in you—because of Nikolai. The home stuff."

"My final mission is to go home," she muttered.

"Exactly. They were always planning to turn you over to Nikolai when your usefulness for Erick Huen and Tippens's research came to an end."

"It's why they didn't kill you outright," Sarge muttered against her hair. "I never understood that. I was thankful, but it didn't make sense."

"How does this help us take Nikolai down?" Wilson asked, for once, his tone not combative.

"I know where home is according to Nikolai's and Tippens's plans. I know what Bronwyn would've done once she got there if she were still under the regimen. We can fool Nikolai into thinking you're still under his control."

Wilson's eyes grew larger. "And then you can find out

where he's keeping the other people under the regimen. His zombie army."

Jenna nodded. "I can show you how you would've behaved—phrases, actions—if the regimen had worked completely and Nikolai had you under his power. I think we can convince him that he's won."

"Then we move in and take him out." Wilson looked over at her. "But it means you'll have to go in alone at first. Are you up for it?"

"Yes." She kept her answer simple even though she wasn't sure the one word was the truth. But until Nikolai was taken down, Bronwyn would never be safe. Neither would Sarge, nor would anyone at Zodiac Tactical. Nikolai would continue to come at her any way he could.

If he couldn't hurt her personally, he'd start hurting the people she cared about.

She looked over at Sarge, his face tight. He obviously didn't like this plan. She couldn't blame him. She didn't like a plan that put her back in Nikolai's power even for a short time.

"I'll do it."

Wilson turned to Jenna. "Give them all the data they need to make her interaction with Nikolai believable. I'll go tell the rest of the team the plan."

He got up and headed toward the back of the plane.

"I really do believe this is going to work," Jenna said. "I can leak some data to Nikolai's organization that will give a plausible excuse for where you've been the past few weeks. Then all you have to do is make him think the programming has worked and you got there as soon as you could."

"You're sure you've got enough details for her to be able to do that?" Sarge's hands tightened around hers. "She'll be by herself with him. Her life is at stake."

"Yes. I know what she'll be asked, and I know how she should respond to prove she's under the regimen. We can get her ready. Plus, I have a gift for you guys. It should be there when you land."

Bronwyn squeezed his hand. "It's better than the wandering-around-Prague plan we had before. It probably wouldn't have worked anyway, just gotten me a bullet in the head."

Of course, there was no guarantee that wouldn't still happen.

"Yeah," Sarge muttered. "But I still don't like it."

They didn't have to like it. They just had to do it.

"Okay." She let out a breath and pulled away from Sarge. "Let's start going over all the details of what I need to do. We don't have much time. And the sooner we get Nikolai, the more lives we'll save."

Including hers.

———

"I don't like this," Sarge whispered into her hair. "Test your comm unit again."

"I'm going to be okay."

It was both a test of the tiny transmitting device—not unlike the one Sarge had given her when she'd shown up at his house that one time—and a reassurance for both of them.

They were in Prague, and she was about to step out of the safety of his arms and walk to where her programming would've taken her if she were under Nikolai's control.

They'd spent every second until they landed going over the details of how she needed to behave. Answers to trick questions Nikolai would ask as fail-safes.

Jenna had leaked data that she had been held in isolation at a military base in Nevada for the past few weeks. Only recently had she been moved and placed under civilian psychiatric care.

She kept the details loose from there. It was completely feasible that once she was in a mental hospital rather than a military brig, she would be able to escape and do what her programming demanded: return to Prague.

They made sure her entry into the country was known. Now they had to see if Nikolai would take the bait. He wouldn't come pick her up himself unless they got ridiculously lucky, so she would be taken to him, and have to be face-to-face with him alone for at least a little while.

"You don't come for me unless you have to." She hugged him closer. "Let me do some good. Let me get as much info as I can."

They all knew that Nikolai probably had a plan in place to eliminate his zombie army if he was arrested. She needed to find out where they were.

"I'm not letting anything happen to you."

"Get those women out first, then come for me. Wilson is right in wanting to make sure that happens."

He cupped her cheeks and kissed her. "Outlaw and I will be ready no matter what asinine decisions Wilson makes."

Mark Outlawson had been Jenna's gift for them. He'd shown up not long after they'd landed. At least now she knew someone had Sarge's back while he had hers.

"Let's go." Wilson walked over and tapped her on the shoulder. "If your computer guru is correct, you have to be out on Radlická Street right at noon. That's the first security measure we've got to cross. If we don't get you out there on time, we have to wait twenty-four more hours."

Bronwyn looked up at Sarge. "I love you." She should've said it earlier, not when they were rushed and Wilson was standing so close she could hear his breathing.

Sarge rubbed his thumb against her lips. "You tell me that again in a day or two when this is over and I have you naked in a bed somewhere."

"Deal."

"I'll see you soon, Pony Girl. Believe it."

She did. She believed it with every fiber of her body. If she didn't, there was no way she'd be able to do this.

She turned and walked out from the back room of a restaurant where they'd been holed up and outside into the dreary Prague weather. She didn't shiver or show any reaction to the cold dampness at all.

Someone under the regimen would not be aware of the discomfort.

She walked straight ahead until she arrived at Radlická where it met a secondary road. Then stood, as directed, near the edge of the street.

People walked around her on either side, not paying her much mind. She felt conspicuous, but to most people rushing along with their own lives in the middle of downtown, she wasn't doing anything except being in their way for a second before they passed.

Bronwyn stood, completely still, staring straight ahead. That was what her programming would have her do. She had no doubt Nikolai had someone watching this corner at noon every day to see if she arrived.

She kept her hands by her sides, forcing herself not to clench them to stop their shaking. Of everything, her hands were most likely to give her away. Someone under control of the regimen would not have shaky hands.

The longer Bronwyn stood, the harder it became. For the first time, she wished she could escape her mind and let her body float out of itself.

We're going to get through this, Pony Girl.

Sarge was with her. Both in her mind, where she needed him, and at her back, where she needed him too.

"Yes," she whispered without moving her lips. "We'll make it through this."

She believed it.

Then a car pulled up at the curb, and she was yanked

inside, taking her away from her salvation and back to her nightmare.

CHAPTER
THIRTY-EIGHT

BRONWYN DIDN'T RECOGNIZE either of the men in the car. The one who grabbed her used a wand over her torso and limbs to check for weapons or recording devices, but he didn't come near her throat or the tiny, clear transmitter pressing against her vocal cords. He immediately restrained her hands.

"Say your words," he said in English.

She stared straight ahead. "I exist only to obey orders. My final mission is to go home."

"And where is home?"

"At the feet of Nikolai."

Both men snickered, but she carefully kept her face blank. Someone under the regimen would have no reaction to the humiliating phrase.

Sarge had nearly lost his temper when Jenna had told them about the trigger phrase and the corresponding response. She'd found it in Dr. Tippens's notes. He'd argued against it as a response phrase, insisting Nikolai use an alphanumeric code, but Nikolai had refused.

Nikolai's need to lord his power over her had definitely worked in their favor. Jenna would've probably never found some random code in Dr. Tippens's notes, but that phrase had caught her attention.

The men switched to Czech, but she still understood perfectly.

"I can't believe she actually showed up," the driver said. "I'll miss my daily coffee as I wait for someone I never thought would arrive."

"Why do you think Nikolai is so obsessed with her?" The man in the back with her trailed a finger up her arm. She kept her fingers clenched together and showed no response. "She is attractive but not worth so much trouble. Maybe we should find a place to pull over and try her out."

The driver chuckled. "Maybe Nikolai wants someone who doesn't pretend not to see his scars. Look at her, she's a robot."

"She looks close enough to flesh and blood for me." He slid his hand up her thigh.

She grabbed the wandering hand, twisting it to the point of breaking even with the cuffs on. "Nikolai only."

The man howled, and she let go. The driver laughed. "Maybe not completely a robot, Jarek."

Bronwyn didn't know if her actions would be part of her programming, but it was a risk she was willing to take. She wasn't going to become a plaything for these two on the way to Nikolai.

Jarek huffed back against the seat. "Bitch."

But at least he left her alone.

The roads of Prague were vaguely familiar. She'd mostly walked and stayed in the same two-mile radius growing up. They weren't going back to the old neighborhood, that was for sure.

They were heading outside of the city, not in the direction that intel put Nikolai's residence.

"North," she muttered softly. She hoped Sarge and the team were following their vehicle closely enough to realize they weren't going in the direction they'd expected. Or that this would at least give them a clue.

"That's right, bitch," Jarek said. "Nikolai is having us take you to the place where no one ever leaves except in a body bag."

Thankfully, he was too busy laughing at his own joke to see her flinch. She had to get her actions under control, or she was going to give herself away. Especially once she was in front of Nikolai.

Bronwyn wished she could have had Sarge's voice in her ear rather than him only being able to hear her.

You do. I'm here.

Maybe it was her mind projecting his voice, but he was in her heart. It gave her hope. Strength.

But the closer they got to Nikolai, the harder it was to stay calm. By the time they pulled up to the doorway, she didn't think she was going to be able to go through with it.

Do you want a future? Then you have to do this.

This time, it was her own voice inside her head. And it was right. If she wanted a future with Sarge, if she wanted to protect him, then this was where she had to make her stand.

And you're not alone.

Sarge.

She probably needed to talk to Dr. Rayne about all the voices in her head.

Jarek yanked her out of the car and pushed her inside the door and down a narrow hallway. Bronwyn focused on breathing. There were no windows anywhere around her, and the concrete walls and sterile floors reminded her of her personal hell. She wouldn't be able to escape the place on her own.

You're not on your own.

They finally stopped in front of a door, and Jarek knocked. She sucked in a breath, glad her hands were still restrained so she could clench them together to hide their shaking.

The door opened, and Jarek led her inside. She stared straight ahead, but she could count three men out of the corner of her eye. Then the one who was right in front of her looking out at something through an interior window.

Nikolai.

He turned to face her, and keeping her face neutral was maybe the hardest thing she'd ever done. The burn scars on his cheek and chin were even worse than the pictures she'd seen from after she'd escaped.

Scars she'd given him and he'd demand payment for.

"You found her." He walked toward her.

Jarek nodded. "Yes, sir. She was at the location right at the time you said she'd be there."

Nikolai passed out of her vision as he circled around her. Bronwyn knew a blow could come any minute. A literal knife in the back.

Steady. These are the most important minutes.

That voice was a mixture of hers and Sarge's. But it was right.

"You look different from when I last saw you in person." Nikolai passed back around so she could see him. That made it easier. "Of course, I've seen footage of you with Erick and Dr. Tippens—screaming, crying, begging. That was nice. But not the same as seeing you in person. I wish I could have been there."

He leaned forward so his face was directly in front of hers, his breath hot against her skin. "I'll look forward to the screaming, begging, and crying in person."

Be strong, Pony Girl.

Bronwyn remained expressionless. The only thing that gave her away were her hands, but nobody was looking at them.

Nikolai backed away, eyes narrowed, still studying her. "She said everything correctly?"

"Yes." Jarek nodded enthusiastically next to her.

"Say your words," he said to her.

"I exist only to obey orders." Saying these words by rote was easy. She'd had so much practice in the lab. "My final mission is to go home."

"And where is home?"

This was harder. "At the feet of Nikolai."

He broke into a big grin. "Yes, I definitely like the sound of that."

The four other men in the room chuckled.

Nikolai walked slowly around her again. "But look at you, all the feisty is gone with you like this. I want to see Bronya, not this robot." He leaned closer to her ear. "Release code four-two-seven."

She kept herself still. Jenna had gone over a release code number, but that wasn't it.

Did she have it wrong? Had it changed? If she didn't move, would he know the truth?

Jenna hadn't steered her wrong thus far, so she held.

Nikolai stepped back and studied her. "Just checking. One can't be too careful. Release code two-one-two."

That was it, the one Jenna had given her. Two hundred and twelve, the temperature at which water boiled. Since she'd burned him with boiling liquid… Trust Nikolai to have a meaning behind everything.

Bronwyn allowed her emotional mask to fall away, to let all the terror she was really feeling show. She unclenched her hands—they were shaking so hard tremors moved up her arms.

She moved away from Nikolai, something she'd wanted to do since she first saw him. Jarek grabbed her arm to keep her in place.

"There she is." Nikolai trailed a finger down her cheek, and she flinched. "There's my little runaway. I've been waiting for this moment a long time."

"Nikolai? What? No. How did you—?" It was easy to inject the terror into her voice.

"You've always been under my power, little Bronya. You just didn't know it." He touched her cheek again, exactly where the scar was on his own face. "So smooth. Maybe not for long."

"Let me go!"

"I don't think so. I think you owe me a little more than one pound of flesh. And I intend to collect however I see fit. You will be under my control until you die." His smile was pure evil. "Which probably won't be too long. I do have other, more important things to do besides toy with you."

The shaking in her hands was starting to cause tremors through her whole body. She prayed Nikolai wouldn't try to apply the regimen on her right now because there was no way she'd be able to go back to being a fake robotic.

He laughed. "You're scared. I like that. First fear, then pain, then death. That's what you have to look forward to, Bronya."

She forced her chin up, the way the old Bronya would've done. Hopefully, some of that feisty girl still existed inside her. "Because I made your face hideous?"

Bronwyn heard the intake of breaths of the men around them. They hadn't known.

His backhand knocked her to the floor. He grabbed her by her hair and yanked her back up to her feet. "Trying to get me to kill you quickly, Bronya? It won't work."

No, she didn't want him to kill her, but she did want him off-balance enough to keep talking.

"How did I get here?" She brought her tied hands to her stinging cheek, glancing around at his men who were watching the show unfold in front of them. "How did you do this?"

"It was in the works before you left. Before Father died. Mosaic was expanding and needed leadership and manpower in Europe. I had funding for their brain experiments. You allowed me to kill two birds with one stone."

"I don't understand."

"I provided them with subjects for Tippens to experiment on. Including you—although we had special parameters for you. In return, I now have three dozen mindless clones willing to do anything I say. For example, I used one in Hamburg recently."

"That was you?"

"Yes. The perfect vessel for terrorism. All young women, trained and willing to kill without blinking. None of them are on any law enforcement watch list. You all look so young and innocent. Lovely and guileless. Women who can walk into places most people can't." He trailed a finger down her cheek once more. "Of course, you won't be able to do that much longer. Your features will be too distinct."

She knew that meant she'd have her own scars. She let out a whimper. His men snickered.

"The best part is, I can send you out, and you'll still come back to me. Every single time, you'll come back to the feet of Nikolai no matter what I do to you."

"No."

"Oh yes. I have to admit, I thought Erick had lost you. It was part of the reason I didn't show up to help him a few days ago like I was supposed to. Then I had him killed so he couldn't talk. I can't have the police figuring out I'm the head of Mosaic in Europe."

She couldn't do this. She needed to get out of there. The walls were closing in on her. Nikolai and his men filled up her vision.

"Let me go."

"I'll never let you go, little Bronya, my feisty one. My face will be the last thing you see before you die."

LISTENING to what was happening to Bronwyn was throwing Sarge back into his own personal hell. Granted, this time, he knew where she was, but she still felt too far out of reach.

Nikolai taunted her with the fact that he could have her perform sexual favors with his men then still come crawling back to him.

"She's not going to make it much longer," he muttered to Wilson.

He shook his head. "She's terrified, but that works in her favor right now."

Sarge didn't want her terrified. And he especially didn't want her anywhere near Nikolai Novotný and all his nefarious intents toward her.

They were less than a mile from the compound where Bronwyn was with Nikolai, but they might as well be hours away. He could kill her a hundred times over in the five minutes it would take them to infiltrate the building.

And even if he didn't kill her, the other things he could do…

"We need to go in," he said to Mark in a low voice.

He shook his head. "She wanted this chance. Bronwyn knows more than anyone what Nikolai is capable of. But it's worth facing him to help get those other women released. It's worth facing him so the two of you can have a future together."

Mark was right, but he didn't like it. "I would walk through any hell for her if it meant she wasn't hurt or afraid anymore."

"I hear that."

He got the feeling they weren't talking solely about Bronwyn.

"Why isn't she getting the data we need about the other victims?" Wilson asked.

"Stand down, Wilson." Sarge gritted his teeth. "She's doing the best she can."

"Well, her best might cost a lot of people their lives."

He wanted to punch Wilson in the face—again—but he was telling the truth. Bronwyn might not be able to get the info they need.

"Chances are the other women are in that building," he said. "Look at it. It's a fucking compound. I say we move in now and take our chances."

Move in now, and get Bronwyn out.

"No. We wait and see what information she can get."

A cry from Bronwyn drew their attention back to the speaker where her transmissions were broadcast.

"Goddammit, he hit her again." Sarge stood from his seat in the back of the cargo van. "I'm going in there."

Wilson moved in front of the door. "No, you're not. She knew the risks."

"We thought he'd be taking her to his house. Someplace we could get in quickly. This is not what she signed up for. Get out of my way."

"Don't make me draw my weapon."

"Don't make me break your nose again, Wilson."

"You guys, shut the fuck up and listen!"

Wilson and Sarge both turned back toward Outlaw at his words.

"You can hit me all you want, Nikolai. But I still think you're a liar. You don't have an army. You can barely keep me here, forget anyone else."

"She's baiting him," he muttered. It was dangerous. If it backfired…

Acid burned in his gut when Bronwyn cried out again. He couldn't see what was happening, but he knew it wasn't good. "I'm going to enjoy scarring you the way you scarred me."

He'd heard enough. "Get out of my way. I'm going in, with or without you." He wasn't going to sit here and listen as Bronwyn suffered.

"There." Nikolai's voice came through the speaker. "All of my little slaves, just like you."

"Are those walls…dirt?"

He locked eyes with Mark. If the walls where the other women were being held were dirt, then they weren't in that building with Bronwyn.

"For now. Soon, this building will be ready to house them. Look closer. You know where that is."

A long moment of silence passed before Bronwyn spoke. "Your father's secret wine cellar. Where I hid from you when he died."

"And I found you there, didn't I?"

Bile rose in his gut. He didn't have to guess what had happened in that cellar after Nikolai found her.

He'd never wanted to kill anyone as much as he did this bastard.

Come on, Pony Girl. Get us the info we need so we can get you out of there.

"I can't believe you're keeping that many women hidden in that wine cellar in Havlíčkovy sady. Under the fountain."

She'd done it. She'd gotten the information.

Wilson was immediately on the phone, calling in support. They had the location of the missing women.

Nikolai chuckled over the transmission. "Every time I walk in that park, I think of our time together."

Bronwyn, wisely, didn't respond.

"She did it! Let's go." Wilson was already climbing toward the driver's side. "We've got to move now. Once Nikolai knows we're on to him, he'll have the women moved or killed. We're the closest ones. We can't call Prague police because at least some of them will be on Nikolai's payroll."

"No." Sarge wasn't leaving Bronwyn.

"McEwan, we have to. We'll get the women out then immediately come back for Bronwyn. She's doing okay. She only needs to survive another hour."

That was a fucking eternity.

"No. I'm not leaving her." Not again. Not ever again. This would not be one more time he would look back on and think he shouldn't have left her. "You guys go. I'll get Bronwyn out."

Wilson scrubbed a hand down his face, for once looking sincere. "We don't have the manpower to support infiltration in both places. We have to go with what will benefit the most people. I swear on my life we will immediately come back for Bronwyn."

His life didn't mean anything to Sarge. Only hers. "Take your team and get the women out. I'm going after Bronwyn now."

"You'll die," Wilson said. "Like you keep telling me, we're all on the same side. I don't want to lose someone on my team."

"He's right, Sarge." Mark put his hand on his shoulder. "You won't make it alone."

He didn't care. "I'm not leaving her. If I die, it will be getting her out."

Mark turned to Wilson. "You and your team get to the wine cellar. Sarge will make sure Bronwyn gets out, and I'll make sure he's still alive when he does."

————

Timing was going to be key to their survival. Nikolai may be a sadistic bastard, but he wasn't an idiot. Once he got word the hidden wine cellar was under attack so soon after sharing the data with Bronwyn, he was going to put two and two together quickly.

And put a bullet in her brain.

He had to be in place before that happened.

Their two-man infiltration team wasn't pretty. There was no finesse whatsoever as they burst through a back door and began moving way too quickly down the main hallway.

"This is going to get us killed," Mark said as they dipped their heads around a corner and saw a few guards at the far end.

"I don't know what else to do. I've got to make it to Bronwyn before Nikolai gets word of what's going on. He'll kill her."

"He'll kill her just as fast if he gets word there's someone in the building shooting his men."

Mark was right, and he had no idea what to do. "Fuck. I need two minutes to get to that southeast office."

He nodded. "I can buy you two minutes. Make them count, brother."

Before Sarge could ask his plan, he'd jogged down the hall toward the guards. "Hey, excuse me," he called out. "Is this the building where we meet up for the Vltava River Cruise? I think I might have come to the wrong address."

The man had guts; he had to hand it to him. It wouldn't fool the guards for long but long enough.

He snuck around behind Nikolai's men as Outlaw

continued his role as lost tourist. He was almost to the office when he heard gunfire back from his direction. Sarge's jaw hardened as he gave up any pretense of stealth and pushed for full speed. He prayed his friend hadn't lost his life to buy him these seconds.

He got to Nikolai's office and kicked the door in. Time slowed as he evaluated the threats. Nikolai. Three other men. Bronwyn standing to the side, still alive. That was the most important thing.

Time snapped back into place. He didn't hesitate, rushing forward to knock the gun out of the hands of the first man while he was in the process of drawing it. A spinning kick sent another man's gun skidding across the floor. With two steps, he was at Nikolai, knocking his weapon before he could fully aim it.

But he wasn't going to get to the fourth guy in time. He blocked the punch Nikolai threw and waited for a directive to freeze or maybe a bullet straight in the back.

It didn't come.

Sarge spun, kicking out at one of the first two thugs, and saw that Bronwyn had taken care of the last man's gun. Her hands were still restrained in front of her, but she was holding her own. He gave her a grin and continued his spin to fight the three he was in charge of. She would take care of the one on his six.

But they were only a few more seconds in when Nikolai stepped back and spoke up. "Bronwyn, protocol activated immediately. Say your words."

He blocked another punch, expecting to hear Bronwyn tell Nikolai to go to hell.

"I exist only to obey orders. My final mission is to go home."

His heart sank at her words. He spun to see what was going on and caught a punch in the jaw for his lack of focus.

Bronwyn was still, no longer fighting, her gazing staring out blankly ahead of her.

She was gone. The robot was back in her place. And Nikolai had a gun in his hand once again. Sarge stopped fighting.

Nikolai walked toward him. "You. The American. I remember you from years ago. I remember having my men beat you to the ground to see if I could get a reaction from Bronya."

His hand holding the gun slammed into Sarge's midsection. He doubled over, air disappearing and pain exploding through his gut. "If she had begged me not to hurt you, I would've killed you right there. But she didn't seem to care, so I let you live. My mistake."

His eyes were on Bronwyn as he righted himself. She was still staring blankly ahead. The chances of him being able to take the gun from Nikolai, fight off three of his men, then get her out of there if she was resisting were zero to snowball's chance in hell.

He had no idea what he was going to do. Nikolai still had that gun pointed at him and…

Wait.

Had Bronwyn moved the slightest bit closer to Nikolai?

That might not mean anything, but…

She did it again. While he was continuing his monologue about how he never should've let Sarge live the first time and would rectify that mistake.

He looked at Bronwyn's hands clasped in front of her.

They were shaking.

She definitely wasn't under the influence of the regimen like Nikolai thought. She was biding her time.

The best way he could help her get a chance to make a move was to draw attention away from her.

"Has anyone ever told you that you talk too much?" He

shook his head at Nikolai. "I meant to say that to you the first day I met you."

That got him a punch in the face from one of his men. He turned to that guy. "Come on, you've got to be thinking it too. Nikolai likes to hear himself talk."

Bronwyn moved another half step closer to Nikolai. She was making her way. Sarge hoped he didn't shoot him first. He was counting on the fact that he would consider a bullet too quick of a death for him.

And God, he hoped Wilson and his team had gotten those women out of that wine cellar or this was all for naught.

"You think I talk too much?"

Nikolai—nothing if not predictable—nodded to his men. Fists flew at him from all directions. Sarge didn't use a tenth of his close-quarter combat skills to stop them. He let them beat him until he was lying on the ground. He'd have a couple cracked ribs and wouldn't be able to see out of one swollen eye in a few minutes, but hopefully it would be worth it.

Nikolai called off his guys. "Seems like my men are always beating you to the ground."

She was almost in position to make her move. She needed a little more time.

Sarge started to laugh.

Nikolai didn't like that at all. "What's so funny? Do you think I'm not going to kill you?" He pointed the gun directly down at him.

"No, I'm sure you plan on it." He shifted his weight, the groan escaping him not fake but definitely meant to make them think he wasn't going to be getting up any time soon.

"Then what is funny?"

Sarge shook his head and continued to chuckle. "Zodiac Tactical made the same mistake you did. We thought that Bronwyn's strength was in her nimble fingers, her ability to steal and pickpocket, to blend. We all missed the obvious."

His eyes narrowed. "And what's that?"

"Her greatest strength is her mind. She's smarter than all of us."

"I'll remember that when she begs for her life and I kill her anyway. I'll remember that she's smarter than me as she falls to the ground. She's mine."

Bronwyn moved faster than he'd ever seen her, even at the top of her game. She chopped Nikolai in the wrist, grabbing the gun from his now-numb fingers. She shot all three of his men before they could get their weapons from the floor.

He'd planned on jumping up to help her, but she hadn't needed his help at all.

"I will never be yours," she spat the words in Nikolai's face then sent him reeling with a sharp punch.

She rushed over to him. "Are you okay? I'm sorry. I was pretending to be under the regimen, but I wasn't sure if you understood. I needed to—"

Sarge kissed her with lips that were already swollen. "I know, Pony Girl. Once again, you were doing what you had to do to survive. This time, for both of us to survive."

"How?" Nikolai whined, wiping blood from his nose where she'd hit him. "How did you break the regimen?"

Bronwyn didn't look at him as she helped him to his feet. "Because I'm not alone anymore. Because unlike those other women you targeted—unlike the person I was before—I have a team, a family who made sure my mind was clear and my back was covered before coming here. You will never have any control over me again."

Nikolai's face turned nearly purple with rage. He reached down and pulled a knife from his boot and rushed toward them.

His intent was clear. Sarge reached to push her behind his body, but she pulled away. She brought up the gun with both bound hands and shot Nikolai three times in the chest. He fell dead to the floor.

Her hands weren't shaking the slightest little bit.

CHAPTER
FORTY

SIX MONTHS *Later*

When Sarge woke up, Bronwyn wasn't in bed with him.

It wasn't unusual that she'd woken up early. Sleeping was still a tricky thing for her. Even with Mosaic completely gone —Erick and Nikolai dead and the other two leaders having fallen not long after—it didn't change what they done to her.

Twenty-two women had been rescued that day in Prague. Wilson may have been an asshole, but he'd gotten them out and taken a bullet while doing it. Many of those women were way worse off than Bronwyn, but they were at least all alive and receiving medical help.

Outlaw had been shot, too, once his lost tourist act had failed. But he'd survived and had taken four men down with him as he'd bought Sarge the time he'd needed to get to Bronwyn.

He was now in Wyoming working with the Linear Tactical guys on a special project centering around Jenna and her past.

Bronwyn was still healing. For the most part, her hands still shook. They were both coming to accept that might permanently be a part of who she was. Even though she'd done an admirable job of stitching her pieces back together, that didn't mean she hadn't been broken.

Her broken pieces were the most beautiful part of his life, and he would treasure each and every one for the rest of his days.

He knew where she was, so he didn't hurry as he rolled out of bed. Although he was surprised that she had gotten away from him without him waking up at all. They still slept like a couple of octopi, entwined as much as two people could be.

They both slept better for it.

Sarge got dressed and padded into the kitchen. The coffee had already been made, so he poured two more mugs and made his way outside.

They'd moved a few months ago about an hour outside of Denver. He'd given up his house with the view of the Front Range—Landon was currently renting it. After he'd gotten out of the hospital, stairs had been a bit much for his body to handle. He'd needed a place all on one level.

Sarge had needed a place with more land.

The house he and Bronwyn had moved into didn't have a fabulous view of the Rockies, but it had a few acres. He knew that was where Bronwyn would be now, out in the fenced-in area.

Watching Mac and Cheese.

Once life had settled down after they'd returned from Prague, she'd asked if she could go visit the alpaca and alpaca-at-heart sheep back at Resting Warrior.

It had been Lucas's idea that they find a way to bring the animals back to Colorado. They weren't trained as service or emotional support animals, but they were both those things to Bronwyn.

So they'd found a place that had acreage and a small barn. A couple months later, Cheese, the sheep, and Mac, along with two other alpacas she'd named Peanut Butter and Jelly —because why not?—had become part of their family at their new home.

Cheese was currently following Jelly around. Mac and Peanut Butter ignored them both, chewing on grass in the gentle light of the dawn.

"Are the four food groups doing okay out here?" He handed her a mug where she sat perched on the fence rails watching the animals.

"Yeah. Cheese won't leave Jelly alone. Mac couldn't care less."

Sarge smiled. "Is Jelly being aggressive toward Cheese?" They'd been a little concerned that the other two alpacas wouldn't be as tolerant of the sheep as Mac had been.

"Nah. Just annoyed."

"Understandable." He rubbed a hand down her back, and she leaned toward him. "And you? You doing okay? It's a big day."

She blew out a breath. "I'm scared."

"Your tutor doesn't think you'll have any problem at all. She said she'd never seen anyone complete the GED work so quickly."

It took most people six months to a year to pass their high school equivalency exam. Bronwyn had aced it in a little over six weeks.

Color him not surprised.

The blue eyes—still taking his breath away as much as they had that very first day—pinned him. "Maybe I should wait. Maybe I shouldn't start a program that's both a bachelor's and master's degree combined. Maybe my professors are going to realize I'm a fraud."

He slipped his hand into her hair and pulled her in for a kiss. "Maybe you're going to complete this program with flying colors, get your PhD. And become a literature professor like your mom."

She hadn't been interested in remaining an active Zodiac employee. Although he hated that she thought it was because she couldn't do that sort of work as well anymore, her being out of danger suited him just fine.

"I'm scared," she whispered again.

"It's okay to be scared." he kissed her again then turned back to the animals. "First days of school are scary. But I know you're still going to go, and I know you'll succeed."

"I will succeed," she muttered.

Sarge grinned without looking at her. "Then one day when you teach your own college literature class, I'll take it. And we'll tell our kids how we were the second generation of literature professor and student."

"Our kids?" she whispered.

"Is that okay? Is it okay that I want to marry you and have kids of the human type running around, not just alpaca kids?"

A smile lit up her face. "I want that too. But not today. Today, I have to get ready for school."

"I love you, Pony Girl."

She took his hand, and they turned from the gold of the dawn to walk back inside. The light wouldn't stay gold; it would change as the sun came up.

It was what Robert Frost had been referring to in that poem quoted in *The Outsiders*. The one Ponyboy recited as he and Johnny watched the dawn.

Nothing gold can stay.

They got to the door, and Bronwyn turned to him. "I used to dream about what my life would be when I grew up. I never once considered it would be this wonderful or with a man I would love as much as I love you. My own personal cranky hero."

She grinned and bolted inside.

"Don't make me late on my first day," she called over her shoulder, laughing.

Oh, she knew he was going to do his damnedest even if it meant he had to drive her to campus himself so she made it on time. He dashed inside after her, the sound of her laughter everything that had meaning in my life.

Frost had been wrong.

Their gold would stay.

• • •

The Zodiac Tactical series continues with **CODE NAME: LIBRA**.

ALSO BY JANIE CROUCH

All books: https://www.janiecrouch.com/books

LINEAR TACTICAL: OAK CREEK

Hero Unbound

Hero's Flight

Hero's Prize

ZODIAC TACTICAL

Code Name: ARIES

Code Name: VIRGO

Code Name: LIBRA

Code Name: PISCES

Code Name: OUTLAW

Code Name: GEMINI

GILDED EMPIRE (as MJ Crouch; series complete)

Broken Crown

Damaged Kingdom

Fierce Monarch

Vicious Throne

RESTING WARRIOR RANCH (with Josie Jade; series complete)

Montana Sanctuary

Montana Danger

Montana Desire

Montana Mystery

Montana Storm

Montana Freedom

Montana Silence

Montana Rain

LINEAR TACTICAL SERIES (series complete)

Cyclone

Eagle

Shamrock

Angel

Ghost

Shadow

Echo

Phoenix

Baby

Storm

Redwood

Scout

Blaze

Hero Forever

INSTINCT SERIES (series complete)

Primal Instinct

Critical Instinct

Survival Instinct

THE RISK SERIES (series complete)

Calculated Risk

Security Risk

Constant Risk

Risk Everything

OMEGA SECTOR SERIES (series complete)

Stealth

Covert

Conceal

Secret

OMEGA SECTOR: CRITICAL RESPONSE (series complete)

Special Forces Savior

Fully Committed

Armored Attraction

Man of Action

Overwhelming Force

Battle Tested

OMEGA SECTOR: UNDER SIEGE (series complete)

Daddy Defender

Protector's Instinct

Cease Fire

Major Crimes

Armed Response

In the Lawman's Protection

ABOUT THE AUTHOR

"Passion that leaps right off the page." - Romantic Times Book Reviews

USA Today and Publishers Weekly bestselling author Janie Crouch writes what she loves to read: passionate romantic suspense featuring protective heroes. Her books have won multiple awards, including the Romance Writers of America's coveted Vivian® Award, the National Readers Choice Award, and the Booksellers' Best.

After a lifetime on the East Coast, and a six-year stint in Germany due to her husband's job as support for the U.S. Military, Janie has settled into her dream home in Front Range of the Colorado Rockies.

When she's not listening to the voices in her head—and even when she is—she enjoys engaging in all sorts of crazy adventures (200-mile relay races; Ironman Triathlons, treks to Mt. Everest Base Camp...), traveling, and hanging out with her four kids.

Her favorite quote: "Life is a daring adventure or nothing." ~ Helen Keller.